The Home Corner

Ruth Thomas is the author of two novels and three collections of short stories. Her first collection was short-listed for the John Llewellyn Rhys and the Saltire Society First Book Awards, and her second received a Scottish Arts Council Book Award. *Super Girl*, her first collection with Faber, was longlisted for the Frank O'Connor International Short Story Award, and her novel *Things to Make and Mend* received a Good Housekeeping Book Award. She is currently a Royal Literary Fund Writing Fellow at the Royal Conservatoire of Scotland, and lives in Edinburgh with her husband and children.

The Home Corner

RUTH THOMAS

faber and faber

First published in this edition in 2013
by Faber and Faber Limited
Bloomsbury House, 74–77 Great Russell Street,
London WC1B 3DA

Printed and bound by CPI Group (UK) Ltd, Croydon, CR0 4YY

The right of Ruth Thomas to be identified as author
of this work has been asserted in accordance with Section 77
of the Copyright, Designs and Patents Act 1988

This is a work of fiction. Names, characters, places and incidents either are
products of the author's imagination or are used fictitiously. Any resemblance
to actual events or locales or persons, living or dead, is entirely coincidental.

A CIP record for this book
is available from the British Library

ISBN 978-0-571-23061-7

FSC
www.fsc.org
MIX
Paper from
responsible sources
FSC® C101712

2 4 6 8 10 9 7 5 3 1

For Charlotte, George and Archie,
and for Mike

When they said the time to hide was mine,
I hid back under a thick grape vine.

And while I was still for the time to pass,
A little grey thing came out of the grass.

He hopped his way through the melon bed
And sat down close by a cabbage head.

He sat down close where I could see,
And his big still eyes looked hard at me,

His big eyes bursting out of the rim,
And I looked back very hard at him.

'The Rabbit', by Elizabeth Madox Roberts

I

The seasons seemed to come and go that year without me really noticing them. They just rolled on. Sometimes I wondered if that was how my predecessor had seen them, too; if Miss Ford had ever looked up at the pure blue sky one September afternoon, and thought *Jesus, it's autumn*. Or if she'd used to sit on a bus from her home to St Luke's and back in a kind of trance. I hardly even registered the children growing taller, or the sums getting harder, or the seasonal fruits on the lunch menu changing from rock-hard winter oranges to small Scottish strawberries. I used to take sandwiches in for lunch, myself: I packed them in the pale green lunchbox I'd had at high school. Cheese and pickle most days, a wee carton of juice and an apple. I ate sitting on the same chair in the staffroom, looking out of the same window at the same view. I was stuck, I suppose; I was fixed, and I didn't know how to alter things. *This month is: JUNE. Today the weather is: SUNNY*, I remember it saying one day on the weather chart that Mrs Baxter kept propping up on the Nature Table – but it's funny how you can read a statement like that and not take it in. How you can almost want to disagree with it.

I hadn't arrived at the start of the school year; I'd been offered the job late in the autumn, a replacement for Miss Ford, who had not, apparently, quite *cut the mustard*. Susan Ford was a kind of ghost at St Luke's, an absence, a person whose spectral shoes I was filling. There was a gap on the staffroom wall of fame where *Miss Ford's* photo had been. I remember wondering if my recruitment had been a case of desperate measures, because I was clearly never going to be ideal either, as classroom assistants go. My job offer had been typed on pale letterheaded paper bearing St Luke's emblem of a fat owl sitting in a tree, and its motto, *Veritas et Fidelis*.

Truth and Fidelity.

Dear Miss McKenzie, Mrs Crieff, the school's headmistress, had written, *Following your interview at St Luke's yesterday afternoon I am delighted to inform you . . .*

– and it had been quite hard to believe that I'd passed something; that I hadn't failed, the way I'd flunked all my Highers the previous year. It had felt strange that I would have a role and an income and a place to go. By the time I started, we were already halfway through November. Harvest Festival had come and gone, and so had Halloween and Eid and Sukkot, and we were on our way to Diwali and St Andrew's Day. We had, as Mrs Crieff said, ticked a lot of the *festivals boxes* that term, both secular and religious.

St Luke's was one of those sandstone Victorian places built to last. There was a door marked *Boys* and another marked *Girls*, and standing outside the main door was one lone silver birch tree. The playground was pretty much a sea of tarmac apart from that tree. The only other form of decoration was a stone relief, placed high on the front wall, of a small child and a crouching, cloaked person showing the child a book. I used to think that the cloaked person looked quite off-putting, like Death or the Spirit of Christmas Yet to Come. But I suppose it was just one of those educational things that you saw sometimes on old buildings. A lot of other things about St Luke's had changed, of course, since it was first built. For instance, the old janitor's house that had once stood alongside had quite recently been knocked down and replaced with four small modern houses, known collectively as Janitor's Close. The houses in Janitor's Close were identical, with sloping, chalet-style roofs and creosoted lean-tos for the rubbish bins, and porches with frosted glass. At playtimes, the children used to peer across at the houses, now sectioned off from the school behind a new wall, and discuss who might live in them, like wondering if there was a troll lurking beneath a bridge.

The playground, in the mornings, always looked very grey and hard. And sometimes the mothers – still standing there after their children had gone in and the doors had closed behind them – made me think of teenagers hanging around a swingpark after dark. Loitering; waiting for something – though it was hard to tell for what. To be reunited, maybe, with something they'd let go of by mistake. It was mainly mothers, in the playground. Some of the fathers only turned up once a fortnight or so. This had been quite a shock to me at first: I'd always assumed that times had changed, that we'd moved on from the days of dads in offices and mums at home. But this was not the case at all. The St Luke's dads were like needles in haystacks. There was one man in particular, the father of a little girl called Emily Ellis, who stuck out by his absence. He was some sort of specialist in something, some consultant, I'd been told, and when he *did* turn up at school, he always looked as if he had somewhere to be that was more important.

'Chop chop,' I'd heard him say once to Emily when she was taking a long time getting her shoes on in the cloakroom. 'Chop chop', he'd said, standing there with his arms folded and a frown on his face. And I don't know why, but I'd felt like punching him. I'd only been there a couple of weeks, and it just seemed such a mean thing to say to a wee girl struggling with her shoes. 'Chop chop' was what people in authority said. It was what my old Brown Owl had barked at me on Brownie nights when I'd taken too long – I'd always taken too long – getting out the papier mâché toadstool for the fairy ring. 'Chop chop, Luisa McKenzie!' she'd used to say, clapping her hands.

I'd once heard Mr Ellis tell Emily to pick her feet up, too, when she'd tripped in the playground.

If you picked your feet up, Emily, that kind of thing wouldn't happen.

He certainly never helped her with her shoe buckles,

or commiserated for long over her bleeding knees. That was my job, or Mrs Baxter's, or some other woman who happened to be around.

'He's quite pleasant underneath it all,' Mrs Baxter had told me once, damning him with faint praise. She often did that, when speaking about the parents. 'A few weeks ago,' she'd added, 'Mr Ellis donated a fair stash of his own money to the school library.'

Yes, he had *personally* provided the cash for several new *Biff and Chip* books, as well as a series of hardbacks about the universe.

'I think he spent over £100 in total,' she'd said.

'Bit of a dark horse, then,' I'd replied.

I still couldn't think of Mr Ellis as a generous person, though, or even as someone who particularly liked books. But then, there were a lot of people at St Luke's who were surprising. And in any case, I no longer trusted my ability to judge character.

*

Just inside the school gates was a large wooden board upon which were listed the school's Golden Rules. All the primary schools had them. I used to read them as I hurried in every morning. I hurried because I was nearly always late. But I still read them – the rules – instinctively, compulsively, the way I read the backs of cereal packets at breakfast, as if they might mysteriously have changed overnight. They never had, of course.

We are honest!
We are kind!
We are patient!
We are fair!

It seemed to me that you could put a 'not' in every one of these statements and they would still work. The children mostly ignored them, anyway. Especially the bigger boys trading football cards in the playground. Really, those rules were about as meaningful as my old high school motto – *Per Ardua ad Astra* – had been. Which had been no help at all. I was already nineteen by now, and I had not risen through adversity to the stars. *You know*, I sometimes felt like saying to Mrs Crieff, *after I flunked all my exams last year it was either a job here, or working as a sous-chef, or being a florist: those were really the only options available to me!* And Catering had almost won, in fact: I liked cooking. But on the day I'd signed up at my local training college I just hadn't been able to picture myself standing behind a huge aluminium tin of mashed potato, a hairnet on my head; or stirring a great vat of gravy in some two-star hotel. So a classroom assistant was what I had become. It was as if somebody had lifted me, like a little Playmobil figure, out of the life I'd once envisaged and plonked me down again in the wrong setting. *There you are, Miss McKenzie.* And they'd put me in the kindergarten! They'd put me in the school! – when I'd actually wanted to be in the artist's studio with the easel, or in the cafe with the ice-cream sundaes, or at least sitting in the little cinema with a friend and a bag of popcorn. I wasn't even wearing the right kinds of *clothes* any more – I was wearing strappy sandals and a cheesecloth shirt and stripy linen trousers! I was wearing kindly, slightly dowdy clothes appropriate for someone twice my age! – when once, a few months earlier, I'd have dressed head to toe in black. And just a few years before *that*, I'd have been wearing a blue and white striped dress and been at primary school myself.

I used to try to have mature, teacherly conversations with Mrs Baxter, or to crack knowing jokes with the lollipop man, but quite often I just used to find myself saying all the wrong things and hurrying on. Likewise, I used to try to be in by 8.30, but sometimes I was not in till nearly nine, and then I used to have to run, breaking one of our own Golden Rules in the process. Classroom assistants were supposed to be calm, dignified people who always walked and knew just the right, encouraging things to say to the children. But I was not; I did not: I was not a good example at all.

'Good morning, everyone,' I would say brightly when I arrived, slightly out of breath, at the classroom door. And the children would all look up from their little tables.

'Good Moorr-ning, Miss McKenn-zie,' they would reply in the droning note that schoolchildren have used down the ages. And because the use of first names was frowned upon, for some reason I could never work out.

'Ah: Miss McKenzie,' Mrs Baxter would add, a little

curtly, like a big, irked robin, from her side of the room. Mrs Baxter and I worked together, Monday to Friday, seven hours a day, and it could be a bit of a trial, for both of us. We inhabited a Portakabin at the far side of the playground, with our class of twenty-nine. To get there you had to walk the length of the school, past the secretary's office and the medical room, past Mrs Crieff's office, through the dinner hall, past the gym, up and down three short flights of steps and then back out again into the playground. Then you had to walk past the bike shed, past a bin shaped like a frog and the lone silver birch tree, and up a ramp.

Welcome to Our Classroom, said a sign when you eventually got there. It was stuck to the Portakabin's front door. *Today we are talking about*, it added, in smaller letters; and beneath this sentence Mrs Baxter would sometimes stick a label with a word on it, often quite an abstract one like 'sunshine' or 'happiness' or 'holidays'. Less often, we would talk about things like 'frogs' or 'trees' or 'shoes'. I remember that we were looking at colours that term, that particular summer term, and that last fortnight, for some reason, was yellow. This was an opinion I disagreed with, being one of those people who attributed different colours to different things. That fortnight to me, for instance, had so far been a kind of greyish-mauve.

Inside the classroom there was a smell of plasticine and sun-warmed milk and plastic plates. There was a rectangular fish tank on a shelf, the water a little murky and containing three small, orange fish. Ranged around the windowsills were twenty-nine yogurt pots each containing a yellowing, overheated plant. Blu-tacked to the walls were pieces of work that Mrs Baxter and I had deemed to be of interest in some way over the course of that term, and worthy of display.

Letter to an Alien, one group of pictures was entitled. We had done outer space in May.

Dear Alien
    I am John. I lik the culr yellow. I am six. Wat is lif lik on yur planet?

There were several other sheets of paper too, as you headed further into the room. Some of them were funny, and some could make your stomach suddenly flip over with a strange kind of sadness.

Ones I had a coin and I spent it –

it said beneath a display entitled *Discoveries We Have Made.*

Ones I wen to Afrika and I saw a jiraffe
Ones I saw a man who was bald.

(*Is this kind, Spike?* Mrs Baxter had written under the bald-man sentence. I'd stuck it up anyway, because it had made me laugh.)

The children's coat pegs were in three rows, just to the left of a small collection of wooden furniture we called the Home Corner. Each child had a peg there, with their name above it and a picture of an animal beneath. I don't know who'd decided on the animals – who'd thought that Sam Bridges should be given a hippo, or Emily Ellis a bear. That was just the way it was. On my first day in post the previous autumn, I'd had to help the children locate their names. There were a lot of names, and I couldn't imagine how I would ever learn them all. Had Miss Ford learned them all? Or was that one of the ways in which she had failed? Mrs Baxter had made it easy for me, though. She'd written them all down in marker pen on a sheet of sticky labels, and all I'd had to do was pair them up with the children and stick them onto their jumpers.

'Here's *you*! Here's your *name*!' I'd exclaimed brightly, as if I was having a lot of fun; and I'd peeled the labels off the backing sheet and stuck them on.

'You've put mine on upside down,' a little boy had observed.

'So I have!' I'd continued, seamless and upbeat. And I'd peeled the sticker straight off again and put it back on the right way up. Some of the children could read already and some of them couldn't: that was one of the first things I hadn't anticipated, as a classroom assistant.

'That's better,' the little boy had said, whose name, I'd discovered, was John Singer: a plain name to suit his plainness of speech. 'But why am I a tortoise?'

'Sorry?'

He pointed to the picture he'd been allocated beneath

his coat peg: a cartoonish pale-green creature beneath a shell, with two timidly bulging eyes.

'Most other people have got bears and lions and elephants,' he said. He was taller than the other children, a bit older perhaps, and lankier-limbed. His hair was very straight across his forehead. He was wearing glasses, and to help keep them on he had a Band-Aid over the bridge of his nose.

'Why am I a tortoise?' he said.

'Well . . .' I replied. My mind was a blank. I was not used to speaking to six-year-olds; to crouching at a helpful eye level and being the one with all the answers.

'Maybe,' John said, 'it's because my mum has a tortoise. She's got a Russian tortoise called Tolstoy.'

'Ha!' I said. *A six-year-old who knew about Tolstoy!*

'Maybe Mrs Baxter knows about my mum's tortoise.'

'Yes,' I replied. 'Maybe that's why.'

Although having a tortoise as a pet is frowned on nowadays, isn't it? I felt like adding. *I wouldn't tell Mrs Crieff about Tolstoy if I were you: she might confiscate him.*

I remember that John Singer had sighed then, and looked again at the tortoise picture. Perhaps he was thinking about his mother, happy at home, gazing into some fern-filled tortoise tank.

'I don't really mind being a tortoise,' he said.

'Good,' I replied.

But I couldn't help wondering if such things, such arbitrary decisions – a picture above a name – might sometimes have a kind of resonance in a person's life.

Maybe John Singer would grow up guarded and introspective, just because someone had once stuck a picture of a tortoise above his coat peg.

'How are we getting on, Miss McKenzie?' a voice asked suddenly, making me jump, and I looked up. It was Mrs Crieff, precipitating herself through the doorway of the Portakabin. She never knocked on doors.

'Yes,' I said, still kneeling, paralysed for a second at the shock of her appearance, 'we're getting on fine, thanks, Mrs Crieff.'

And I remember feeling, even on that very first morning, that I'd said the wrong thing. That I *was*, in some way, wrong.

Mrs Crieff gazed at me. She had silvery hair, cut in an origami-sharp bob. Her blouse was olive green. Her eyes were the palest grey.

'Great,' she said.

'John and I were –'

'I see,' Mrs Crieff ploughed on. 'So. Getting to know everyone's name OK.'

'Yes,' I croaked. I wondered what else to say.

'I was just thinking,' I said finally, 'that there's a lot of gemstone names in this class, aren't there?'

Because, actually, there were. There were several gems amongst the girls that year, including a Ruby, a Jade, two Ambers and a Topaz.

'Gemstone names?' said Mrs Crieff. Mrs Crieff was known, amongst the parents, to be *one of the best Heads in Edinburgh*. It was just a fact. It used to make me think of the French Revolution, and all those heads tumbling into baskets. 'Gemstones?' she mused.

'Yes,' I said, my voice strangely high and upbeat suddenly; it did not seem to belong to me.

Mrs Crieff considered for a moment, her expression a little pained. She sometimes looked as if she couldn't imagine ever having a real reason to speak to you. Maybe only if you were someone offering her something, like a shop assistant or an air hostess: maybe she'd ask you for a box of matches in a corner shop, or a packet of peanuts on a flight to Bruges.

'Yes, I suppose we *have* got quite a few gems this year,' she conceded after a short pause. 'Quite a little jewellery box . . .'

Beside me, John Singer sighed wearily. Mrs Crieff ignored this.

'Morning, Morag,' she observed instead to Mrs Baxter, who was standing a few feet away, a box of Octons in her hands. And without waiting for her to reply, she swept back out of the Portakabin.

There were no Beryls in the class, of course, I thought, as I watched the door close behind her. No berylliums. Or even Agates. It was funny, how some gemstones could fall right out of favour.

*

I'd been sacked from the only other job I'd ever had, the previous spring: I'd been booted out of a gift shop called Moonchild. And along with various other things that had happened to me that past year or so, I'd found this a difficult thing to take on board. Moonchild had only been a *gift shop*, after all! It had only been a hippy gift shop located in a basement off the High Street and it was supposed to have been a doddle, working there – the kind of job girls like me were supposed to do with their eyes shut. I'd worked there Tuesday to Saturday, from two in the afternoon to six in the evening, and sometimes we only got seven or eight customers the whole afternoon; tourists, mainly, who would stroll in with their cameras and hats and rustling rain macs, look slightly baffled and stroll out again. I'd imagined, briefly, that I might have been happy there; that I might have found the place that was right for me. All day I would be submerged beneath a gently forgiving fog of patchouli and rose oil and joss sticks, and it would follow me, that scent, even after I'd locked up for the night; it would trail after me, like Pig-Pen's little dust cloud. The shop had been filled with soothing, forgiving sounds, too: with the jangle of silvery wind-chimes and the clatter of bamboo ones; with the splashing of the little stone fountain my boss Sondrine switched on every morning; with 70s folk music on tape. I spent my time standing behind the counter listening to Joni Mitchell and Steeleye Span ('All around my hat,' Steeleye Span sang in their robust way, 'I will wear the green wi-hi-llow . . .'), and occasionally selling a tie-dyed blouse or a mood ring or a sea urchin. The sea urchins stood in a display cabinet, behind a small hand-written sign:

Pretty to look at,
Lovely to hold,
But if you break it,
Consider it SOLD!

There was something ironic about that sign, but I didn't like to think about it too much.

'Hi there,' I'd say to the people wandering in, and I'd let them browse. I was discreet, as shop assistants go. Un-pushy. The main problem was, I'd kept over-ringing the till: there was always a discrepancy at the end of the day between what was in the till and what it said on the receipt.

'I can't understand how you can be doing this, Luisa,' Sondrine had mourned at the end of one afternoon, her wide, smooth brow furrowed with concern. 'I don't get how you can be so . . .' – and she paused – '. . . unfocused about everything.'

'I've not always been unfocused,' I replied. Because I hadn't. I'd once had a mind that operated with clarity and purpose. It was just that something, during my last few months at high school, had begun to unravel. 'Well, I'm sorry, Luisa, I really am,' Sondrine had continued, her frown deepening. 'There were also', she added regretfully, 'those two . . . breakages the other week. Those sea urchins you broke . . .' Which was quite true. In the three months I had worked at Moonchild, I was the only one who'd actually broken any of the sea urchins. None of the customers had broken anything. 'I mean,' Sondrine continued sorrowfully, 'I just can't really overlook things like that any more.'

And then she'd sacked me. She was less of a hippy than her appearance suggested. And for a while after that, my downward spiral had gathered pace. I'd returned home that evening in my invisible cloak of patchouli and incense, gone up to my bedroom and just sat looking out through the Velux window at the sky. I don't know how long I sat there. Hours, maybe. Days. *All around my hat*, I thought, *I will wear the green willow*. It was only when my mother, a few weeks later, suggested I do some sort of course – something *vocational* in nursery nursing, teacher training – 'Something, sweetheart,' she'd said heavily, 'that might get you back on *track*' – that things had begun to alter. Not necessarily, though, in the way she'd imagined.

*

I'd had to report to Mrs Crieff's office mid-morning, I remember, on my first day in post. It was the same morning we'd had our discussion about gemstones; a Monday, November, and raining a cold grey rain.

'Ah: Luisa,' she'd said when I turned up at her door. And she seemed oddly pleased to see me, as if our earlier conversation had never happened; she'd already moved on from *that* conversation. 'So: welcome!' she proclaimed, somewhat hammily, and she stepped back and ushered me into her office.

'Thanks,' I said, feeling quite cowed, all over again, by the slightly military green of the blouse she was wearing, and also by that silvery-grey hair, cut with such precision and as coarse as a badger's pelt.

We both headed across the room and sat down at either side of her desk. Mrs Crieff adjusted the angle of her chair and smiled across at me.

'OK,' she said.

And then she proceeded to go over what was expected of me in the job. The dos and the don'ts. It was like a sort of presentation, the kind you might use an overhead projector for. She used a lot of words like *positive, upbeat, role model, happy, nurturing.*

'Yes,' I interjected occasionally, 'I see . . .'

Although I didn't, really. I didn't think any of those words applied to me. And Mrs Crieff did not refer to my predecessor at all, not once, the whole time I was sitting there: Susan Ford appeared to be *persona non grata.* I supposed that I represented a clean slate.

'Super,' Mrs Crieff encouraged from time to time, after I had begun to speak about the many ways in which I was hoping to excel in the role of classroom assistant. 'Smashing.' But I couldn't help thinking of all the ways in which I might not be super or smashing (or perhaps only in a sea-urchin sense); of all the ways I might, in the coming months, fail to impress. And I regretted the fact that I was not a girl who threw herself into things: I'd never been that sort of girl. I wasn't going to be like the resilient Mrs Baxter with her songs and games; or the metropolitan Mr Temple in P6, whose merry innuendos I'd already encountered at my interview; or the lollipop man with his jokes and his mad yellow jacket.

There were plenty of people like that at St Luke's, I could see; people who knew the words to things; who cracked jokes and who knew who they were. But I was not going to be one of them.

'Now. This', Mrs Crieff said somewhere towards the end of our conversation, and handing me a green piece of paper, 'is an information sheet Mrs Baxter and I have drawn up.'

'Right'

'It should hopefully give you some idea of what's . . .' – she paused, and looked briefly and regretfully at the blank rectangle where I suspected Miss Ford's picture had been – '. . . expected of you, in the role.'

'Thanks,' I said, taking the paper from her and looking down at it. The information it contained appeared in the form of a grid – a kind of spreadsheet involving a lot of elongated rectangles, with headings shaded in pale grey. Some of the words on the far right of the sheet had disappeared, or been chopped in half.

Classroom Assistant Post
St Luke's Primary School

The role of Classroom Assistant is many and vario
One day you may be planting seedlings in our wildlif
garden

[this was, I already knew, a set of wooden barrels in the playground]

the next you might be preparing costu
for the school nativity play. Life here a
St Luke's is a –

– and here the text ended abruptly, and was replaced by
three columns of words

Classroom Assistant: Daily Tasks.
Supervising individual/group activity
Observing individual/group activity
Talking with individual/group
Referring to teacher's plans
Recording observations
Housekeeping tasks
Preparation of resources, materials
Preparing snacks
Displaying children's work

'How does that look to you?' Mrs Crieff asked, her head
cocked to one side. And, briefly, she closed her eyes. She
was one of those people who closed their eyes at crucial
points in conversations.

'Yes,' I said, 'it seems . . .'

It seemed to me like a cross between being a secret
agent and an overbearing mother. I moved on to the next
list.

Ideal Classroom Assistant Responses and Strengths

Responses:
Give support
Explain
Praise
Smile
Encourage
Listen

Strengths:
Diplomacy
Ability to work on own initiative
Mediating skills
Punctuality

I was aware of Mrs Crieff opening her eyes again and looking at me. This list seemed a little more normal at least – I could *smile*, I could say *'Well done'* – although the third and final column, entitled 'Managing Behaviour', was more worrying:

In instances of pupil dissent, the following methods should be applied.
  Return pupil to task in hand
  Intervene
  Ask for quiet
  Reprimand
  Refer to teacher
  Remove from room

'Hmm,' I said.

I couldn't recall when I'd ever *intervened*. I'd certainly never removed anyone from a room! It was the sort of thing I could only imagine bouncers and police officers doing.

'You see, one of the things Mrs Baxter and I thought would be important this year,' Mrs Crieff said, smiling her curious smile, '– because we felt this would provide a better sense of the children's own learning experience – is to give you your *own* set of tasks. Your *own* challenges. Your own *project*, if you like . . .'

'Right,' I said, a small wisp of apprehension flickering up my chest, like a tiny plume of smoke.

Mrs Crieff stopped talking and looked at me. I looked down at her desktop. It was the sort you might imagine a Newton's Cradle perched upon, and an intercom for communicating with your secretary. It seemed to represent achievement, in some way.

'So, tell me,' she prompted. 'Looking at this list, Luisa: can you tell me if there are any particular skills here you would like to develop? To improve upon? Which could be your first, if you like, *goal*?'

I refocused on the piece of paper.

'A *goal* . . .' I said. I thought of the netball posts at my old high school, the school I had left under a cloud, and the words seemed to lift off the page and float around.

'Well,' I said, 'my housekeeping skills could probably do with a bit of . . .'

'Ha!' Mrs Crieff interrupted, a little mirthlessly. 'Now, when we say *housekeeping skills*, Luisa, we're not expecting you to do the hoovering and mop the floors! That's the *janitor's* job, of course. That's Mr Raeburn's job.'

'Mr *Raeburn*?' I asked.

'Yes,' said Mrs Crieff, sternly. 'Housekeeping skills,' she continued, 'in a classroom context, are things like tidying up the work areas. Making sure the scissors go back in the box: that sort of thing. No, Mrs Baxter and I were thinking more in terms of *personal skills*. Things that can be developed in your work as a classroom assist- ant. That we can perhaps . . . help you to foster, Luisa. Professionally.'

'Of course. Well . . .'

I could feel my heart beating. I wondered about the things Miss Ford might have highlighted as personal skills. I cast my eyes down the list again.

Diplomacy
Ability to work on own initiative
Mediating skills
Punctuality

Well, I was already being diplomatic: being diplomatic seemed to be more of a hindrance than a skill. And I didn't know what was meant by mediating skills. And I was not a punctual person: I seemed, lately, to have lost that ability.

'Ability to work on my own initiative?' I suggested, like someone querying a dish on a menu.

'OK,' Mrs Crieff replied in an upbeat voice, and writing this down. 'Super. So, could we make that your first goal? Your first little aim in the post? Your project, if you like, for the rest of term, leading up to Christmas? Which will be upon us, I'm afraid to say, in the blink of an eye.'

'I know,' I said, and we both fell silent. I thought of Christmas – of the roast turkey my parents and I would be sharing with my grandmother and my Uncle Rob and Aunty Doreen and all their successful children – and I suddenly felt very tired, as if I could just lie down on Mrs Crieff's wiry, pan-scourer floor tiles and go to sleep. Mrs Crieff was rising from her seat now, though. 'So . . .' she was saying, moving forwards and upwards and knocking together her plastic files and bits of paper, like a newscaster coming to the end of a bulletin. I took this as my cue to stand up and pull my coat on; to begin my return back down to the Portakabin. 'So, I'm intrigued,' Mrs Crieff said as we both approached the door. 'What was it about working in a school, Luisa, that particularly appealed to you? I didn't get a chance to ask you at our interview because it was all such a . . . rush. However.'

And she stopped talking.

'Well,' I replied. I was aware of all the thoughts in my head taking off and scattering into the air, like a flock of startled birds. I felt bereft of anything to tell Mrs Crieff about my interest in the job; anything that was not, in some way, a lie. *It appeals to me because it fills an absence*, I felt like saying; *it's an alternative to doing what I was supposed to have done.* I looked out through the window and down at the school playground, at the flimsy grey-walled Portakabin to which I would be returning. The lollipop man was slowly battling past it in his fluorescent yellow jacket, defying the November winds with his *Stop! Children* sign.

Mrs Crieff was peering at me. The smile on her face had become slightly stiffer.

'Well,' I heard myself say, 'I suppose I thought, for one thing, that it might be a way I could use my interest in . . . art'

'*Your interest in art?*' Mrs Crieff repeated, bug-eyed, making me instantly regret what I'd just said. Why had I mentioned art? I'd not intended to mention it at all! I might as well have dragged in all kinds of other ambitions I'd once had and had managed to screw up in some way! – Love! Freedom! A career! Life in another city! *There are any number of reasons why I'm sitting in your office talking to you, Mrs Crieff,* I could have told her, *and none of them bear any relation to the job.*

I began a new tack.

'I was going to do geography, you see, at university,' I said. 'That had been the plan for quite a while. And then . . . I changed my mind again, at the last minute, and thought I'd do . . .'

Mrs Crieff's eyes seemed circular with amazement. My voice: my voice was like a dried-out reed stem, small and hollow and thin. I thought of my days spent working in Moonchild, and of my days at school before Moonchild. And I felt like apologising for wasting everyone's time and running out to catch the bus home.

'Thought you'd do what?' asked Mrs Crieff.

Oh God.

'I just realised', I whispered, 'that I'd rather do some-thing, y'know, more real and . . . grounded . . . and . . .' – I could feel myself sweating – '. . . something . . .' I floundered.

'. . . *more grounded than art?*' Mrs Crieff boomed. Because really, what was there that was more grounded than art? What was more real than a pencil and a piece of paper and drawing what was in front of you? Art *was* the ground! – it was the patch of ground I never should have left!

'Yeah,' I said. I gulped, and quickly wiped the palms of my hands against my thin cotton skirt. It was a new *working-girl* skirt I had chosen with my mother in Top-shop, and I didn't know now why I'd bothered. Clothes I bought for special occasions had a bad habit of letting me down. 'Yes,' I continued. 'More grounded, in some ways, anyway. I thought working with children would be more . . . real.'

'Oh well: fair enough,' Mrs Crieff chirruped, oddly content with this mangled explanation, 'And I'm *de-lighted* to hear you have an artistic streak, Luisa! That's just what we need in our classroom helpers! I also think', she added, 'that you'll find working with the children here is very *real*.'

'Whe—' I began.

'Very good,' Mrs Crieff concluded. 'Super. So: back to work! And we'll meet up again in a couple of weeks, at the beginning of December.'

'Yes,' I said. 'Ha ha. Thank you very much.'

'By the way,' Mrs Crieff added, as a kind of after-thought – like Columbo turning in the doorway before dropping some bombshell about a murder – 'did you know we're neighbours?'

'Sorry?'

'We live on the same street. I'm at number 25.'

'Sorry?'

'I live on the same street as you,' Mrs Crieff articulated, patiently. 'At number 25 on our street.'

'Really?' I said.

This information filled me with a new kind of despair. I tried to think which house was number 25, but I couldn't: all the houses on our street had suddenly merged into a kind of blur in my head.

'I just noticed it, when I was looking over your CV. *Oh*, I thought: *Miss McKenzie lives on my street!* I'm just down the hill from you. You're the house with all those rose bushes, aren't you?'

'Yes,' I said. 'My mum . . . likes roses. Especially the scented ones.'

'Indeed. So, I'll be keeping an eye on you after school as well!'

'Ha ha,' I said. 'Yes.'

I felt slightly sick. I lifted my shoulder bag from where it had been dangling on the back of my chair and walked across the room to Mrs Crieff's big wooden door. I opened it and headed straight downstairs, down three flights, and progressed along a pale-grey corridor and in-to a room in the basement, marked *Female Staff Toilets*. Some woman I didn't know, a short, stout woman who was, I supposed, a colleague, was standing there at the hand-dryers.

'Wet day,' she sighed, shaking water from her fingers.

'Not dry.'

And I could see my new life at St Luke's acquiring a sense of eternity, a great expanse of time billowing and spiralling like a sea haar into the future. I could see my life sliding along in a succession of terms and holidays, of work-time and lunch-time and home-time and observations about the weather. Already I envied my predecessor Susan Ford, and her decision to leave. But I couldn't do that; I couldn't just leave, because I'd already left a school once – and I knew that on the other side of leaving there was sometimes just a big gaping hole.

'Ah, well,' said the woman, 'upwards and onwards. Or Golden Time won't happen at all.'

And she walked out.

There was a smell of disinfectant in the toilets, a medicinal sort of smell that reassured and upset me at the same time. I went and stood for a while by the big white Twyford sink and the paper-towel dispensers and the sign that said *Now Wash Your Hands*. It was cold, the window wide open in the middle of November.

*

The funny thing is, I couldn't remember much, that year, about my own days at primary school. I couldn't recall the routines or the rooms, or even the teachers at Rose Hill Primary. Only a few recollections would surface sometimes, from the maelstrom of chalk-clouded blackboards and school lunches and Chinese burns and cheery songs played on the guitar. I did have two quite vivid memories, though: the first was of falling over once in the playground and watching, amazed, as two circles of blood bloomed like flowers through the knees of my red tights; and the second was a vision of a wooden painting easel. That easel, in particular, lingered in my mind. Someone had set it up for me one day and placed a row of plastic paint pots in the tray beneath it. And I remember that I'd just stood and looked at it. I must have been five; and I'd just looked and looked at it. The paints had been red, yellow and blue, and there'd been a thick paintbrush sticking through the lid of each pot. I recalled a kind of smock, too – blue, with rolled-up, elasticated sleeves – and somebody taller than me placing a paintbrush into my hand.

'What are you going to paint, Luisa?' a voice had asked me from some high, cloudy place.

'I'm going to paint a rabbit,' I'd replied.

I was very excited about that, I remembered: about the smock and the paintbrush, and the idea of a rabbit. About painting a rabbit into existence. The voice, I supposed, must have belonged to my very first teacher, a woman named Miss Gazall. Although Miss Gazall was actually a lot woollier in my memory than the easel and the paints. All I remembered about her was that she'd worn red a lot, and her hair had been as straight and black as an Egyptian pharaoh's. And at the end of the year she'd pinned a metal badge on my cardigan that said 'Well Done'.

I had stretched out my cardigan and tucked down my chin to peer at it.

WELL DONE

It had seemed like a kind thing to say.

2

It was much later that school year – a Sunday afternoon, late June, when I was shopping at Safeways with
my mother – that I bumped into someone I'd once
known at school. A girl named Stella Muir. Stella had
once been a friend of mine: we'd both attended St Cath-
erine's of Siena High, state school on a slope on the
south side of town; and for a time we'd been oddly
close. For a few months we'd been inseparable. We
hadn't seen each other for a long time by then, though,
the day we bumped into each other in Safeways. Not
for almost a year.

'Lulu!' I heard someone say, and I turned from where
I was standing (pretty vacantly, it has to be said, beside
the cheese counter), and there she was.

'Hi!' Stella continued, in the bright, strangely accusa-
tory way she had, 'How are *you*? What have you done to
your *hair*?'

Which was a fair enough question, as my hair was
quite a different colour from when Stella had last seen
me. Generally it was mouse-brown, but I'd just dyed it.
I'd dyed it the day before, in fact. *Marron foncé*, the dye
was called: *a lustrous auburn shade that will bring out
the beauty of your natural colour.*

'Hi, Stella,' I said. There were a lot of reasons why I was not pleased to bump into Stella.

'So: Wow! I mean: God! Did you get it done professionally?'

'Sorry?'

'Your hair.' Stella's eyes were greener than I remembered, and her jaw more angular. 'Are you going for a kind of . . . punk look?'

'Oh,' I said, putting my hand up to my hair. It felt coarse, like something lacquered. It did not have the subtle quality I had been hoping for: it was really a lot more pink than that. I could feel myself blushing, chameleon-like, to match it.

'Well, I just thought it was time for a change,' I said. 'It's OK having . . . colourful hair if you work in a primary school. People don't mind you looking . . . bright.'

Stella gazed at me. Her own hair was as naturally blonde as it always had been, I couldn't help noticing, but now it seemed even smoother and more perfectly styled. Clipped prettily against the side of her forehead was a silvery hair slide; a hard, glittering rectangle of diamanté.

'I thought you were working in a shop,' she said.

'Not any more,' I said. 'I work in a school now.'

'A school? How funny.'

'Hmm,' I replied, regretting the new territory I'd just dragged us both into.

'So, what are you doing there? In the school?'

'Being a classroom assistant,' I replied, in a strangely breezy voice.

31

Stella didn't say anything for a moment.

'Well, that's unexpected,' she said finally.

'Yes.'

'Which school?'

'St Luke's.'

'Really?' Stella replied, in a remote sort of way. She seemed not to have an opinion about St Luke's; maybe she hadn't even heard of it. 'So what's it like there, then?'

I glanced across at my mother, who was standing a few feet away from us, deliberating over the yogurt display. My mother, over the past year, had shown a lot of forbearance about the peculiar, altered course of my life. A lot of tolerance and kindness. She was a kinder, better, wiser person than I would ever be; which suddenly irritated me more than I could articulate. She was wearing her Scholl sandals that day because it was June and hot outside, and her blue flowery blouse. *Oh, Mum.* And I wanted to run across and hug her, and at the same time criticise her for her fashion sense.

'Well,' I said to Stella in a low voice, feeling, somehow, the need to whisper, 'it's OK. It's not too bad.'

'Cool. So things have worked out OK then? After . . .'

'Yeah. St Luke's is a great place to work,' I interrupted, a curious tightness in my throat. 'As it turns out. I mean, if you're a classroom assistant you get to spend most of the time playing with plasticine anyway, and chucking glitter around . . .'

I trailed off. This statement was not even true. *I spend hardly any time*, I thought, *playing with plasticine or glit-*

ter. I spent a lot more time at St Luke's filling in Mrs Crieff's record sheets and answering strange questions about God and death and the colour of the sky. That was what little children asked you, I'd discovered. '*Miss McKenzie, when people die'*, one little boy had said recently, '*do they go to heaven in their minds?*' '*In their minds?*' I'd replied, intrigued. *Do they go to heaven in their minds?* And I hadn't been sure how to answer.

'So,' Stella said. She looked oddly irked: she had the sort of expression someone has when they're querying the price on a till receipt. 'Well, that's cool, about your job: that you still get a chance to do arty stuff. Because you've always been arty, haven't you?' She glanced at my pink hair again. 'You were always doing all those . . . wacky pictures. In Art.'

'Yes,' I said, 'I was'; and at the mention of Art – that lost thing in my life – I felt something strange happening in the space behind my ribcage. A sensation of vertigo. A kind of closing in. It was the same feeling I got if I stood at the edge of a tall building or a cliff, or sat in the swinging carriage of a Ferris wheel at the fairground. And I recalled a paragraph in a school textbook that I'd queried once during a history lesson: '*Palaeolithic man was an accomplished artist'*, it had begun, '*who, for leisure and enjoyment, would paint pictures on the walls of his cave . . .*' 'But excuse me', I'd said, putting up my hand, 'what about Palaeolithic woman?' Because I'd had more confidence in those days; and because maybe it was Palaeolithic *woman* who'd painted pictures on the walls of the cave! Maybe it was *the women* who'd been the

33

painters, while the men had just gone out and dug traps for animals to fall into! Had nobody thought of that?!

'Well,' I said now to Stella, 'I suppose Art was not to be.'

And we both stopped talking and looked down at Stella's wire basket, as if it might hold something more useful for us to talk about. But it just contained a circle of Coeur de Lion Camembert, some bottles of beer and a packet of John West prawns.

'It's funny,' Stella said. 'I never would have pictured you working in a school, Lulu. You're the last person I'd have thought would end up teaching.'

'Yes,' I conceded. It *was* quite a ridiculous state of affairs. It would once have seemed about as likely to me as parachuting out of a plane.

'I –' I began.

'Oh, there's your *mum*!' Stella interjected, looking over my shoulder. 'Oh, that's so *sweet*, Luisa, going on a shopping trip with your mum! I always liked your mum,' she added rather wistfully. She seemed to have placed me into some kind of category now. *Finished*, perhaps it was called. Or *History*. And I realised how slight our friendship had been; how it had never really been a friendship at all. How it had probably been something else entirely.

'I usually help with the shopping on Sunday,' I heard myself saying. 'My parents and I halve the bill,' I added – a small, private fact I immediately regretted revealing. 'Seeing as I'm still hanging around at home rent-free,' I continued (*shut up! shut up!*), 'it's, you know, the least I . . .'

34

'So the salary's not bad then, at work?' said Stella. She'd always had that ability: to cut to the chase.

'Not bad, no. It could be worse. It's an income. How about you anyway, Stella? How are things going at vet school?'

Because Stella's career, unlike mine, had gone according to plan after we'd left school. It had gone neatly in the right direction. While I'd spent the past year or so of my life selling wind-chimes or sitting at low tables grappling with glue sticks, Stella had been studying veterinary science at university. It was what she'd always wanted to do. It was a profession she had been working towards since the age of twelve.

'Yeah, it's great,' Stella said, smiling at me – or rather, not at me, but at some unseen, unknown thing that was better. 'It's fab,' she said. 'It's brill.'

'Great, that's . . .'

'I'm just here buying stuff for dinner tonight, actually,' she added, 'for my body buddies.'

I looked at her. 'Your what?'

'My body buddies. My dissecting team. That's what we call each other.'

Stella's voice had adopted the slightly combative tone I remembered from school.

'There are six of us,' she continued, tucking a strand of hair around her left ear, 'and we're all really close. Even the lecturers. When we first got together last year we all really hit it off, so we decided we'd make dinner for each other.'

'I see,' I said, even though I didn't, at all. I didn't

understand how liking people meant you had to cook dinner for them.

'One of us cooks for the others,' Stella said, 'every Sunday. Once every six weeks. That's the way it works. It's this kind of rota. It's brilliant.'

'Even the lecturers?' I asked. It sounded complicated, having buddies; having friends in rotas. 'Do the lecturers cook dinner, too?'

'. . . and it's my turn tonight,' Stella said, ignoring this. And then she stopped talking.

'Well,' I ploughed on, 'that makes sense, working in a team like that. And being friends. That sounds very . . .' – I couldn't think of the right word – '. . . organised.'

'Yeah, it's great,' Stella confirmed. 'I mean, five Sundays in a row, you don't have to make dinner. Plus: your social life's sorted.'

She smiled at me, and I wondered how else to respond. *Why would you want to eat dinner with people you'd spent all day dissecting animals with?* I considered saying. *And why did we ever think we were friends, Stella?*

'So did you get your hair dyed recently?' Stella asked.

'Yep. Yesterday. I did it myself. From a packet.'

'Really?'

'Hmm'

For some reason, I was suddenly very aware of the supermarket we were standing in. It seemed to have become rangier and whiter and more inane than usual. It was filled with a low kind of buzzing noise – a noise of boringly sensible human activity – and illuminated with a white, unreal glow. And the unreality of it all somehow suited the conversation Stella and I were having. It was as if we'd just encountered each other on some strange, nameless planet we'd both arrived at, and were no longer sure how to communicate with each other. On all the shelves and in all the display cabinets there were rows and rows of immaculate, attractive packages. Pristine, cellophane-wrapped packs of basmati rice and ramen noodles and polenta. Of Earl Grey tea and Lindt chocolate. And they were like Stella, those packages, I felt. They were well presented. They were going into people's baskets and trolleys and making themselves useful. Whereas I was like the stubbornly unwrapped lumps of celeriac. I was the sticks of pink rhubarb poking garishly out from the fruit crates.

Above our heads, at the level of the sprinklers and the secret-eye cameras, a woman's weary voice began, mantra-like, to drawl an instruction.

'Colleague announcement: would Donald Crawford please go to the staff office,' she sighed. 'Would Donald Crawford please go to the staff office . . .'

'Aren't they funny, those announcements?' I said. 'I always wonder about those, do you? I always wonder if Donald Crawford's maybe done something wrong.'

Stella regarded me.

'No,' she said, 'I never wonder that, actually, Luisa. I couldn't give a monkey's about people like Donald Crawford.'

'Oh,' I said.

And now my mother, still in a kind of trance by the yogurts, looked up, noticed me standing there with my former friend, looked momentarily flustered, and smiled.

'I'm going to say hello to your mum,' Stella proclaimed. 'Hi, Mrs McKenzie,' she called out.

'*Hello, Stella*!' my mother called back, sounding delighted – *maybe she* is *delighted*, I thought – and she pushed a small tub of Ski yogurt back onto the shelf and wheeled her trolley over to us.

'How are *you*, Stella?' she asked, arriving slightly rosy-cheeked, as if at the end of some bracing walk.

'I'm fine, thanks,' Stella said, politely.

'Long time no see.'

'Yes.' And she paused for a moment. We all did. Paused for thought.

'So I was just telling Luisa', Stella said, 'about this system I have with my body buddies.'

'Oh yes?' My mother looked a little worried.

'Yes,' I interrupted. 'Stella has these people called body buddies, Mum, that she meets up with every five weeks. They have dinner together every Saturday. One of them makes dinner for the other four. Isn't that a good idea?'

Stella shot me a look.

'We meet every *Sunday* night, in fact,' she said levelly. 'Today's *Sunday*, Luisa. And there are actually six of us. And we *meet* every day – we see each other every day, over our . . .' – and she stopped. It would have been funny, I thought, if she'd said 'over our dead bodies', but she didn't, quite. 'Anyway,' she said, 'the point is, we're all best pals. Your body buddies always are.'

And I'm not, I thought. *I'm not your best pal*. And I thought of two other friends I'd once had at school –

of Mary Wedderburn and Linda Daniels – older, truer friends I'd abandoned without a backward glance – and felt guilty.

My mother was standing there looking at Stella, her smile polite and kindly and also a little scared. Stella was a lot taller than her now, it occurred to me. I could remember a time when she had been shorter. She'd come round on a Shrove Tuesday once, when we'd first got to know each other, and had eaten pancakes with us, and been shorter.

'Well, it's lovely to see you, Stella,' my mother concluded. 'You're looking very well.'

'Thank you.'

But mainly Stella just looked irked, as if she didn't at all want to be standing in Safeways with a former schoolfriend and her homespun, Scholl-sandal-wearing mother. She was peering down into her basket again, as if some new item might magically have jumped into it since the last time she looked; or been spirited away.

'So, Luisa was telling me all about St Luke's,' she said.

'Was she?' my mother asked, pleased. Because she *was* pleased about my job. *It's the sort of thing that will lead on to other things,* she'd said when I'd first got it. Even though – as I'd pointed out – everything *did* lead on to other things. That was just what life was: a series of things leading on to other things.

'Yes,' my mother said now, 'well, it's a really . . .'

'Anyway,' Stella interrupted, 'I suppose I'd better get on with the shopping. I'm doing Thai fishcakes, for my sins,' she added – a statement that utterly depressed me,

39

because it was one of those cheerily bland things people say when they have run out of anything else. It never had anything to do with sins; it was just what people said.

'It's this really fiddly recipe,' Stella added as my mother smiled, said goodbye and wandered away with our trolley. 'It's got prawns in it. I don't know why I chose it now.'

'You didn't have to choose Thai fishcakes though, presumably,' I snapped, because I couldn't resist it suddenly, and it saddened me, to see my mother dismissed. 'I mean, presumably no one forced you to make Thai fishcakes, Stella?'

But she was already beginning to move on too, with her basket.

'Oh, and by the way, Stella,' I continued in a sudden rush, because I knew it was now or never, really, and I suspected I might never see her again anyway – the odds were against it – 'by the way,' I said, as my mother rounded a corner and disappeared down the cereals aisle, 'how's Ed?'

Stella stopped.

'Who?'

I looked her. *What do you mean, 'Who?'* I thought. *How do you mean, 'Who?'*

'Oh, you mean *Ed*!' Stella exclaimed. She was already several feet away from me and had to raise her voice slightly. 'Ed from school, you mean? Ed McRae?'

'Yes,' I said, feeling oddly light-headed. *Of course Ed from school, of course.* And I felt almost like a person who wasn't there at all any more: some hollow, husk-like thing, a waning moon, a dried pod of honesty. The super-market was very white and sad and celestial. 'I mean,' I said, 'are you and . . . Ed still . . .'

Stella looked slightly entertained.

'God, no!' she said. 'That's ancient history! That was never going to work. God! That was over a year ago! Have you still got a thing about Ed McRae?'

'Sorry?' I asked.

'That all ended ages ago. Practically as soon as we all left school! God, that was just a bit of a fling!'

Something curious was happening to my heart: a kind of blanching. My heart, as well as my head, had started to hurt.

'No, I haven't seen Ed for months!' Stella confirmed cheerfully. 'He's going out with some girl in Bristol now, anyway, as far as I know. Some fellow architect.'

I didn't know which words to form. Something felt as if it was falling away. 'It's funny,' I croaked eventually, 'be-cause last time I saw you, you were this great . . . item!'

'I *know*!' said Stella, heartily. She seemed to find the whole thing about Ed McRae quite amusing. 'Well, it was really lovely to see you,' she smiled. And she glanced upwards again, for the briefest of moments, at my mad pink hair. Maybe she was envisaging telling her body buddies about it over dinner. 'Glad to hear you're enjoy-ing St . . . thingummy's anyway, Lulu. St Luke's. I'll give you a ring. We should get together for a coffee. It would be nice to have a proper catch-up.'

And she legged it past the salads aisle, turned and dis-appeared. I feared we would probably bump into each other again, rounding the corner of the bread section or maybe even the oriental ready-meals, but she was not there, at the end of any aisle.

'What are body buddies?' my mother asked, as we stood at the checkout beside the little display of bagged sweets, waiting to put our shopping on the conveyor belt.

'I think they're people you hang out with at vet school,' I replied. I could feel my heart racing, the way it had once at the dentist's when I'd been given an injection of adrenaline. It was thudding, the pulse of it in my ears, like the hooves of a tiny, angry horse.

'People you hang out with at vet school?' my mother queried.

But I didn't want to tell her more precisely than that. My mother had a sweetness about her, a kind of faith. She had something, anyway, that I'd already lost. And I didn't want to distress her with images of small animals laid out stiff on a dissecting table. It was Sunday afternoon, and we were going home to eat tea, and tea was going to be what we usually had on Sundays: bread and cheese and crisps and vinegary beetroot and halved boiled eggs and slices of ham. It was not going to be Thai fishcakes and bottles of beer, it was going to be high tea, with cold cuts.

3

The thing about Ed McRae was, he had been an artist. Well, he'd been going to study architecture, but really he'd been an artist. He'd had a light, quick way of talking suggestive of spiritual wealth and material poverty. In the winter he'd used to wear fingerless gloves, and I imagined this was so he could carry on painting, even in the snow. I also thought he swigged Irn-Bru at lunch breaks because Irn-Bru was what he'd been brought up with – not because he was making some sort of ironic statement about the class system. That was one of the first mistakes I made about him.

We used to sit together in art lessons. Our surnames were next to each other in the register; it was never anything to do with destiny. Ed's drawings were very stark and intense, and he kept them in a transparent portfolio which had the words 'Naked Art' written across it. I didn't know what to make of that portfolio. I'd always just carried my pictures around in a black plastic thing which had been impossible to get the stretch of my arm around, and which had buckled shut with a snap. My mother had bought it for me in WH Smith's when I was fourteen. And there was just no comparison, really; already there was no point of comparison in our lives. You could see straight through Ed's portfolio to the perfect pictures it contained: it was like looking at the beating heart of a transparent little fish. It made me think of the fishes residing in a small, lugubrious aquatics shop near our house, called The Age of Aquarius. My own drawings were more colourful than Ed's, but they were not so accurate, or so nakedly displayed. I was just doing art, really, because I liked drawing pictures. That was all it had ever been about for me. Only now, of course, there was also the thrill of Ed McRae sitting beside me every Monday and Thursday, behind a row of castor-oil plants, in a building called the Arts Block.

'Hi,' Ed used to say when he arrived, always a little late, scrunching his long legs beneath the bench we shared.

'Hi,' I replied in a voice so casual it was almost inaudible.

'So, how's it going?'

'Yeah: fine.'

I was never sure what to say after that. A kind of haze descended. I would return to whatever it was I was drawing – some smudged charcoal picture of the view through the window; some big, wobbly still life in chalk, of the castor-oil plants. And I felt transparent, light as air, as if I might float up and out through the window into the sky. I liked feeling like that, though: it was when I was happiest. Above the classroom doorway, presiding like one of God's commandments, was a bare white poster displaying a quote by Henri Matisse. It said: *I wouldn't mind turning into a vermillion goldfish*. I wasn't sure what this was supposed to mean, but the fact that it had been stuck there like a totally sane statement made me happy.

'Got anything planned for the weekend?' Ed would ask me sometimes, expertly framing that week's *tableau* with his pencil, first vertically, then horizontally – and the normal functioning of my mind would go into a kind of freefall. I would feel myself gasping for breath.

'Yeah: you know, bits and pieces,' I would mumble. 'Might meet up with Stella or something on Saturday.'

'Who?'

'Stella Muir.'

'Oh yeah. Cool.'

'Yeah.'

And that was pretty much the extent of what I would say to him. Apart from something like, 'Could you pass me that craft knife, please?' Or: 'Have you got any green ink left?'

'Sure,' he'd reply, whizzing it across the table to me.

*

On art afternoons, Ed had nearly always worn a T-shirt that said *Life's a Bitch and Then You Die*. It was as if he had Life worked out: as if he already knew all its ironies. Even Death didn't seem too big a deal, to Ed McRae. He used to wear the T-shirt under his coat, which he kept buttoned up and only took off when he arrived in the classroom. Mr Carter turned a blind eye to it, preferring the truisms that were Blu-tacked to the walls:

Art is not what you see, but what you make others see.

Edgar Degas

To be an artist is to believe in life.

Henry Moore

Seen that attitude before, pal, Mr Carter looked as if he was thinking when he peered at Ed's T-shirt. *You don't know how many times I've clocked smart-arses like you.*

But I hadn't seen that attitude before. Ed's T-shirt, to me, had just seemed funny. Funny and fresh and strange, like the sentence about the vermillion fish. *Life's a Bitch and Then You Die!* Of course! It had struck me as *so* funny one afternoon, in fact, that it emboldened me to talk properly to Ed for the first time: it reminded me, I said, as we were walking together out of school and along the pavement – it just reminded me of something I'd read in history a few days earlier.

'Oh yeah?'

Yes: it was just something. That made me think of it.

'We were looking at famous last words, you see,' I'd continued, feeling myself blushing, 'and we came across this thing William Pitt the Younger was supposed to have . . .'

'Who?'

'Pitt the Younger . . . what he was supposed to have . . .'

'Oh yeah?'

'Yes.' I had to go on, now. 'Yeah, the very last thing he *said*, apparently, as he lay on his deathbed . . .'

46

'Which was?' Ed asked.

'"I think I could eat one of Bellamy's veal pies,"' I informed him, hearing my voice clanking, loud and ridiculous, from my mouth. I looked down at the pavement – a slate-grey, potholed expanse undermined by tree roots. 'That's what he was supposed to have said, anyway,' I ploughed on, feeling the colour developing in my cheeks. "I think I could eat one of Bellamy's veal pies" . . . And then he just . . .'

I paused, aware of him staring.

'. . . died,' I concluded.

Ed was silent.

'Nice one,' he said after a moment.

'Yeah.' I couldn't think of anything worse.

'Cool. So. Anyway. Better get going.'

'Right.'

'My mum wants me to walk the dog this afternoon.'

'Right.'

And, without saying another word, Ed turned and walked away – he practically bounded, ran! – and then he disappeared around the corner of the road, and that was it. That was that. *Life's a Bitch*, I thought, *and Then You Die*. Which was absolutely correct.

But what happens, I'd wondered, when you don't die? Dying might have been an answer, but it was not an option.

For the rest of that term, in art, I'd sat beneath a new poster that someone had stuck, belatedly, to the wall.

Ars Longa, Vita Brevis.

Though it seemed to me that it might be the other way round. Maybe life was going to be long, and art was going to be short. I'd been perfectly happy, once, sitting there drawing a plant or a bird or a bowl of fruit. But now I couldn't concentrate. I sat very quietly, in the presence of Ed McRae, and tried not to breathe in the fumes of fixative and turpentine. I tried not to breathe too much at all.

*

I discovered later that a lot of what I'd imagined about Ed McRae was not quite true. For instance, he was not impoverished. He lived in a big house in one of the nicest parts of town. People didn't habitually drink Irn-Bru there, or wear T-shirts with ironic slogans on them. They lived there discreetly, charmingly, mysteriously, as if they were the occupants of some enchanted land. It had, I supposed, something to do with wealth. With the easy trappings of it. The McRaes and their semi-detached neighbours all seemed to have at least two cars, and garages to park them in. They all had stained-glass panels in their vestibule windows and subtly blinking burglar alarms. There were no old sweetie wrappers on the pavements, or crisp packets or squashed cans of Lilt, such as could be seen on the pavements around our house. There were no billboards advertising chocolate bars and the latest blockbusters. The front gardens all seemed to contain the same colour of gravel and the same kinds of bench and terracotta flower tub. Little birds hopped obediently about the driveways and sang from the branches of the laurel and rhododendron trees. Everything was calm, ordered, expansive. Even the McRaes' dog kennel was the size, practically, of our front porch! And their living room was so large that all the furniture just seemed to disappear into it, somehow, like space debris entering a black hole. I discovered this when I went to a party Ed held there at the end of that winter term – because I had made it, amazingly, despite my Bellamy's veal pie comment – onto his invitation list. It was a New Year's Eve party, and I had arrived; and as soon as I *had* arrived it was clear, from the number of people there, and the number of rooms in his house, that I was simply one of the multitude. Ed's parents and younger brother were away at some skiing lodge in Fort William, and he had secretly invited half the people in our year – 'a bus-load of folk', he'd said – to see in the bells. There was nothing significant about my having been one of the bus-load. I *did* go there on the bus, although the rest of the bus-load seemed to have been driven there in their parents' cars. I'd spent hours getting ready that evening, applying lip gloss 'for kissable lips' and adjusting the belt of my dress so it sat at the right, cowgirl-ish slant on my hips. It was a dark-blue shirt-dress with little pearlised buttons that Stella had insisted Ed would find irresistible.

'He'll think you're gorgeous in that,' she'd said.

Although when I got there he was nowhere to be seen. And how could he think I was gorgeous or resist the buttons on my dress if he wasn't even there?

I spent most of the party standing in the kitchen with

a boy called Craig Dillard. Craig was in my geography class at school: he was studying geography, like me, and he was going to carry on studying it at university. And everything about geography, that night, had suddenly seemed extremely unappealing.

'I'm going over land erosion,' I remember Craig saying, quite early on in our conversation.

'What?' I asked, clutching onto the enormous glass of red wine I'd poured for myself on arriving.

'I'm going over land erosion,' he said again.

He was tall and thin, Craig, and there was nothing wrong with that; it was just that he kept looming in too close. His eyes were intense, blurry things, like overripe blackberries, and they had a way of boring humourlessly into you. I kept having to look away for light relief. I remember peering up at the frieze stuck around the top of the kitchen wall – a cheerful repeating pattern of lemons – and also at an enormous clock above our heads. It was like a clock you might have found on a Paris railway platform circa 1937, except there was nothing romantic about this one. Its hands just clunked slow and inevitable around the dial.

'Have you revised land erosion yet?' Craig persisted.

I gulped some more wine from the glass I was holding and wondered where Ed was. My heart already felt full of his absence. I was in love, that was the problem. *I got here at nine*, I thought, peering up again at the clock, *I got here at nine, and it's still not even ten*. And already I had drunk too much. I was aware, standing beneath Craig's stooping figure, of movement and colour at the edges of my vision, and of a jumbled clatter of words falling without meaning into my ears. He was saying something now about *basalt*. About basalt and granite and limestone quarries. About quartz. About pearlite. I thought about the buttons on my dress. And where was Ed? Where was the host of this party? There were a lot of dark rooms off the hallway with the scent of cigarettes emerging from them and the sound of music and low conversation, and I felt as if I was standing in the wrong house; a house that was never supposed to have me in it as a guest. It was impossible to make out *who* was in those rooms, so I remained in the kitchen which was at least reassuring – being a kitchen – despite having Craig Dillard in it.

'Za' clock uppair ackerchy working?' I asked, my heart a lead weight of disappointment.

Craig didn't reply. He just stared, as if mesmerised.

Now I wondered if the red wine had coloured my lips. They often went a kind of burgundy colour if I had not applied enough lipstick. Or lip gloss – if I had not put on enough lip gloss that evening. My lips went like that in the winter. Maybe that was why Craig was looking at them. Nothing did appear to be wrong with the clock, in any case; it was probably, I felt, more likely that something was wrong with *me*. Or possibly with Time: maybe Time, that evening, had developed a strange, elastic quality. It had begun to seem like a lost weekend now, the party at Ed McRae's house, a kind of timeless cave. I felt like Persephone, having eaten the pomegranate seeds and unable to find her way back out.

I swayed and swigged wine and listened to Craig talking about pearlite and put my hand by accident onto a hot slice of pizza that someone had put down on the kitchen table.

'You all right?' asked Craig, his face looming in with concern.

'Yes,' I said, 'I'm fine' – although I had in fact scalded my hand quite badly, I realised; on the fleshy part of it, beneath the knuckle of my little finger.

'Want to run it under a tap?'

'No thanks,' I said, dabbing tomato sauce off my palm onto the edge of Mrs McRae's tablecloth. Because I was determined, for some reason, to stay exactly where I was. I felt that if I did that, nothing too bad would happen.

'So, what universities are you putting on your UCCA form?' Craig asked after a moment's pause, as the minute hand of the clock moved slowly, slowly towards the number seven.

'What?' I asked, still dabbing, and I looked up again. Craig's blackberry eyes were swimming alarmingly in and out of focus.

'What universities –' he began very clearly.

And that was the moment when Ed McRae had finally – finally! – appeared in the kitchen. There he was, transported from somewhere else, holding an opened bottle of red wine.

'Hi, Luisa. Top-up?' he asked, striding towards me.

I was so overcome by his presence that I couldn't speak.

'When did you get here?' he asked.

'I don't know,' I said.

He looked at me.

'Thank,' I added, holding my glass out like Oliver Twist with his tragic little bowl of gruel.

'*Thank*?' Ed asked, staring at me too, and grinning. Ed and Craig, both. Grinning at me.

'-ks,' I said.

'Oh: "*thanks*".'

And, wordlessly, he poured more wine into my glass, right up to the top, glanced briefly at my small suggestion of cleavage; at the silver button that coincided with it, and then walked back out of the room.

'So, where were we?' asked Craig. 'What were we talking about?'

I felt a kind of weariness, like a low mist, come rolling into my head.

'Oh yes: about the UCCA form.'

I didn't reply. I stood against the warmth of Mrs McRae's Aga for a while – or maybe it was for a long time: it had become hard to tell, with the way the clock was behaving and Time having altered its nature. I stood there, anyway, with Craig Dillard, and watched the rest of the party happening a long way away without me, through the open kitchen door. Somebody, I noticed – Mrs McRae perhaps – had wound swathes of silver tinsel around the stair banisters and hung bunches of mistletoe from all the doorways leading off the hall. And it was all silver: silver and white. Mrs McRae (or whoever it was) had even gone out into the front garden and continued the festive theme out there, with silver lights in the trees.

I had never known that kind of house or garden, or that way of living. Lights in the trees would have horrified *our* neighbours. And I thought suddenly of my mother, who always got out the same concertinaed paper bells every December from the same battered cardboard box marked XMAS and hung them in our porch. There was also a concertinaed robin in the box. It was put up with the bells, its feet brushing the heads of visitors when they came to the house.

Ed was standing in the hall now, telling people a joke, and everyone was laughing. Oh, because he was a funny boy! He was funny and quick and creative and beautiful. And sitting, wise and beautiful too, in the glass arch above the McRae's front door, was the moon. 'Look at the moon,' I announced to Craig. The moon, and Ed McRae, seemed suddenly more important than anything I'd ever seen. I wanted it to be just me and the moon and Ed McRae. I wanted to paint a picture of them. And I knew for an absolute fact that I did not want to study geography for as long as I lived. I didn't want to leave school and study it at university, as I was supposed to do. Because studying geography appeared to lead to claims on the land: to hacking lumps of rock out of the earth. Basalt and quartz and pearlite. It led, eventually, to people like Craig Dillard going up to the moon in rockets and trudging around it, defacing it with their moon buggies and their gauges and flags and probes and their stupid moon boots. Geography was not for me.

I was aware of Craig still peering at me, rather anxiously, from his gangly height. Maybe he could see

54

something troubling or enlightening, or maybe he was just short-sighted. 'There's really nothing wrong with me, Craig,' I wanted to say, 'nothing at all. I can see everything very clearly, in fact . . .'

And, smiling, I turned and saw that, in the hallway, Ed McRae was plonking his arm around a girl's shoulders. And the girl was Stella Muir. She was standing there, her hair pretty and newly washed and swept into a cooperatively wispy ponytail. She looked straight through me. And I suppose that was when I first realised that friendship means different things to different people. And that to some people, it doesn't mean very much at all.

'So, what are your second and third choices on your UCCA?' Craig persisted, scooping a large handful of Bombay mix from a pure white bowl and tipping chickpea noodles into his mouth.

'My second and third choices?' I asked.

'Are you putting any Scottish yoonies down?'

'Sorry?'

'Are you all right?'

'Sorry?'

There was a smell of burnt garlic and cigarettes. Someone was being sick in the McRaes' downstairs toilet. Someone else was beginning a countdown from ten. Stella had disappeared now, and Ed was wandering around with a plastic Addis bucket.

'. . . London?' Craig said.

But I couldn't think. I couldn't remember what I'd put on my UCCA form. I couldn't think what UCCA meant, or why I'd ever wanted to study geography, or had Stella Muir for a friend. I looked up and noticed that the McRaes had a shelf in their kitchen about six feet long and filled from one end to the other with spice bottles; and I wondered whether Ed had ever got those spice bottles down off that shelf when he was a little boy, and made biscuits with his mother.

'. . . seven . . . six . . . five . . .!' people were saying now in a kind of chorus, because it was nearly the New Year – Jesus, it was nearly the month I was turning eighteen, nearly the year I was supposed to *become* someone! And now there was nothing to do and no one to kiss, because even *Craig* had disappeared, had evaporated into thin air, just at the moment when our conversation might have had some point.

But then, quite suddenly, hovering in front of me, there *was* someone. There was a person, taller than me, peering, moving in close. '. . . four . . . three . . . two . . .' people were chanting. And without any warning, before I'd even properly registered who this person was, he grabbed me. He grabbed me, pulled me towards him and put his mouth against mine. And I had no time to know what to do about this, I didn't even have the ability to speak, now that Ed McRae's mouth was pushed against mine. He was wearing his *Life's a Bitch* T-shirt and it smelt incongruously fragrant, like a baby's newly washed babygro, but his mouth tasted slightly metallic – of iron and Irn-Bru and beer and liquorice and cigarettes, and his tongue was warm and wet and rude, and his hands were sliding, flat-palmed, down my thighs, and despite the shock of this – or perhaps because of it – we'd gone on kissing and kissing.

'Are you feeling OK? Shall we go somewhere quieter?' I remember him whispering after a while in a voice of sweet concern, and he took my hand and led me out of the room.

We went straight upstairs and into a living room. I remember being amazed that the McRaes had not one but two living rooms, on separate floors. *Maybe they even have another one*, I thought; *a flight further up*. This one had two checked sofas in it and a Christmas tree decorated with fake apples and silver angel hair. There was also a fireplace, in the grate of which stood a huge vase of twigs. There was a small Persian rug, a framed painting of a harbour and one large, empty bowl positioned, perfect and simple, on a round mahogany table. And that was all there was. It was a beautiful room. I remember how Ed had peered around it for a second before quietly, almost reverentially, closing the door again. His mother would maybe have disapproved of us going in there. Then he led me wordlessly out again, back along the carpeted landing, through a door and into somewhere a little less magnificent. A utility room. I think it must have been a utility room because I remember a pile of dirty washing and a tumble dryer, and an economy-sized box of Persil and a big woven basket like something out of *Ali Baba and the Forty Thieves*. Ed said something then, but I can't remember what it was. I don't quite recall, either, where I sat, or lay. Maybe on the pile of washing: I was pretty drunk by then. I have a vision of Ed pushing a wooden clothes horse against the door handle, though, for privacy's sake. There was still the sound of music downstairs, a lot of bass notes and a lot of hilarity and screeching. And I remember wondering, as he loomed in to kiss my burgundy lips and to undo, at last, my pearlised buttons – whether he'd ever played houses under that clothes horse. It would have suited him, I felt: he would have been a sweet, imaginative, home-loving boy. But then maybe I had misunderstood the sort of person he was. It was the beginning of misunderstanding things.

4

My mother drove us home from the supermarket. I sat in the passenger seat and looked out through the window. *Kellogg's Raisin Splitz: There's Raisin in the Middle*, announced an advert on a bus stop. *Wispa: Bite It and Believe It*, said another that was stuck to a wall. An old, thin man with a Bejam bag and a walking stick slowly traversed a pedestrian crossing. He came to a complete halt for a moment and waved his stick at our car, as if it was a beast that needed taming. *Get back! Get back!*

'What a funny man.'

'Yes.'

Although I felt he was probably, in some ways, the sanest person on the street. Two young women walked past the car as we waited for him to get to the other side of the road. They were both wearing short white T-shirts, stretched tight across the bust and proclaiming, in glittery writing, the words *Gorgeous Babe*. They were both *Gorgeous Babes*.

'So, that was funny, bumping into Stella,' my mother said, as we slowed to a halt at another set of lights.

'Hmm.'

'Why did she call you Lulu? When did she start calling you that?'

'I can't remember,' I lied.

'I do hate it' she said, 'when people change a pretty name into something ugly.'

'It's not ugly,' I snapped. I don't know why I was defending Stella Muir: I suppose it just seemed preferable to agreeing with my mother, who was often, in an irksome way, right. I could actually remember *exactly* when Stella had started calling me Lulu. It had been during an afternoon we'd spent once in our school library, looking up people's names in the *Guinness Book of Names*. There'd been all kinds of interesting ones with profound meanings to them. Hannah, for instance, meant 'blessed', Emma meant 'universal', Astrid meant 'divinely beautiful' and Stella meant 'star'.

'Lulu,' I remembered Stella reading out. 'Native American name meaning "rabbit".'

She'd looked at me.

'How funny.'

I hadn't replied for a moment. Then I'd said, 'You're the only person who calls me that, though, Stella. And Lulu's only *short* for Luisa. Which has nothing to do with rabbits.'

'How funny,' Stella had said again.

Maybe I am quite rabbit-like, I thought now, as my mother and I drove along. *Maybe there is a touch of the rabbit about me.*

'What is that van *doing*?' my mother asked.

And we both watched as a large white van, slowly being manoeuvred down a side street, crunched with a kind of inevitability into the side of a bin. A man walking past

began to shout and wave his arms, as if the van had re-
versed into *him*.

'What is it *doing*?' my mother said.

'It's reversing.'

'Yes, but into a bin!'

The Roof Company, it said on the side of the van.
*Flat-Roof Specialists. All Other Roofing Work Under-
taken.*

'Well, oh dear,' my mother said, driving on.

I sat back against the sticky plastic of the car seat and
tried not to think about Stella and her body buddies and
her bottles of beer, and the way her life was progressing the way people had always expected it to – how it
was like some smooth, correctly laid path leading up to
a pretty front door – and how mine was not. My life was
more like a lot of tracks running across each other on
Portobello beach.

*

'*Have you talked to anyone about this? Have you told
your mother?*' the doctor had asked me when I went to
see him, a few weeks after Ed's party. It was early February by then and my time of the month had come and
gone, had arrived and departed: *the Curse*, as Mary Wedderburn had used to put it, had not made an appearance.
Which was, of course, the real curse. I'd gone to my own
doctor first, one afternoon after school; and then a few
days later I'd had to go to another place – a clinic, a
white, flat-looking building located behind a car show-

room and a furniture warehouse on the far side of town. I'd had to take the bus there, and then another bus, and then another. It had taken me almost an hour to get there, and it had been dark by the time I arrived at the door. I'd told my mother I was going to Stella's house for tea.

'*So your mother is aware of the situation?*' the clinic doctor had asked me, in his consultancy room.

'Yes,' I'd lied. 'She knows about it.'

'Good. Because it's always a good idea, in . . . cases like this . . . talking to your mother. Even though technically now, at your age . . .' – he petered out and peered across the room at a large, parched-looking yucca plant that someone had stuck into a pot full of pretend pebbles – 'technically, we don't need your parents' consent.'

'No.'

'And how about the . . . ah . . . your . . . boyfriend?' he'd continued, scooting across the room on his little wheeled chair, picking up a pen and scooting back again. He seemed oddly coy for someone in his line of work. 'Have you spoken to him?' he asked, glancing up.

'Yes,' I said.

I *had*, in fact, spoken to Ed, accosting him scarlet-faced the previous week behind the Physics shelves in the school library. 'Hi. Just thought you should know I'm *up the duff*!' I'd whispered rapidly, almost merrily, as if mentioning some homework assignment he might not have heard about. And he had stared at me, stared and stared and looked quite unhandsome suddenly – quite sour-faced and angry. Then, in a low voice, he had said, 'Jesus Christ.'

62

I'd looked at him.

'Do your folks know?'

'No,' I'd said, 'they don't.'

'Do you want money?'

'No. I just have to take a pill. One pill, and then another pill. I have to go to this place and take these pills. You can do it like that now. It's on the NHS. I'm eighteen,' I added, apropos of nothing, really.

'Jesus. Well, God, yeah, just get on with it. God. Jesus.'

And he'd picked up a book he'd temporarily placed on a shelf and walked out of the library. And that was that. That was all. He didn't say sorry, I remember.

*

'You should think yourself lucky, that you live in the twentieth century,' the next doctor had said when I'd gone back the following week. There had to be at least two doctors: it was one of the rules. And I'd had to return to check that the pills had worked. 'It's also fortunate,' the doctor had said, 'that we got in quick. A lot of girls in your position make the mistake of . . . delaying. And then find it's too late. And if we'd left it much longer we'd have had to have gone down a more . . . distressing route.' This doctor was a big-faced man called Dr Birdseye. ('Like the fish fingers!' he'd quipped, on introducing himself. Although his own fingers had been more like sausages.) And I *did* think myself lucky that the pills had worked. The pills didn't always work, Dr Birdseye said, but these ones had. So it was all over. Over and done with. All rather painful and unnecessary, of course. But next time you'll know better, hmm? Or at least start using contraception.

'Yes,' I'd replied. Yes, it *was* painful, I could have added. The pain, in fact, had been intense. And the amount of blood had frightened me, flowing and flowing for days, like a rebuke. I'd thought of Lady Macbeth. I'd thought maybe I would die. 'Thank you,' I said to Dr Birdseye. And I'd risen from my chair, headed past the yucca plant to the door and gone back out into the Reception bay. Things seemed to wobble slightly, in and out of focus, as I walked through it. Beneath a small table there was a box of wooden building blocks and a plastic, flip-up farm-animal game and a dog-eared book entitled *Ted Goes to London*. On the wall above the desk there was a child's drawing of two mad-looking people with huge, purple smiles and outstretched sticks for arms.

I was miles away from our side of town. I didn't really know where I was at all. It was as if that clinic had just appeared out of nowhere, and would go back to nowhere after I'd left. Everything was just white and cold and strange and I walked away from it as fast as I could. I remember that I did stop off at a chemist's before I reached the bus stop, to buy another huge packet of Kotex towels. I didn't know when the bleeding would ever stop. 'Will you want a bag for that, Love?' the chemist asked. *Well, who wouldn't?* I thought. *Who wouldn't want a bag for that?* There was a picture on the bag of a cheerful-looking cartoon woman encircling her children with her arms. 'Caring for your Family', it said beneath the picture. *There is no way I am ever going to tell my mother about this*, I thought, putting it in my schoolbag. And walking to the bus stop I cried and cried. But apart from that – apart from the crying and the pitch-dark bus journeys and the pain and my mother's ignorance and the huge packet of Kotex that I hid in my clothes drawer – I suppose I blanked most of it out. Stella was the only person I ever confided in, one freezing cold day in March as we were standing on a netball court in our green nylon tabards; and she hadn't even seemed particularly surprised.

'Oh *Lulu*,' she'd soothed. 'Never mind: worse things happen at sea.' Which was this odd phrase she'd used sometimes, and which never seemed to have anything to do with anything. I think she'd just picked it up from her father, who'd been a ship's steward, she'd told me once; in the 1950s. *My dad says that sometimes*, she'd said, *and he should know.* And it was around this time that everything I'd been sure of began to alter, anyway; that things began to disintegrate. I remember that a few weeks later that term all the pupils in my year had to go and see a visiting careers advisor, to discuss our futures. We'd all been given a leaflet and a questionnaire to fill in entitled '*Your Career: Your Future in Your Hands*', and I remember it was then that I began to wonder if I *had* a future. Stella had one. And Ed had one. All the sensible people had futures. But mine seemed to have gone a peculiar shape – scattered, unfocused; to contain things that no longer had anything to do with me. *My future,*

I thought, *is not in my hands.* And sure enough, when my exam results came back later that summer, I was discovered to have achieved three Ds and an E. In art I had a B, based on coursework. But where was a lone B in art going to get me?

'What *happened*, Luisa?' my headmaster Mr Deane asked, pop-eyed, at an 'emergency debriefing' session the school laid on every year, for all its failed students.

'Well: oh dear,' my father confirmed, standing there in his slippers in our cool hallway when I returned home that day. A lot of people had said things like that, that week. *'What happened?'* and *'Oh dear.'* Other words, like 'university', 'student accommodation' and 'London', seemed to have adopted a hollow, clanging quality, like someone wandering around a field ringing a big cracked cow bell.

Stella called round at the end of September, to say goodbye. She was off with her rucksack and her umbrella plant and her CD player, off up to the other side of town, to start her course in veterinary science. And goodbye seemed the right thing to be saying.

'So what are you going to do now?' she asked, peering at me.

'I don't know,' I replied.

Stella tutted. She seemed strangely cross. My secret trip to the doctor's the previous February was something that had happened a long long time ago, to someone else; it was something with a beginning, a middle and an end.

'D'you think you'll do retakes?' she said.

'No.'

'Why not?'

'Because if I was going to do retakes I should've signed up for them by now, shouldn't I? And anyway, there's no way I'd ever retake geography.'

'You've got decent O-grades, though, haven't you?' Stella pointed out, a frown briefly puckering her forehead. 'You could always do something with them. I mean, it's not as if you haven't got maths and English.' She stared out, across our front lawn. 'You could do a course at the Open University or something.'

I was silent. The words 'Open University' hung in the air between us. *Nobody our age studies with the Open University, Stella!* I wanted to yell. *The Open University happens at two in the morning! It's for shift workers and posties! It's for mothers, up in the small hours with their babies!*

Stella sighed and yawned.

'So. Anyway,' she said, 'I'm going to have to go now.' She paused. 'Ed's coming round soon.'

I felt a strange, fizzing kind of heat somewhere inside my head.

'Ed's coming round?' I said.

'Yes,' Stella replied.

'Well,' I said, 'how very odd. How very odd,' I said again.

Although Stella *had* briefly mentioned him, I reflected, the last time we'd seen each other. But only in the amusing context of the way he dressed. Only to berate that awful T-shirt; those scruffy trainers; that weird see-through portfolio, that funny trenchcoat. Now the T-shirt and trainers and portfolio and coat seemed to have become less amusing. The clothes he wore and the things he carried seemed to have become acceptable in some way. 'It's not as if you were ever going to get round to anything, is it?' she snapped now. 'I mean, nothing ever happened, did it, after the . . . thing that happened at his party?'

I couldn't think how to reply to this. The words failed to form. But something had already begun to shift, to become slippery, like compacted ice. Nothing seemed quite stable any more.

'. . . and anyway,' Stella was going on, 'how about Craig Dillard?'

I stared at her.

'What?'

'I thought he was pretty keen, wasn't he? You two seemed to be pretty much an *item* last term! Always sitting together in geography!'

'An item?' I said.

I thought of an item of luggage; of a great, heavy, unclaimed suitcase, revolving slowly round an airport carousel. And it struck me how friendship, of any kind, might never be more than two people occupying the same space at the same time. That was all it might ever be about – like the closeness of two people standing side by side in an airport, waiting to reclaim their luggage.

'Anyway, you were never going to get your act together with Ed, were you? I mean, I'm really sorry about what happened and everything,' Stella was saying, 'but that's just the way it is.'

And she turned and walked towards the gate. She was going to study veterinary science in a week's time, and it was unclear what I was going to do. She always was pragmatic, though: I remember thinking that as I watched her rounding the corner of the road and disappearing from view. She'd had the ability to grab opportunities when they arose. In netball, for instance, she'd used to leap around scoring goal after goal, while I'd lurked at the side, unsure of my position, wearing a green tabard that said WD or WA. I hadn't known, for years, what WD and WA even *meant*.

*

Half a mile or so before my mother and I got home I leaned forward and switched on the car radio. Someone was singing a song.

'All we are is dust in the wind . . .' they were singing, '. . . dust in the wind . . .'

'Cheerful,' my mother said.

And I switched the radio off again.

We drove the rest of the way behind a magnolia-coloured ice-cream van. It kept stopping abruptly. It had a drawing on the back, of a huge flattened palm.

Mind That Child!

it said, above the hand.

'I remember when you used to run out for the ice-cream van,' my mother said.

'Yes.'

'What tune was it, it used to play?'

'"Greensleeves".'

'Yes. Not a very ice-creamy tune,' she said, turning the car up the hill and onto our street.

'What is an ice-creamy tune?' I asked.

We often spoke like that, that summer. It was like someone yelling something at you across a huge field: you could hear their voice, but you couldn't make out what they were saying.

*

Our house was a bungalow with an upstairs. Technically, it wasn't a bungalow at all; it was, as I'd once written in a school essay, *an anomaly*. It had retained its essential bungalow nature, though. It was low, and the windows were wider than they were high. In my childhood drawings, our house was the slightly mad, square building that small children often draw of their home. Only, in my case, the off-centre windows and the precipitous roof and the out-of-scale flowers were pretty accurate. My drawings had certainly captured *something*, my parents' friends used to say politely, peering at my work over my shoulder. There had been *something* about them: yes, there was definitely something about the down-on-its-hinges gate and the oddly asymmetrical little willow tree. Unlike some people's houses, our house did not have room for artful display. There was a lot of clutter and not much space to put it in. Even the introduction of quite a small bowl on the kitchen table would have taken up valuable inches. The people who'd lived there before us had put the staircase in some time in the 70s; they were also the people who'd given the house its name: it had once been plain old 37 Salisbury Crags Rise, but they'd decided to call it 'Pumzika', which meant 'tranquillity' in Swahili, apparently. As none of us spoke Swahili, though, I suppose it could have meant anything. It could just have meant 'bungalow on a hill' for all we knew.

Ed McRae came here, I thought, as we pulled up into the drive. And I thought of a visit he had made – one, solitary visit – in the innocent interlude between our terrible Bellamy's veal pie conversation and the New Year's Eve party.

'Your bungalow has an upstairs,' he'd commented, as we plodded in through the front door.

'*Well, ten out of ten for observation!*' I should have retorted. But I hadn't, of course. I'd never said anything to Ed McRae that I should have said. And I tried now, as my mother turned off the car engine, not to think of the awful, silent ascent Ed and I had made up the stairs; or of the childish, cat-print bean bag he'd sat on in my bedroom; or of the sombre discussion we'd had about a film we'd both recently seen – some story about a Russian rock band who'd all sported quiffs and winkle-pickers. Or how, in the middle of this conversation, Ed had suddenly started to sneeze, having developed an allergy to something in my room – to the carpet, maybe, or the bean bag, or maybe to me. I couldn't actually remember much else about the afternoon at all. I suppose I'd blanked it out.

I pulled the door handle and got out of the car. Some sparrows were perched high up in our little cherry tree, making their summer, suburban sound, but they all ceased, as if they had been switched off, when we slammed our car doors shut. 'Home sweet home,' my mother said. She had said this for so many years that it had become a truism rather than fondly ironic, which was what I think she intended.

We took the shopping bags out of the boot and plodded with it all up the front path. Then my mother unlocked the door, and we stepped in. The hallway smelt, as it always did, of the washing drying on the pulley and of honey and fried onions. It was home. And I loved it and I hated it. It was like a poem by Catullus that I'd learned once at school, 'Odi et amo':

'I hate and I love. You ask how this can be . . . I do not know – I just know – and it tortures me . . .'

I had to keep the hate part of it to myself, though. There was no one I could talk to about that.

'So,' my mother said, 'let's unpack and get tea organised.'

'Yeah. I'm just going up to my room for a bit,' I said. 'I'll come and help in a minute.'

And I sprang upstairs.

*

My room was full of things I had outgrown. The bean bag Ed McRae had once sat on was slumped in a slightly abject way in one corner of the room, and my old flowery duvet was flopped across my bed. Standing on my pine bookshelves was a half-empty bottle of moisturising cream I'd bought when I was sixteen, and the Mr Men tin I'd had since I was nine, and a sea urchin Sondrine had given me the day I left Moonchild. 'No hard feelings, Luisa,' she'd said, handing me this hard crustacean shell. Which I'd thought was quite funny. The sea urchin stood now on top of a little plastic bag which contained a small amount of fine soil and had a label on it saying, *Congratulations: You Now Own a Piece of Texas.* Stella had given it to me after she'd been on holiday there once. It was the sort of thing Stella had used to give people.

The clutter on my bookshelves had begun to resemble a kind of archaeological dig, it occurred to me. It had historical layers. I walked over and peered at a blackand-white photograph that was perched at the back, behind my alarm clock. It was of me as a baby, the print framed within narrow white borders. Sometimes, looking at that picture, I would try to remember how I had once been, how I had once viewed the world. But it was impossible. I was just a puzzled, pale-faced infant peering out from my mother's arms. *Baby Luisa, June 1976*, it said on the back, in her handwriting. My mother occasionally mentioned how nice it would have been if other children had come along; if siblings had *turned up*, she used to say, as if siblings were people invited to a party. But I was my parents' only child: that was just the way it was.

On the wall beside my bookshelf there was a cork noticeboard, on which was pinned a letter my old German penfriend Beate Groschler had once sent me. She'd sent it more than a year earlier – before I'd even started working at *Moonchild*. I'd only ever met Beate twice: once when she'd come to see me in Scotland, and once on a return trip to Germany. But she'd always seemed to be leading a calm, beatific life in Frankfurt, and in the photos she sent her face was always settled and kind. When she was younger, she'd used to send me recipes for cinnamon biscuits and plum dumplings, but in this last letter she'd mentioned a new boyfriend whose name was Frank and who was going to be studying law in Mainz.

I could still remember opening it, the day I came home from my emergency meeting with Mr Deane. I'd read it standing in the porch, my mother's spider plants drooping sympathetically from pots over my shoulders.

'*Hello, Luisa!*' Beate had written, her greeting encircled in a little heart. '*How are you? I hope good. We are cracking up on Friday. When do you crack up?*'

And I had started to laugh. Which might, in a way, have answered her question. And then I'd gone upstairs and pinned the letter onto my noticeboard, and it had stayed there ever since.

One of the few concessions in my room to my St Luke's job was something John Singer had made for me a few weeks earlier. This was a figure created from green cartridge paper. It had crescent-moon-shaped stickers dotted all over it and it consisted of six circles – head, body, four limbs – all secured by split pins. There was a drawing of a face on the biggest circle at the top: two misaligned eyes and a mad, lopsided smile. Written along one arm, in green felt-tip pen, it said:

missmckenze

I quite liked it: it was a sweet gift. Also it was a truer likeness, I couldn't help thinking sometimes, than my own reflection in the dressing-table mirror. Because I couldn't quite see myself any more – I couldn't see what other people might be able to see. I couldn't even tell if I was pretty or plain. The best I could make out, through half-closed eyes, was what the French called *jolie laide*. My face was pale and quite thin. My hair, illuminated by the sunlight coming in through the Velux window, had recently turned Ribena pink. It was what my old physics teacher would have called magenta. 'You mix magenta with yellow to get red,' I could remember him saying to us once, 'and with cyan to get blue: *disco colours*!' But it was clear that dyeing your hair did not alter anything: it did not cause the world to open out before you like a dance floor.

I hung around upstairs for a while and listened to the sound of my mother unpacking the shopping. I'd got into the habit that summer of skulking upstairs while my mother was in the kitchen being practical.

'. . . some of that nice peppery ham we had a couple of weeks ago . . .' I heard her saying to my father, and then the kitchen door closed.

I lay down on my bed and closed my eyes. A small breeze trickled through the open window and across my face. I was aware of a cloud floating past, darkening the room for a few moments. There was the sound of two children on the pavement outside, shouting something about the correct way to throw a ball.

*

When I went downstairs, it had turned five. The kitchen seemed squarer than normal for some reason and was full of a bright, wavering sunlight, like the light in a swimming pool or an aquarium. From the fruit bowl in the middle of the table rose the smell of cantaloupe melon. There was half a Dundee cake on a melamine plate. Outside, swifts were calling, dipping and diving in the huge blue sky.

My mother had unpacked all the shopping, I noticed, with shame. She had stashed it away in the cupboards, while I'd been hanging around upstairs like Greta Garbo.

'You were quick,' I said.

'You were slow,' retorted my father, who was sitting at the table.

And there was a moment's lull, as if the room was drawing breath. I leaned against the message board on the wall, against the Family Organiser that my mother had pinned there the previous January. It had illustrations on every page depicting happy families through the seasons. The green and blue squares relating to my parents' lives were full of event *(Dinner with Sue and Malcolm; to cinema; book tickets for Skye...)* The orange squares relating to mine were a series of blanks.

'Hungry, sweetheart?' my mother asked, the way she always did.

76

'Not really,' I replied, my voice emerging small and stuck from my throat.

My mother looked at me.

'Have you got hay fever?' she asked, sympathetically.

And I moved away from the wall, causing the Family Organiser to swing on its hook and dislodging a postcard. *Having a great break*, I read, as I stooped to pick it up. *Weather not bad. Food quite good. Went to the Maspalomas dunes today. Love, Wendy and Ron.*

But why had Wendy and Ron bothered to write and tell my parents that? What *were* the Maspalomas dunes, anyway? My mother always pinned up the cards their friends sent – an organised trait I'd not inherited. I always just lost them. Or kept them, then threw them away at the wrong time. I'd discarded nearly all the letters Beate Groschler had sent me, for instance, keeping only the first couple, in which she'd told me she played the piano and had blue eyes and liked swimming; and the last one, when she'd enquired when I would be cracking up.

'Maybe you could set the table,' my mother said. 'We'll need forks. Because there's going to be coleslaw.'

'Right.'

And I paper-clipped Wendy Williams' postcard back up and began to plod about the room. I went over to the cutlery drawer, clattered out the knives and forks and crashed them down on the table. I placed plates into the spaces between.

*

'So, we met an old schoolfriend of Luisa's in Safeways this afternoon,' my mother reported brightly to my father, once we were all sitting down at the table, contemplating tea. 'Do you remember Stella?' she continued. 'Friend of Luisa's? She used to come round quite a lot a couple of years back, when . . . before . . .'

And her voice adopted a sudden note of regret, and she stopped talking.

'Stella?' my father queried vaguely, picking up his fork and pronging a slice of ham with it. 'D'you mean the one who got all the As?'

I looked across the room and out through the window. My heart felt curled up, unyielding, like a walnut in a shell. My mother glanced across at me and lowered her voice slightly. 'Anyway,' she said, 'she's studying to be a vet now . . .'

'Is she?'

'Yes: and she seems to be having quite a time, doesn't she, Luisa?'

'Yes.'

'She's obviously very . . . busy with things, anyway. Has quite a busy . . . schedule . . .'

I am sitting in the same chair I sat in when I was five, I thought. *I am sitting opposite the same picture on the wall.* I'd painted that picture for my mother when I was small: it was a kind of explosion of flowers with the words *Happy Days Are Coming* written underneath. My mother had liked it circa 1982, and put it in the frame, and there it had stayed. And ever since, *Happy Days Are Coming* had been in my head when I sat in the kitchen, like a kind of truth you don't question.

'Anyway,' my mother said, 'she was certainly full of the joys of spring.'

It was like trying to fit into a place I was too big for. It was like being the freakishly large Alice in *Alice in Wonderland*, my limbs poking out through the doors and windows.

'Was she?' my father said, looking, suddenly, a little lost. Neither of my parents had mentioned my recent change of hair colour; not once, since I'd appeared in the kitchen, transformed, the previous evening. They'd just glanced at it, as if it might imply something more worrying. The beetroot slices, sitting in a bowl in front of me, were pretty much the same colour as my hair. *'It's a very odd thing / As odd as can be . . .'* I thought, remembering another poem from school – *'That whatever Miss T eats turns into Miss T . . .'* – and then I speared a slice of beetroot with my fork and put it into my mouth.

'So, all set for school tomorrow?' my father asked as we progressed onto the fruit salad.

'Yes,' I said, levelly. 'I'm reading with the Fantastic Foxes tomorrow. Then I'll probably be helping out in the Home Corner.'

'The Fantastic Foxes? What's the Fantastic Foxes?' asked my father, and my heart sank.

'It's a reading group,' I explained. 'We also have Excellent Elephants, Terrific Tigers and Cool Cats.'

'Oh, have you? And which one's top?'

'Sorry?'

'Which one's the top reading group?'

'That's not the point, Dad. That's *why* they've been given those names. So you can't *tell* who's top.'

'Hah!' my father said. 'But surely it's going to be obvious, isn't it? Surely if one group's reading *War and Peace* and another group's reading *Peter and Jane*, everyone will know!'

I looked down at my plate.

'Nobody's reading *War and Peace*,' I mumbled. 'Or *Peter and Jane*,' I added.

And when I looked up again at my father his expression was one of utter blankness. It often was, that summer. I suppose he'd presumed, like everyone else, that I would have flown the coop. That I would have stretched my wings and flown. But there I still was! – there I *was*, living at home with them when I should have been somewhere else!

'And what's a Home Corner again?' he asked.

'A Home Corner', I replied, 'is a corner of the room that's like a little kind of . . . home. It's got a cooker and a sink and a washing machine and an ironing board,' I ploughed on, feeling suddenly upset for some reason. 'And a table. A little table and chairs. And crockery. I mean, it's basically a Wendy house,' I concluded, 'like the one I used to have when I was little.'

'You never had a Wendy house,' my mother said.

'Didn't I?'

'No.'

'Oh.'

I gazed across at the Dundee cake.

'What was that thing I used to play in, then?' I said. 'I remember I used to play in some kind of . . .'

'That was the clothes airer. That's probably what you're thinking of. That nice old wooden one we had, with the canvas straps. I used to turn it on its side for you and hang the travel rug over it.'

'Oh yes,' I replied, embarrassed. And I thought of the laundry room Ed McRae had taken me to in his house – I couldn't help it – and then I did remember it, our old clothes airer, I remembered it with a sudden, sharp nostalgia. I was transported back to that place that had been just mine, and the scent of the heavy, tartan wool, and my bears lined up in a row: Clive, Catface and Red Bear.

'Anyway,' my mother went on, 'it's nice, the things they have in schools now. Schools are so much better equipped these days, aren't they?'

'Yes,' I said. I put a half-strawberry into my mouth and swallowed it. Then I sliced a piece of cake in half and swallowed that. From the living room, the clock on the mantelpiece began its tinselly rendition of the Westminster chimes.

'So: coffee?' my mother suggested. 'Why don't you go and sit in the living room,' she added to my father, 'and I'll bring coffee through in a minute.'

'Can't help with the washing-up?' he replied, already getting up and legging it towards the door. It was a kind of routine they had.

'No,' my mother said, 'you go and sit down.'

'Alright, love.'

And he went to sit in the living room and gaze at the

swifts swooping past the window – the swifts being, in my opinion, the only creatures leading productive lives on our street that summer.

*

I helped my mother to wash up. I folded the damp tea towel (Robert Burns bordered by thistles) and hung it over the radiator. I wiped down the table. Then I went back upstairs, lay on my bed and looked up through the thick, slanting window, up and up at the sky. A plane, 35,000 feet up, appeared at one corner of the frame and began to draw a pure white line through the blue, from left to right. And that was all: just this rectangle of pure blue with a line through it, like a ticked box. I flopped off my bed after a while and went over to the window to look down. If I stood on tiptoe and craned my neck, I could just make out Mrs Crieff's house at number 25. I could see the concrete birdbath on her patio, and the lopsided, busby-shaped cypress hedge at the end of her lawn, and beyond that, the view of the Pentland Hills. Once, two summers earlier, I'd gone on a trip to those hills with my art class. We'd all wandered around with our A3 sketch pads and our tins of pencils and putty rubbers, trying to work out perspectives, and watching as dozens of small grey rabbits lolloped around us in the grass. They'd been funny, those rabbits. They had been more interesting, in a lot of ways, than the lesson on perspective.

'I thought you were out in the garden, love!' my

mother said, coming upstairs after a while to get something from the airing cupboard outside my room. 'You ought to be out getting some sun! What are you doing up here?'

'Nothing much,' I replied, peering down at the bright summer green of our lawn.

'Why don't you ever go outside and *draw* like you used to?' she continued. 'You never *do* any more, Luisa, and it's a real shame.'

'What is?'

'That you don't *draw*! What wouldn't *I* give', she carried on, 'to go and sit in the garden and draw! To just go down and . . .'

'So why don't you then, Mum?' I snapped. 'What's stopping you?'

And her face turned a little pink. Once, when I was younger, she'd attended drawing classes at our local community centre. She'd kept the pictures, stored away in one of my father's old briefcases: charcoal drawings of plastic anemones and earthenware jugs and stuffed Victorian pheasants. I think she'd planned to do something with them. Frame them, maybe, or sell them in a cafe.

'All I'm saying, Luisa,' she said as she stood in the doorway, 'is there's plenty things you could be doing this evening instead of moping about up here! I mean, what about that card, for one thing, that you were going to make for Kirsty?'

'What card?'

'That congratulations card.'

'Oh,' I said.

Kirsty was a cousin of mine. She and her husband lived in a brand-new house in Dalgety Bay and had recently had their first baby, a girl they'd named Aimee Dorothy: *Aimee* because she was loved and *Dorothy* after her grandmother. And I'd told my mother that I'd make them a card: a 'Well Done' card to celebrate Aimee Dorothy's arrival. I couldn't think why I'd said that, now, though. I just said things sometimes, and they were complete lies.

'It might be a nice thing to do,' my mother continued, 'don't you think? If you've got time on your hands . . .'

'Why?'

'Because you like drawing.'

'No I don't,' I said. 'And I'll probably not even meet the baby till she's eighteen or something.'

I stopped talking and looked down at my feet, bare and white against the pale-green carpet. I thought of my cousin. Mrs Kirsty Robinson. The last time I'd seen her was at her wedding, a year earlier. I'd sat at an octagonal table with all her old university friends – a group of people in their late twenties I'd never met in my life before. I remembered that I'd drunk a lot of wine and had proclaimed, during a lull in the conversation, that I'd once floated 2,000 feet above that very building in a hot-air balloon. And all Kirsty's old university friends had just stared at me, their little nests of sugared almonds on the table in front of them.

'The thing is, Mum,' I said, 'I'm not eight any more, am I? I don't need to do things any more like make congratulations cards. I mean, I hardly even know Kirsty, really. We only ever meet at weddings and funerals. And she's already going to be swamped with baby cards.'

My mother's expression had changed, subtly, from something like sorrow to something more like irritation.

'All I'm saying', she said, 'is there's plenty of things you could be doing.'

Which was true: there were plenty of things. So far, though, I wasn't doing any of them.

5

I was late in to St Luke's on Monday morning. The playground was already three-quarters empty by the time I made it through the gates. Only a few of the older children were still left outside, standing around in uneven lines, and some mothers, hanging about in their groups of threes and fours, arms folded or weighed down by babies and shoulder bags.

'Good morning!' I called to them brightly, brightly, over the song I was listening to on my old Walkman. And I strode past and onwards across the tarmac, in my big black shoes. *I am nineteen*, I reminded myself, *and I am wearing sensible shoes. I am saying 'Good morning' and wearing sensible shoes.*

'Hi, Miss McKenzie,' one or two of the mothers said cautiously as I passed them – the sensible quality of my shoes already undermined that morning by the Walkman and the stupid colour of my hair. Some of them didn't like me much: they had not liked me from the word go.

I continued on, the smile cheerful on my face, and looked down at my watch. It was already gone nine. It was already nearly ten past.

'More than a little late this morning,' uttered Mrs Crieff, appearing at the main doors as I was heading towards the steps. Because Mrs Crieff was always there, somehow, when I was being at my least impressive.

I paused on the bottom step, removed the headphones from my ears and switched off *The Hissing of Summer Lawns*.

'Hi,' I said.

'Good morning,' corrected Mrs Crieff. Our conversation was already back to front, somehow, and wrong. A sudden gust of wind whizzed around the corner of the school and blew my hair in front of my face. I was conscious of my thin cotton skirt wrapping itself around my legs, and of my big, sensible, classroom-assistant shoes which did not go with it; and also of my Indian bangles, which clattered together as I moved my arm.

Mrs Crieff was wearing one of her silk-effect, dry-clean-only blouses. Her hair remained stationary. Her jacket was so bright and well maintained it looked as if it might bounce if you touched it.

'Overslept?'

'It's just, the traffic was really awful today,' I said.

'Not that *I* noticed,' Mrs Crieff retorted, her gaze flicking disconcertingly to my left hand as I pushed a strand of hair behind my ear. She was carrying a yellow cardboard folder which had 'Assessments' written on it. 'It seemed pretty normal to me. And anyway, I thought you came by bus. I thought you got the 8.32 from the bottom of the Drive.'

'I do,' I confirmed. 'It was just, the bus had to go on all these . . . diversions today. And, you know, I suppose buses are not exempt from . . .' – I hesitated – '. . . traffic jams.'

I stopped talking and glanced down at a wooden tub which stood at the top of the steps. It contained a display of yellow bedding plants. I'd once heard Mrs Crieff call them Black-Eyed Susans, though I'd always known them as Busy Lizzies. My mother called them that, and I was pretty sure they *were* Busy Lizzies.

'Well, it's nearly quarter past. You've pretty much missed assembly, anyway,' Mrs Crieff said. 'It was Reverend Johnston today'; and when I looked up again, she was frowning. *In all honesty, Luisa,* she'd said to me at our last meeting a couple of weeks earlier, *you're going to have to up your game, if I'm to tick all the boxes on your assessment form.* 'Up my game?' I'd asked. *Yes. In terms of your levels of commitment. I mean, we can hardly tick the punctuality box!*

'You're not forgetting our meeting at eleven this morning, are you?' she said now, in a flat voice.

'No, I'm not,' I replied. Although I *had* forgotten; up until that moment I'd forgotten completely. I'd been meaning to put it in my diary, this meeting where I'd declare all the ways in which I'd upped my game; and then I hadn't.

'See you at eleven, then,' Mrs Crieff said, progressing down the steps. 'In my office,' she added, as if I might not have worked this out.

I watched her carry on across the playground with her yellow cardboard folder, past the silver birch tree and the frog-shaped rubbish bin, and disappear around a corner. She always left the scent of perfume in her wake: one of those acerbic ones with a scary name. It had top notes of something like petrol and blueberries.

I pushed the Walkman and headphones into my bag. And then I carried on, on my zigzag journey through the school, towards the Portakabin. I was late, I was late, and Mrs Crieff didn't like me. Mrs Crieff had causes for concern. And what more was there to say? I tried not to imagine what she might have to tell me at our meeting – and also, more worryingly, on Friday, the last day of term, the day that marked the end of my trial period. Because you can try, and not succeed. You can try, and fail, despite your best intentions.

*

The walls of the Portakabin were rattling slightly in the breeze as I approached. I clattered up the ramp past the collection of scooters and trikes, pressed the security code on the keypad, opened the door and plodded along the linoleum and plasticine-scented corridor to the classroom.

Mrs Baxter was alone. She was kneeling on the floor as if praying, and surrounded by a lot of empty egg boxes. Empty egg boxes – empty cardboard boxes in general – were a fact of life at St Luke's.

'Hi, Morag,' I said in my breezy Monday voice.

'The children are almost back from assembly,' she replied balefully. 'You really should try and get here earlier, Luisa.'

Then she looked up and did a quick kind of double take.

'What in God's name have you done to your hair?'
'Oh yes, my hair,' I replied. 'Well, it was just a bit of an experiment. I thought it was one of those wash-in, wash-out things, you see, only –'

'– it didn't wash out,' Mrs Baxter concluded. *Boom, boom.* We were a bit of a double act, me and Mrs Baxter.

'Well,' I said, 'no, it didn't.'

I didn't add that I'd tried to wash it out many times over the course of the weekend; that I'd given up after the seventh attempt, watching the pale-pink foam disappear down the plughole. And I couldn't help thinking now that my peculiar hair might be something else that counted against me, on Mrs Crieff's form.

'Anyway, it's good having a change sometimes, isn't it?' I said, ploughing on into the main arena of the classroom. *The body of the kirk,* as Mrs Baxter called it. Here, beyond the sand tray and the rocking horse, there was a large green cupboard with a label on it saying *Mats.* The mats were one of my tasks that morning; they had been, for the whole term. I opened the door of the cupboard and pulled out twenty-nine of them: twenty-nine foam-filled rectangles of red and yellow and blue. Then I carried them, stacked, in seven trips, back and forth to the centre of the room and began distributing them in a large, orderly circle on the floor. It was like setting up a fairy ring. I always placed them in the same recurrent order: red, yellow, blue; red, yellow, blue; red, yellow, blue. I sometimes liked to create order out of chaos.

'So: nice weekend?' Mrs Baxter asked, plodding through the circle in her flat shoes to pin the day's snack menu on the noticeboard. Mondays were breadsticks and raisins.

'Pretty good, thanks,' I lied. 'How was yours?'

'Fab. Doug and I spent nearly all of yesterday at the garden centre.'

'Really?' I said.

Sometimes the things Mrs Baxter told me she'd done at the weekend were so unlike anything I'd do that it left me almost speechless. She'd once told me she bought a Marks and Spencer's ready-meal every Friday night – 'come rain or shine' – which she and her husband always ate while watching *Bergerac*. And somehow, when she'd said that, I couldn't imagine her ever having experienced uncertainty about anything in her life. Uncertainty or regret. I'd pictured the last time I'd gone to a garden centre myself, the previous Christmas, with my parents. I'd thought of the sinister reindeer animatrons that had swayed their heads in time to 'Jingle Bells', and the rows and rows of bright red poinsettias.

'We stayed for tea. Because they do teas and coffees there now. And soup. And we got some lovely begonias,' Mrs Baxter said.

'Did you?' I didn't even know what begonias looked like.

'Some really super ones. All sorts of bright colours,' she added, her eyes darting up to my hair again.

Mrs Baxter had recently become a grandmother: she'd brought in several photographs of a red-faced, angry-looking baby to show everyone in the staffroom. 'Isn't he a poppet?' she'd said.

'Yeah, he's really cute,' I'd replied dutifully, peering over her shoulder at the picture.

'My daughter's had his handprint cast in silver. This teeny wee handprint. She's getting it put on a pendant.'

'What a nice idea,' I'd said. Because, really, what else was there to say? I didn't want to think about babies. I wanted to be as far removed as I could possibly be from a life involving babies' handprints cast in silver and strung onto pendants. I didn't want to imagine what kind of emotion made you want to do things like that. 'So, that's the menu up,' Mrs Baxter said now, stepping back from the noticeboard and smoothing her skirt flat with the palms of her hands.

'Right,' I said brightly, as if happy – happy about Mrs Baxter's begonias and the snacks menu and about life in general! – and I went to check on the goldfish in their green tank. Bunty and Bobby and Billy. *Hello, fish.* They were all still alive. Then I adjusted the weather chart on the wall: *Today it is: Sunny.* There was not much option anyway as Mrs Baxter and I had lost nearly all the clouds, like distracted TV weather forecasters.

By now it was nearly nine thirty. I could hear the children, back from assembly, beginning to line up outside the classroom door. 'Monday, Monday, so good to me . . .' Mrs Baxter hummed as she opened the door and they began to wander in – she was a big Mamas and Papas fan – and now she clasped her hands together, an expression of determined happiness on her face. I stood and watched the children find their places in the room, and wondered if there was anything I could add to Mrs Baxter's interpretation of Monday. But I'd never particularly liked Mondays. Mine had always been less like the Mamas and Papas' version and more like the Boomtown Rats'. I cleared my throat and was about to say something – something falsely cheerful about the start of the week – but Mrs Baxter had already started speaking. Really, I was not quick enough at this game.

'Good morning, boys and girls,' she said to the children in her optimistic voice, 'let's not push and shove.'

'Hi, everyone,' I added dutifully as the children began to take their places on their foam mats.

Mrs Baxter strode across the centre of the circle and sat down on the teacher's chair beside the window.

'Everyone?' she remarked, in a questioning kind of way, and there was a sudden hush. 'Everyone?' was a kind of command. It meant, *We should all be sitting down now.* And there *I* was, Miss McKenzie, standing up: my chair was round the other side of the circle, and I was not beside it. I clomped towards it now, like the last person in Musical Chairs, and sat down opposite Mrs Baxter. Mrs Baxter gave a smile of great fortitude. Then she breathed out and clapped her hands together.

'Where are people's Listening Ears this morning?' she enquired, above a new crescendo of voices.

'Hush, now,' I added. And at the sound of my voice, several children looked up at me, as if they'd never clapped eyes on me before.

'Miss McKenzie,' said Emily Ellis quietly, 'why is your hair pink?'

'Well –' I began.

But Mrs Baxter already had her finger to her lips. 'Shush,' she was saying. 'Shush. Have you got your Listening Ears, Emily?'

Emily did not respond.

'Because we haven't all come to school this morning to talk about Miss McKenzie's hair, have we? What are we supposed to be saying at the moment? Good . . .?'

'. . . *mooo-rning*, Mrs Baxter,' the children intoned. 'Good mooor-ning, Miss McKenn-zie,' they added.

'Now: is everyone sitting nicely on their bottoms with their hands on their knees? And is our circle nice and neat?' Mrs Baxter asked. There was a small hiatus of shuffling and rearrangement. 'Very nice. Good.' She looked around the circle. 'Now, over to you then, Miss McKenzie.'

This was my cue. 'OK,' I said, standing up, opening a cupboard in the wall behind me – a different one from the mats cupboard – and pulling out a large blue teddy bear. The bear's name was Talking Ted, and he made an appearance every morning.

'Good morning, Talking Ted,' I said to the bear, and I handed it down to Emily, who was sitting nearest me in the circle. He was always passed to the left for some reason, like a bottle of port. He was there, Mrs Baxter had explained when I'd begun the job, to teach children how to converse properly, how not to interrupt: nobody was allowed to interrupt anyone in Circle Time if they were holding Talking Ted. It was like the conch shell in *Lord of the Flies*.

'Have you got anything you want to say, Emily?' I prompted.

Clutching the bear, Emily Ellis peered at me. She had a way of looking at you sometimes – they all did.

'Yes, Emily,' Mrs Baxter added from her chair by the colour chart, 'do *you* have anything you'd like to tell us this morning?'

Because Emily usually did have something interesting to say. The previous week she'd announced that she knew who the son of God was. 'Really, Emily?' Mrs Baxter had asked, looking both uncomfortable and fascinated and leaning forward in her chair. 'Yes,' Emily had said. 'His name is Edith.' And there had been a pause, a lull – a tiny rending, almost, in the fabric of time – while Mrs Baxter had worked out what to say. She was mute now, though, Emily, as she clutched the bear's big blue ears. It was funny how Talking Ted could sometimes have a silencing effect.

'Anything to say, poppet?' Mrs Baxter asked, her head slightly to one side. 'Hmm? Nothing to . . .'

'Yes,' Emily said abruptly, just as we were all ready to move on.

'Oh, good,' Mrs Baxter replied, sounding a little rattled. 'What's your news then, Love?'

'I've got a new Barbie!' Emily announced.

'Ooh,' said Mrs Baxter.

'My dad gave me her. I'll go and get her,' Emily added, suddenly excited. And she chucked Talking Ted face down onto the floor, got up, broke out of the circle, hurried across to the plastic tray she'd been allocated in the

95

corner of the room, removed something from it and returned to her place.

'Here she is,' she proclaimed, holding out a small plastic doll. We all peered at it.

'Well,' Mrs Baxter said unsurely, 'she's very nice.'

'She's my bestest ever,' Emily said. 'My dad gave me her,' she said again.

The doll was one of the smaller Barbies, and she was sitting, I saw now, in her own little plastic car. Her arms were holding the steering wheel in an alarmingly rigid way. *If she was driving that car in real life, Emily*, I felt like saying, *she'd leave the road in seconds.*

'Well, she's lovely,' Mrs Baxter said chirpily. 'Is she your new favourite, sweetheart? What's her name?'

Emily smiled and considered her doll.

'Her name's Jenny,' she said.

'And where did your dad get her from? Somewhere on his travels?'

'No. He bought her in Jenners.'

'Ooh,' said Mrs Baxter.

'We went there on Saturday,' Emily confirmed. 'Me and Daddy. We bought her in Jenners and that's why she's called Jenny. She doesn't have hair that pulls out, though. There weren't any of those left.'

'Oh dear,' I said, my voice coming out louder and more cynical than I'd intended. I peered at the Barbie. She was immaculate and blonde, with a retroussé nose and perfect bust. She reminded me of Stella Muir. I couldn't help thinking that.

'Well,' said Mrs Baxter, 'that was very kind of your

dad. Wasn't it, everyone?' she continued, addressing the rest of the circle. 'To buy Emily a brand-new doll.'

And we all fell silent in contemplation of Mr Ellis's kindness. Though he'd never struck me as the sort of man who would buy anyone a Barbie doll. He'd always looked to me like somebody who wouldn't tolerate cheap tat, just as he barely liked to acknowledge the existence of nineteen-year-old classroom assistants, or the need for sympathy when his wee girl fell and grazed her knees. *And why would you want a doll, anyway*, I felt like saying to Emily, *with hair that pulled out from the top of her head? A Barbie doll is as plastic as the box she's packed in.*

'So,' Mrs Baxter said, breaking our reverie like a minister coming to the end of silent prayer; and Talking Ted was passed on. He stopped briefly at a boy called Jamie, who informed the class that his mother had just had a baby weighing 10lbs 8oz – 'Goodness gracious me!' Mrs Baxter said – and at Zoe Jacobs, who was going to Florida on a plane on Thursday. And then the bear reached Mrs Baxter.

'So, now *I've* got Talking Ted,' she said in her big, educational way, '*I'm* going to remind everyone about an *exciting event* that is happening *tomorrow*. Now,' she continued, peering down at the children, 'can anyone tell me what that is?'

The children looked at her. There was no response. Then Solly Calman put his hand up.

'Yes, Solly?'

'A wizard's coming, with a rabbit.'

97

'Haa,' said Mrs Baxter, deflated. Already, it seemed, her Monday was not quite panning out. Nobody was meant to be getting Barbie dolls out of their trays or talking about wizards and rabbits. I hardly knew about the wizard myself: I hadn't been paying much attention when Mrs Crieff had told the staff her plans for the week. All I knew was that he was part of some end-of-term celebration – some jamboree she'd decided to have.

'Well, you're quite right, Solly,' Mrs Baxter said now, 'because, yes, we are going to be having a wizard here this week, on Thursday. A magician, in fact. He's coming to our end-of-term party, isn't he? Which is very . . .' she added flatly, 'exciting. Because the wiz— the magician is going to be very special, isn't he? But', she continued, raising her voice above the renewing volume, 'I actually wanted to tell you about something else, this Circle Time. *What* have we got happening *before* the wizard?'

She was virtually shouting now. The children stopped talking and regarded her. Positioned directly behind Mrs Baxter's head was a poster depicting a happy worm in an apple, exhorting children to *Eat Fruit*. Outside the window a mean-eyed herring gull hovered and squawked in the purest summer sky. *I could have been living in London now*, I thought, glancing up at the gull. *I could have been living a completely different life.* And I tried not to mind that I was, instead, sitting in a Portakabin in my home town, surrounded by five-year-olds.

'I'm not going to ask people who click their fingers at me,' Mrs Baxter cautioned, 'or anyone who is not . . .'

And then Emily, still holding the Barbie doll, put her hand up. Emily was as sharp as a tack.

'I know what we're doing, Mrs Baxter: we're going to the Scottish Waterways Visitor Centre,' she said in a quick little voice.

'Yes, Emily, that's right,' Mrs Baxter replied, relieved. 'You can put your hand down now. Because we are indeed, children, going to the Scottish Waterways Visitor Centre.'

Yesss, some of the boys hissed, as if somebody had just scored a goal in football. Though I suspected they might not actually know what the Scottish Waterways Visitor Centre was; that they might have confused it with Waterworld at the far end of Great Junction Street – a very different kind of place, involving flumes and a wave machine.

'Settle down,' Mrs Baxter called. 'Now, the reason I'm telling you about the trip is so you can remind your mums and dads to make you a packed lunch tomorrow.'

'Yes,' I confirmed to the children sitting near me, and they all looked up at me again in surprise.

'Are you going to bring a packed lunch, Miss McKenzie?' Emily asked. 'Are you going to bring crispspsps?'

'Well, maybe not crisps,' I whispered back, 'maybe . . .'

'Miss McKenzie, where are your Listening Ears?' Mrs Baxter asked.

*

After Song Time that morning it was Undirected Play, the part of the morning I was supposed to supervise. Nearly all the boys went straight to the boxes containing the Hot Wheels cars, while the girls headed for the Home Corner. That was just how it was. At the sand tray two boys, Mungo and Zac, were creating a kind of cliff like the white cliffs of Dover and tipping cars over its edge.

'Hello,' I said, going over to them, 'what are you two doing here?'

Mungo and Zac ceased their work in the sand for a moment.

'We're pushing the cars over the cliff,' Mungo said.

'And the cows. This cow has just died,' Zac added, pointing to a small plastic cow, its four legs as stiff as pokers.

'I see,' I replied. Sometimes, I felt about as far away as I could possibly be from the mind of a five-year-old. But then something would remind me. The toy cows we had in the Portakabin were exactly like the ones I'd used to play with at home when I was little. They stood on identical patches of pretend grass. And when I looked at them, time seemed to fold up, like a telescope.

'That's a shame, that it died,' I said to Zac. 'Maybe it can come back to life later.'

Zac frowned.

'No,' he said, 'it's dead. It was meant to die. It was part of the game.'

'I see,' I said, feeling bleak and standing up straight again. And then I moved away, in the direction of the Home Corner, which seemed at least a kinder place to be, that morning. Although, as I approached it now, I noticed that Emily Ellis's new Barbie doll was lying prone and bare-breasted on top of the cooker. Her little car was nowhere to be seen.

There were five girls in the Home Corner, making pretend biscuits at the table.

'You look busy in there,' I said, stooping down at the gingham-curtained window. Sometimes, I felt like Mr Jackson in *The Tale of Mrs Tittlemouse*, too big to squash through the door.

'We *are* very busy,' said Emily Ellis, who was standing at the table, a plastic mixing bowl in her hands. 'We're making biscuits. Would you like a biscuit?'

'Oh: yes *please*!' I said, with the kind of enthusiasm I had learned to perfect.

'Here you go, then,' she said. And she passed me an invisible biscuit through the window.

'Thanks,' I said. 'Yummy.' It was like standing at the school serving hatch at dinner time.

'Is your mummy coming with us on the bus tomorrow?' I heard Jade asking Emily as I was pretending to eat.

'No, my mum's going to be busy tomorrow,' Emily replied insouciantly, returning to her mixing bowl.

'Didn't you want your mummy to come, then?'

'I don't mind,' Emily said.

'Is your mummy going to be making cakes for the end-of-term party? My mummy's going to be making butterfly cakes for the end-of-term party. Is your mummy going to make some cakes?' Jade persisted, like some looped recording.

'No,' Emily retorted. 'My mum's going to be making sausages on sticks.'

'Ha!' I laughed. I quite liked the sound of Mrs Ellis.

'Oh, it's just like a little life, isn't it? Like a little version of real life,' Mrs Baxter exclaimed, sweeping past at that moment and glancing in through the window. And I stopped laughing. I looked through the door of the Home Corner. Everything inside it was made of wood. There was a wooden cooker, a wooden sink and wooden pots and pans. There was a wooden food mixer and a wooden toaster and wooden slices of toast.

'I suppose it's a bit like *The Little House on the Prairie*,' I said.

And Mrs Baxter looked at me. She looked, and glided on.

'Miss McKenzie,' Emily Ellis called out now, from inside the little house, 'I've got something to tell you.'

'Have you, Poppet?' I asked; and Emily appeared again at the window. She leaned right through and propped her elbows against the painted-on flowers. The gingham curtains were like some in Mrs Crieff's house, it occurred to me; her house at 25 Salisbury Crags Rise. I could never resist gawping at them on my way home in the afternoons.

'What I have to say', Emily said, 'is: Mindy Moo is here today.'

'Is she?' I asked.

'She just got here,' Emily continued. 'She just arrived. Her car broke down this morning, which is why she's late.'

'I see.'

Mindy Moo was Emily's imaginary friend, and she was quite a character. She was a bit disaster-prone, which made me feel a bit better, somehow. Also, she had an imaginary getaway car – a little blue one – which she secretly parked right beside Mrs Crieff's Rover in the staff car park. I would have liked a getaway car like that. Sometimes she drove to England in it to visit her grandmothers, and sometimes she went to Tesco's and sometimes she just thought s*od it* and got a car ferry and headed off to Africa or America. She was quite a feisty girl. Usually, though, she just hung loyally around school with Emily. She would go for a wander, ending up in the school kitchens with the dinner ladies or upstairs in Mrs Crieff's office. I have no idea why she was called Mindy Moo. When I imagined her, though, I thought of someone Betty Boop-ish – sassy, with big round eyes and perfectly styled, jet-black hair. Like me, on my good days. Not the sort of girl to screw things up.

'So how's Mindy Moo today?' I asked; and Emily considered, gazing clear-eyed through the Portakabin window.

'She was a bit wild today,' she said. 'She tied a knot in my shoelaces and I fell over. I said: "Mindy Moo, untie my shoelaces at once, or there'll be no pudding and no stories."'

'Really?'

'My dad says that sometimes, too.'

'Does he?' I said. 'What – when he talks to Mindy Moo?'

'No!' Emily retorted, exasperated. 'I mean, he says that about pudding and stories.'

'Oh.'

'He doesn't know about Mindy Moo.'

'Ah.'

But then I supposed he wouldn't, Mr Ellis being far too uptight, as far as I could see, to believe in people like Mindy Moo. In invisible things, like spirits and spooks and fairies. He looked like the sort of person who would not clap his hands at a *Peter Pan* panto; who would just let Tinkerbell die.

'My dad's got a new mobile phone,' Emily continued, apropos of nothing.

'Has he?' I said. But I wasn't inclined to talk about Mr Ellis any more. He was just a man I didn't like much. He had an important job and wore a pair of brogues with a spiral of dots on the toes, and that was all I really wanted to know about him.

*

The first hour of the day always went quite quickly. There was a pleasing kind of routine to it. We chanted the two times table at ten and read a story at half past, and by the time it was quarter to Mrs Baxter had already begun roaming around the room like a weary buffalo on a prairie, bellowing something about Tidy-Up Time. I looked at my watch. It was ten to eleven. Ten minutes until my meeting with Mrs Crieff.

John Singer had been sitting on the outside of the

Home Corner for most of the morning. It was where he often sat: it was his place, and sometimes the sight of him there made me feel sorry. So before Tidy-Up Time began in earnest, while the girls in the Home Corner were finishing their waterless washing-up, I went over to him, to help him put together a jigsaw puzzle he was doing – a picture of a rocket with an insanely happy astronaut waving through the porthole.

'Hi John,' I said, kneeling down beside the little table.

John ignored me. He was concentrating hard, breathing through his mouth.

'Hi there,' I tried again.

'Hello.'

'How's the puzzle going?'

'Fine.'

He clicked a piece into place.

'He looks very . . .' – I couldn't think how to describe the mad spaceman – '. . . cheery.'

John sighed and connected two sections of puzzle together, giving the moon a face. The moon was smiling too. Everything was smiling, even the stars.

'Miss McKenzie,' he said.

'Yes, John?'

'There was something I wanted to talk about in Circle Time. But I didn't talk about it.'

'Oh dear,' I said, and I hesitated. When John Singer said something like this you never really knew what tangent you might go off at. 'Well,' I said in as wise a tone as I could manage, 'why don't you tell me now? About what you wanted to—'

'I was going to say', he interrupted, 'about a bit of Fool's Gold I've got.'

'Oh. Have you got a piece of Fool's Gold?'

And he looked at me. I don't know why I spoke like that sometimes, in that stupid, echoing way, like some bat in a cave.

'Yes,' he said, patiently. 'My mum got it for me from the museum. Do you know why it's called Fool's Gold?'

'No? Why *is* it called that?' I asked, hoping I sounded intrigued, instead of merely stupid.

'Because fools think it's gold.'

'Ah.'

'Only it's not. It's just a bit of rock.'

He spoke the truth, John Singer – he was *faithful and true* – and sometimes it could be a bit devastating. We returned to the puzzle in silence.

'Miss McKenzie?' he asked again after a moment; and a kind of apprehension flickered back into my heart, like a relit gas flame.

'If something gets between you and gravity,' he said, 'guess what happens?'

'Hmm. If something gets between you and gravity? Well,' I replied, 'I really don't know.' Because I didn't: I really didn't know what happened to you if you got on the wrong side of gravity.

John sighed and looked out through the window. He stared out across the tarmac at the waving leaves on the silver birch tree.

'You float up into space,' he said. 'And sometimes you never come back down.'

I waited for him to continue, but it seemed he had said everything he wanted to say.

'Well,' I said after a moment – sensible, unflappable Miss McKenzie – 'I never knew that. It's time to tidy up, now though. Shall we slide the puzzle into the box and you can come back to it after lunch?'

'No, let's just scribble and scrabble it all up,' he replied, pouncing on the puzzle with his fingers and breaking the picture up.

'Oh,' I said, 'OK.'

'It's more fun.'

'OK.'

He could do unexpected things, John. He had been *going through a difficult time* over the past few months, Mrs Baxter had confided to me one lunchtime. 'He's not had an easy time of it, poor wee sausage, what with all the changes at home,' she'd said, delicately poking a stray strand of coleslaw into her mouth. And I suspected his parents were getting divorced, because he was always talking about them in different contexts – his mother taking him out to the zoo or for hot chocolate in a cafe, his father forgetting to put his lunch box into his schoolbag – things like that. Quite a lot of the St Luke's parents seemed to get divorced. It seemed to be an occupational hazard. And Mrs Baxter had been on the point of telling me more about the Singer family's situation when Mr Temple from class P6 had suddenly bounced into the staffroom with some charity raffle tickets to sell – 'I'll buy five, Mark,' Mrs Baxter had said in her flat, unperturbed way – and when we'd resumed our conversation she'd spoken about something completely different: I think it was about someone's time-share apartment in Mallorca. Or Maspalomas, maybe. And I hadn't had the nerve after that to wheedle it out of her, about the difficult times John Singer was going through. Difficult times were best kept private, anyway, in my opinion. Everyone had difficult times, and they were best kept under lock and key.

*

I set off for Mrs Crieff's office while the children were still having their snack. I slunk out of the Portakabin and hurried back across the playground beneath the lightly falling rain. Back indoors again I ascended the main staircase two at a time, aware of my heartbeat thudding in my ears.

Mrs Crieff did not seem overjoyed to see me.

'Luisa,' she said, opening her door and giving me one of her on/off smiles.

'Now, as you know, the reason we're meeting today', she continued as we both plodded across her office and sat down on either side of her enormous desk, 'is so we can remind ourselves of your work over the past few months here.'

'Yes.'

And so we can talk about your . . .' – she paused – 'ongoing role with us.'

'Right.' My voice stuck. I cleared my throat. 'Right,' I said again.

Mrs Crieff picked a piece of paper up off the desk and pushed it towards me.

'Now, these are all areas I've not been able to fully tick,' she said.

'Right.'

Luisa McKenzie, it said on the piece of paper:

End of Year Appraisal: targets to be consolidated
Punctuality
Referring to teacher's plans
Recording observations

There were question marks in green pen beside each of these points. Beside *Punctuality* there was a question mark and an exclamation mark. I thought of the first meeting we'd had in that room the previous autumn, when I'd declared such enthusiasm for the job of classroom assistant. And for a moment Susan Ford floated into my mind again, poor ghostly Miss Ford, who had begun to symbolise all the ways in which I was also failing.

'So,' Mrs Crieff continued briskly, 'as you can see, Luisa, there are still a few areas I've not been able to sign off. Which is certainly not ideal, at this late point in the school year. Though there's nothing that can't be *fixed* here,' she added, doubtfully. 'This *is* the last week of term, but we're not dead in the water yet.'

I thought of a duck, floating motionless on a pond. *I never even told you about Moonchild*, I thought. Moonchild had never even appeared on my CV. And most of the rest of it had been lies, in some form or another.

'So how can I fix things?' I heard myself asking. Because I didn't want to work at St Luke's: I didn't *want* to work there, but I didn't want to get sacked, either. It seemed to me, sometimes, that going to St Luke's on the bus every morning was the only thing that had prevented me from floating away altogether, into outer space, like John Singer's astronaut.

Mrs Crieff gazed at me, as if trying to understand the gulf between us. On the wall behind her were two framed prints which had formed a sort of backdrop to our meetings over the past few months. One of them proclaimed the St Luke's motto, *Veritas et Fidelis*, printed in rather beautiful copper-plate lettering. The other had the words of *The Desiderata* typed on it: *Speak your truth quietly and clearly*, it said, *and listen to others, even the dull and the ignorant: they too have their story . . .* Mrs Crieff had told me once that *The Desiderata* was a sort of mantra for her, a kind of personal prayer, and it had made me want to scream.

'What I mean is,' I began, trying to sound intrigued about my own place in the unfurling of life, and at St Luke's in particular, 'what's the best way I can . . . improve things, before the end of . . . this week? In your opinion?'

Mrs Crieff breathed in.

'Let me put it this way,' she said quickly. 'What I've got here, Luisa, is this form I have to fill in and fax to the council on Friday morning. It's called a Probationary

Year Assessment Form. And as long as the boxes I tick on it are either labelled "Achieved" or "Achieving", you're home and dry.'

'Right.'

'We just don't want any of them, at the end of term, to say "Unachieved".'

'No.'

'It's not really up to me, ultimately – I should stress that. It's just that the form's going to the council. And they're the ones who make decisions about probationary staff.'

'Yes.'

'And I can't, in all honesty, say you've been 100 per cent committed this term, Luisa,' she added, almost chirpily now, like a sprightly little bird, 'or even 100 per cent focused on the curriculum. Can I?'

'No.'

I couldn't quite see the page Mrs Crieff was referring to. I wondered how many of the boxes on it said 'Unachieved'. Maybe they all said that.

'But, as I said, we're not dead in the water. By no means, actually, you'll be pleased to know. We really don't want to *lose you, Luisa*,' she added with a sudden, unnerving intensity.

'OK,' I whispered, my hands clenched into fists on my lap.

'And it honestly doesn't take much to turn "Unachieved" into "Achieving". Just showing a bit more willing would be all it takes! Getting on an earlier bus! Sticking, for the coming week, with the topics the children are supposed to be learning. Maybe, even,' she added, as if inspired, 'you could demonstrate your ability to engage with the curriculum during the school trip tomorrow.' *I mean, it's not rocket science, darling*, she looked as if she was thinking.

'OK,' I said.

'Anyway,' Mrs Crieff continued, changing tack; and she smiled again and leaned forward a little in her chair – 'in more general terms, Luisa, how are you feeling, in yourself, about the job? How are things going?'

I stared at her. She was like the good cop and the bad cop, rolled into one person.

'How are things going?' I asked.

'Yes. Because we have a commitment to you, too, of course. A duty of care. I mean, are you enjoying it here? Is your job matching up to your expectations?'

And she stopped talking. I felt a little stricken. Somebody had asked me the same question a few weeks earlier: Mary Wedderburn had phoned me up out of the blue for a chat – 'Hi Luisa, how're things going?' she'd said – and, for some reason, as soon as I'd put the phone down, I'd started to cry.

'Well, I suppose I didn't have any particular expectations about the job,' I heard myself saying, and a look of sheer incredulity passed across Mrs Crieff's face.

'Really? No . . . particular expectations . . .' she repeated, and she picked up a pen and began to write something down. I waited for her to stop writing and wondered what I was going to say next. Sometimes I wasn't sure what sentence might be about to come out of my mouth. And now there was this new sense, as I sat there – this realisation – that I *did* still want the job, just a little. I did actually want to work there a tiny bit. If only to stop myself becoming another Miss Ford.

'I suppose', I said, in an attempt to limit the damage I'd already done, 'the thing that's exceeded my expectations is all the art projects we've been doing . . .'

'Ah, yes,' said Mrs Crieff, somewhat morosely.

'And the children are great,' I added. 'And Mrs Baxter's been . . .'

'Supportive?' Mrs Crieff asked, looking up, her pen poised.

'Yes, she has,' I said.

'Super,' Mrs Crieff said, ticking something on the form in front of her. 'So the children and the rest of the staff have, in your opinion, been a positive aspect about working here?'

'Yes. I mean, wouldn't it be awful', I said, 'to work in a school and not like the children and the rest of the staff?'

Mrs Crieff peered at me. I peered back. My brain whirred for something to add. As a child myself, I'd once used to worry that my thoughts might be visible in little clouds above my head, and now I could feel the same old idea bubbling up. *What if my thoughts are there, as clear as day? What if she knows what I'm really thinking?*

'Anyway,' I ploughed on, 'I've really been enjoying some of the things we do in class. You know, some of our routines. Like Circle Time, and Show and Tell.'

'OK,' said Mrs Crieff.

'Last Friday was great, for instance,' I carried on, 'because one of the girls brought in a haggis.'

'A haggis?'

'Yes,' I replied; because it was true: Ruby Simpson, whose father worked in a butcher's shop, had brought a haggis in to Show and Tell, smooth and shiny as a large pebble.

Mrs Crieff looked a little pained. 'Hmm,' she said. And my confidence began to ebb again – it just began slipping away as we sat there confronting each other.

'So, perhaps on balance we can say you're *feeling settled in the post*, then?' she said after a moment. 'Will I tick that box, Luisa? I would *like* to be able to tick that box.'

'Absolutely,' I said, glancing down at the two framed photos that sat, side by side, on her desk. They were of Mrs Crieff's grown-up sons. They were both clad in graduation attire with mortar boards on their heads, the tassles hanging studiously. They looked as if they now worked in insurance or banking. Neither of them looked like the kind of boy I would ever be interested in.

'OK,' said Mrs Crieff, 'consider that box ticked.'

'That's great,' I replied.

'So: on to the next question. What you have to tell me now is, what's the best bit about being a classroom assistant?' She leaned a little further forward across her desk. 'And what career developments would you – ideally – like to see in the coming year?'

'Hmm, the best bit . . .' I mused. I didn't like that

word, *ideally.* 'Well, I suppose the best bit is probably some of the things the children say.'

'Oh yes?'

'I mean, they come up with such funny things some-times, don't they?' I continued, sagely. 'Like, today, Emily Ellis . . .'

'Who?'

'. . . Emily Ellis, in my class . . .'

'Ah, yes, Emily Ellis . . .' Mrs Crieff reiterated, and she frowned very slightly and scribbled something down again on the notepad in front of her, as if Emily might have committed some kind of crime. I sat and watched her. I felt my mouth becoming dry. And I suddenly didn't want to tell her my story about Emily – I didn't really want to tell Mrs Crieff anything about anything – but now I'd started I would have to go on.

'So,' I said, 'Emily and I were reading a book the other day – it was this story about a car breaking down on the motorway –'

'Mm-hmm,' Mrs Crieff said, scribbling away.

'– and she suddenly said, "Miss McKenzie, what hap-pens when the break-down truck breaks down?"'

Mrs Crieff looked up.

'How funny,' she said.

'Yes.'

'What a funny thing to say.'

'Yes.'

And I felt quite cold. I felt like someone who has swum too far out to sea without realising it, too far to swim back –

'Yes, it *was* quite funny,' I said, 'the way she just, you know, said it: "What happens when the break-down truck breaks down?" It was just . . .'

But now Mrs Crieff seemed to have switched off altogether. She was looking past me and out of the window, at the trees on the other side of the playground. She looked as if she was listening to something – the wind in the branches, perhaps – or considering some holy set of instructions. And I wondered if, in some unfathomable way, I had just failed my assessment. Maybe I had just said something very bad, and Mrs Crieff would not, now, be able to tick any more boxes. And I would lose my job. And then what would I do? How much further would I fall?

But then, quite suddenly, she snapped out of her reverie. She sighed: it was a snorting kind of sigh that came through her nose, the same sound I'd heard horses make up at the Braid Hills Riding School, when I'd walked past it with my mother.

'Well, children do say such funny things sometimes, don't they?' she said. 'That's what keeps us on our toes, isn't it, Luisa? As teachers.'

And now, without any warning, she was standing up. She was concluding our meeting and rising from her chair.

'Oh,' I said. I grabbed my coat off the back of my chair, picked my bag up from the floor, and stood up, too.

'Well, Luisa,' Mrs Crieff said, striding across to the door. She looked down at her watch. 'Eleven fifteen,' she added, and then she reached out and put her hand on the door handle. 'So, as long as we can turn those two "Un-achieved" boxes into "Achieving" ones over the course of this week, I'm sure the council will be happy to approve a permanent . . .'

'But which ones are they, Mrs Crieff?' I blurted.

And there was a moment's silence. 'Which ones are what?' Mrs Crieff asked in a small voice.

'Which are the boxes that still need ticked? The Un-achieving ones? Because I'm still not quite . . .'

'The Unachieving areas', Mrs Crieff interrupted in a low, measured voice, 'are the same as last time, Luisa. The ones about punctuality and focus. Those are still the areas you need to . . . focus on.'

'Right.'

'However. I've no doubt you'll be redoubling your efforts in those areas before the end of the week'

'Yes.'

'Because we don't want to lose another of our classroom assistants.'

'No.'

'And soon the holidays will be upon us and we can all relax.'

'Yes.'

'And if there's anything you want to come and talk to me about, Luisa, over the next few days, relating to your work here – anything at all,' she said, as she opened the door onto the vast, draughty corridor, 'then do come and tell me. Even if it's outwith school hours.'

'Thank you,' I said, doubting the sincerity of this.

'That's OK,' said Mrs Crieff, closing the door.

I turned and headed down the stairs, my heart a kind of low weight in my chest. I walked past the big *Truth and Fidelity* sign that had been nailed above the dinner-hall door, headed back through the doorway, along the corridor, into the playground and crossed over towards the Portakabin. And for some reason an RE teacher I'd once had at my old school – a bald, quite peculiar man called Mr Sloper – suddenly appeared in my mind. I think it was the sign in the dinner hall that brought him back. 'What is the truth, ladies and gentlemen?' he'd used to ask us, little bubbles of spit forming at the corners of his mouth like cuckoo spit on an ear of corn. '*Quid est veritas?*' Which was something Jesus was supposed to have said. Or was it Pontius Pilate? I suppose I'd never taken much notice in Religious Education.

Dinner was at half past twelve, but Mrs Baxter and I always had to stay behind for ten minutes or so after the lunch-time bell had gone – weary, grown-up drudges – picking up bits of Lego and squashed Play-Doh and sweeping the sand back into the sandpit. I was caught, as I often was, between the desire to salvage everything, every single little plastic wheel and axle, and to just sweep it all into a dustpan and chuck it in the bin.

Mrs Baxter and I made it outdoors at twenty to, clutching our Tupperware lunch boxes and locking the classroom door behind us. The weather had broken, spots of warm rain falling onto our faces as we hurried down the ramp and across the playground.

Mrs Baxter did not ask me about my meeting with Mrs Crieff. 'Humid,' she observed instead, looking up at the clouds above the school roof. They were darkly bright, an almost luminous grey now: they were certainly not the benign sort of clouds we sang about at Assembly.

'I think it suits the end of term though, doesn't it: weather like this,' I replied. 'I mean, these are the dog days, aren't they? The dog days of term.'

Mrs Baxter glanced at me, as if some opinion she'd held about me was regrettably, inevitably, beginning to unravel. Her expression had, in recent weeks, adopted that look.

'I'm not quite sure what you mean by "dog days", Luisa,' she said.

And we carried on in silence across the playground. We headed past the wooden ship that was permanently moored in the tarmac, past the bin and the blasted tree and towards the dinner-hall entrance. Glancing down, I spotted something white lying at the bottom of the steps. It was a piece of checked school paper, torn from an exercise book and now lying in a newly forming puddle. I stooped to pick it up.

A Review of My Progress This Term

it said in computerised font at the top of the page.

This term I learnt how to:

– and then there was a child's handwriting in watery, wobbly pencil –

   1. *I did learn quite a lot about the six times tables but it did not stay in my head.*
   2. *I am still not good at dodging gym balls.*

This year I have enjoyed keeping fit by:
   1. *Sometimes I do walking up hills.*

'Someone will be missing that,' observed Mrs Baxter.

I felt a peculiar fizz of sadness in my chest. I felt suddenly very sad for the child who walked up hills and was not good at dodging gym balls.

'I'll hand it in to the secretary's office,' I said.

'Yes. That would be a plan, Luisa.'

'*Look* at this *beautiful butterfly*!' we heard a voice pronouncing on a classroom TV as we headed in through the main doors. '*Now* let's *fold it* in *half*!'

'What are they *doing* in there?' I asked.

'Symmetry,' Mrs Baxter replied.

6

It's funny how some memories that year were sharp, in focus, while others just receded into the background, waving at me like seaweed beneath the water. I seemed, almost, to recall the wrong things. Or, at least, the things that had gone wrong. I kept remembering, for instance, the day I'd knocked all the sea urchins off that shelf in Moonchild. Also the day of my careers interview in a small, cupboard-like office called *The Resources Room*. I could recall exactly how Mrs Angelli, the careers officer, had stood up when I'd walked into the room, then immediately sat back down with a look of defeat.

'So, you are Luisa McKenzie . . .' she'd confirmed. And then she'd looked down at a piece of paper in her hands. It was evident that the information written on it did not bear much relation to anything she'd been led to expect. 'Now, I have to say I'm a little confused here actually, Luisa,' she'd said, 'because the boxes you've ticked on your questionnaire – "I am a *PEOPLE PERSON*, my favourite pastimes are *DRAWING AND PAINTING*, I prefer being *INDOORS*" – well, they all clearly indicate a career in the arts. They link up directly with the arts box.' She'd blinked. 'But wasn't it your plan to study . . . geography?'

'Well,' I'd replied, 'that was the *plan* . . .'

'But now, here, you've got "Perhaps going to Art College",' Mrs Angelli quoted.

She looked up again. Her mouth had formed a troubled, rounded shape, a bit like the end of a chanter on a set of bagpipes.

'I mean', she said, 'I've spoken to your geography teacher, Luisa, and he was under the distinct impression that geography was what you were going to be doing. I mean, art is a super career for the right person. Art is great. But to be honest, Luisa, there are a lot of young women who want to be artists. And there are scores of ex-art college students flipping burgers out there, aren't there? I'm afraid to say. And signing on the dole.'

I looked down at my hands, which were bunched up into fists in my lap. They were the fists I should have punched Ed McRae with four months earlier. I didn't know what I wanted to do with my life any more: I didn't have a clue. The plans I'd once had – worthy plans relating to coffee bean production and the rubber industry in Brazil, and Europe's changing population patterns – seemed to be sliding away, like something disappearing down a hill. Waiting for me somewhere in London there was probably a little anaglypta-papered room in a bedsit and a group of cheerful, life-affirming friends. But I couldn't picture them any more – the room or the friends or the life.

Mrs Angelli had shifted slightly in her seat. There was a bright pink flowering cactus peeking around the left side of her head.

'You do seem to have got yourself in a bit of a pickle here, don't you?' she said.

I stared down at my knees in their unseasonal black tights: it was nearly May already, the sunshine was becoming warm, and I was still wearing black woollen tights! I had not progressed! I had not moved with the seasons! There was a large, round hole in the right knee of my tights, childish, stretched wide across the whiteness of my kneecap.

'So, I suppose I should just carry on with geography,' I croaked. 'I mean, as you say, there's more likely to be a job in geography . . .'

Mrs Angelli stared at me. It was as if she could see something I couldn't. Some projected life. Maybe she could already see me sitting beneath some upended eggcup mobile in a classroom, surrounded by little children and cutting out shapes with plastic scissors. Maybe careers officers were good at that.

'Chin up,' she said. 'It's normal to get jittery at this stage.' And she leaned forward in her seat and briefly patted my knee. 'And once your exams are behind you and you're in London studying geography, you'll wonder what on earth you were worrying about!'

I was aware that my five-minute careers consultation was up. Some other lost soul was hovering outside in the corridor.

'OK. Thanks, Mrs Angelli,' I said. Because what else was there to say? And I stood up, shook her hand, edged past the photocopier and headed towards the door. Then I walked downstairs, all the way down three flights, to Mr

Jolly's geography room, which was where I was supposed to be that afternoon. We were revising surveying and geological contours that week, and Mr Jolly had told us all to bring compasses for something he called 'mapping purposes'. But when I got to my seat and took my compass out of my bag, I realised I was the only one who'd brought the kind you draw circles with. Everyone else had brought the kind that pointed north. Which said something, I suppose, about the direction I was heading in.

'So, guess what we've just been doing in biology, Lulu?' I remember Stella Muir asking me that day, as we sat together at the cooked dinners table.

'I don't know,' I'd replied, biting into my sandwich.

And she had paused and smiled.

'Delivering rabbit babies.'

'Oh,' I said, my teeth failing, suddenly, to bite.

'Yep, that was what we were doing today,' Stella continued, twisting an overcooked piece of cauliflower rather delicately between her fingers.

And I had no idea what she wanted me to say, what sentence to form about newborn rabbits. About newborn anything. *Don't you remember, Stella?* I wanted to say. *Don't you remember what happened to me?* And I thought of all the lying I'd been doing ever since – all the lying and not telling – and all the plans I'd ever had began to hurtle around my head, like shoals of little fish.

'Hello?' Stella said. 'Earth calling Luisa?'

'Yeah, still here, Stella,' I said. 'On planet Earth.' Although, in some ways, I'd begun to doubt it.

'So. Anyway. It was Mrs Noble's rabbit?' Stella continued. 'And the babies were really ugly. All pink and blind and naked.'

I was feeling slightly sick now.

'How many?' I said.

'Nine!' Stella replied, pushing some more cauliflower onto her fork. 'Nine tiny pink rabbits.'

'Cute,' I said, dutifully.

'No,' Stella replied. 'They weren't cute. I just told you. They were really ugly. And one of them was dead.'

'Oh.'

'They have to have a lot of them,' she continued. 'Rabbits. Kind of survival of the fittest . . .'

And then she seemed to recall something that had happened once, and stopped talking.

'Anyway,' she said, 'it's not that different from drawing them, is it? I mean, you drew some rabbits once, didn't you? Dead ones? In art class?'

I didn't reply. There was nothing to say. I just looked around the dinner hall. I could see my old friends, Mary and Linda, sitting at the packed-lunch tables, eating sandwiches. Theirs had always been a serious, sandwich-eating friendship.

'This cauliflower's overcooked,' I said.

Stella frowned at the gravy on her plate. Then she looked up at me again, and there was something very cool about her expression.

'D'you know what, Luisa?' she said, and her voice was different now, sharper-edged. 'There are plenty of people who might be interested to know what I was doing in biology today.'

It was as if some immutable part of her character was beginning to show through, like the wood beneath a varnished chair. *Or maybe it's me*, I thought. *Maybe I'm the wood beneath the varnish.*

'I mean, at some point', Stella said, 'you're going to have to start showing an interest in what *other people* are doing!'

And I think that was the point when we realised we were no longer friends; that we had never really *been* friends. We'd only ever pretended, and I couldn't even remember why.

Stella sighed, mushed the rest of her cauliflower into a kind of purée and got up from the table.

'Hi, Ed,' she called out.

Because there was Ed McRae suddenly – he happened to be there, right at that moment! – lumbering across the dinner hall with one of the canteen's copper water jugs. He stopped and turned.

'Oh, hi. Yeah. Hi, Luisa,' he added, a little shiftily. His mouth, his lovely mouth, was an awkward line.

Stella turned and glanced, a little regretfully, in my direction.

'Right. I've got maths now, anyway,' she said. 'So I might as well head up there with Ed.'

And she pulled her pretty green cardigan from the back of her chair and went to join him. Ed did look a little embarrassed, I noticed; he even blushed slightly. But I knew he would soon recover his equilibrium. You had to be balanced, after all, if you were going to work with cantilevers and lift shafts and supporting walls for a living. Smiling at Stella, he put the water jug down on one of the used-crockery trolleys, and they walked out together through the swing doors.

I sat at the dinner table for a minute or so. I felt as if I'd had something taken away from me that I'd only just realised was mine. It was early Monday afternoon. One of the table's legs was shorter than the others and it wobbled ridiculously. I felt a lot like crying, but I didn't think it was anything to do with Stella, or even Ed McRae. Maybe it was about nothing more than that poor dead baby rabbit. I got up from the table after a while and pulled my big black cardigan properly over my shoulders. I was going to be one of those complicated girls who went round head to toe in black. I went to the corner of the room with my plate of unfinished lunch, scraped my macaroni cheese and cauliflower florets into the Addis bin the school called 'the scraps bucket', and left the dining room. I just left. I walked up the school drive, waited at the bus stop for the 41 bus and went home. We were allowed to go home that fortnight for something called 'study leave'. Some people used to call it 'study leave-it-out'.

*

The staffroom was quiet that lunchtime. There were just a few teachers wandering around at the far end of the room, quiet and mildly traumatised by their mornings. There was a respectful, almost mournful kind of hush. People didn't like to accost each other too much at that time of day: it was one of those unwritten rules.

Then, after a second, Mr Temple turned up.

Mr Temple was always upbeat. He was always fired up and trendy in his pale suit and Cuban heels. I watched him head straight across to the other side of the room, like a bouncing bomb progressing across a still lake. I saw some of the female staff stiffen, like startled deer, at his approach.

'Ladies!' he said to them in his big voice.

'Hi, Mark,' they carolled.

'Thank God it's lunchtime,' he boomed.

And then he stationed himself by the water urn and began to talk to Mrs Richards. He'd singled her out, the way a lion hunts down a zebra.

Standing beside me, Mrs Baxter tutted. She never thought Mr Temple was funny, she took him very seriously. To me he was just funny. Which was one of the ways I did not fit in.

Mr Temple had taken up the pose now that he often adopted, of significant intelligence. He was a very trim person: short, neat, fortyish, bearded like the king of Spain. Sometimes, in conversation with the younger, pretty female staff like Mrs Richards and me too, on my good days, he even stroked his beard. *He's the sort of person Stella and I would have sniggered about,* I thought; and I felt quite hollow, suddenly, over the loss of an understanding that had once been mine.

As I crossed the room, Mr Temple glanced up over the top of the urn.

'Miss McKenzie.'

'Morning, Mr Temple.'

'Afternoon,' he corrected, rolling his eyes at Mrs Richards. 'Don't they teach you anything, you classroom assistants?'

I didn't reply. I was no good at ripostes; and now I realised with dismay that Mrs Richards had grabbed her chance to get away: she had already made her zebra-like escape and was almost running across the room to speak to Mrs Regan, the school's secretary.

'So, how are you?' Mr Temple asked me, looking slightly irked.

'I'm fine, thanks,' I replied.

'Great. So, any plans for the summer?' he continued, glancing shiftily at my hair.

'The summer?'

'Yes. That interlude between spring and autumn.'

'Well, no. Nothing specific,' I said. Which was true: the summer holidays ahead of me were just a big, wide-open space, as big as an aircraft hangar.

'I'm going to the south of France,' Mr Temple said – a little boastfully, I couldn't help thinking.

'Are you?' I said.

And then neither of us had anything to say. I didn't know what to say about the south of France and I didn't know how to speak to men any more, even funny-peculiar men like Mr Temple – I just didn't know what they expected me to say. And maybe Mr Temple didn't know, either, how to speak to pink-haired classroom assistants who had no plans for the summer.

'Sooo . . .' he began.

'I've just had a meeting with Mrs Crieff,' I blurted, feeling somehow that I should tell someone this, confess it to someone. 'She's doing my end-of-year appraisal.'

Mr Temple raised one urbane eyebrow. I'd heard him making jokes about Mrs Crieff's obsession with appraisals and assessments, but now there was a chance for camaraderie about it, he didn't seem to want to make any.

'I'm not quite sure what she'll be expecting from me in the next couple of days, though,' I heard myself prattling on. 'I don't think', I continued, 'I'm necessarily . . .'

– Mr Temple was frowning vaguely –

'. . . ticking all the right boxes.'

And I stopped talking again. I stood and gazed at the side of the water urn. There was a label stuck to it that said, *Warning: Urn Gets Hot!* I suspected Mr Temple had been the person who'd attached a Post-It note to it a couple of months earlier, saying *Who's Urn?*

He put his right hand in his pocket now and jangled a set of keys. When he moved he always smelled quite strongly of Davidoff: *Cool Water for Men*. It was an aftershave I remembered some of the boys at my old school wearing and it clashed quite horribly sometimes with Mrs Crieff's perfume, the corridors struggling for fresh air in their wakes.

'Mrs Crieff moves in mysterious ways,' Mr Temple said, winking at me, 'her wonders to perform.'

'Sorry?' I felt oddly alarmed: I didn't know what to make of that wink at all.

Mr Temple considered me for a moment. He smiled and stepped forward, and I stepped back.

'Mrs Crieff moves in mysterious ways,' he said again, 'her wonders to perform.'

Which did not enlighten me any further. Also, he did not wink at Mrs Baxter, I couldn't help noticing, who was standing behind me, holding a Custard Cream someone had offered her. At fifty-eight, Mrs Baxter had entered that curious, invisible zone I'd heard my mother speak of. On a different occasion, in Mrs Richards' absence, perhaps, Mr Temple might have begun to flirt with *me*. He might have tried out one of his one-liners on *me*. 'I *like* the hair: very *bold*,' he might have said, his voice a kind of foghorn across the staffroom. That afternoon, though, was evidently not the right moment. Besides, I was perhaps already looking a little too blotchy and a little too weird that week: not quite flirting material. I thought for a moment of Ed McRae, of his overnight switch from ardour to coldness, and about the way I'd behaved around men ever since. How they had scared me. And I wondered if I was already becoming a person who would be discussed by the staff next term. Maybe I was already becoming *Luisa McKenzie, that funny girl we had last year*. The girl who did not tick all the boxes.

'Ignore Mr Temple, Luisa,' Mrs Baxter said in a loud, flat voice, placing the Custard Cream into her mouth, and so I did; it seemed the easiest option. We breezed as a unit past Mr Temple towards the shelf beside the sink, grabbed our coffee mugs and carried on in a kind of arc towards the seats by the windows. Mrs Baxter and I always sat there to eat our lunch. The seats were turquoise – big and sighing and puffy – and people always made a beeline for them. It was a polite, insouciant beeline, but we all still wanted them, those seats.

'So,' said Mrs Baxter contentedly, lowering herself onto a seat so it made its usual sighing exhalation and then she opened up the lid of her lunch box.

I felt jangled by the morning and so I didn't say anything for a while. I just sat there. Sat and waited. Outside the window, on the low branches of a tree, a group of sparrows twittered. Someone hooted their car horn on the road. Mrs Regan, Mr Temple and some P4 teachers moved around conspiratorially on the far side of the room, clattering teaspoons against coffee mugs. I looked down at my lunch box but I wasn't hungry, so I looked up again. On the staff bulletin board beside the door there was a sign for an *end-of-term social* that Mrs Regan was arranging. It would be taking place in a local tandoori restaurant at the beginning of the holidays. *A chance for us all to let our hair down!* Mrs Regan had written in biro at the bottom. I tried to picture myself in a fortnight's time, sitting in a tandoori restaurant with other members of St Luke's staff. I envisaged the little silver bowls full of steamed rice, the heated, fragrant hand wipes, the wine glasses sloshing with Chianti. There was a plan, P3's Miss Leonard had said, to go clubbing afterwards in The Ritzy. I thought of cavemen with clubs; of those strange, low-hatted men in *Wacky Races* hitting each other over the head. I *had* signed up for the evening – Mrs Baxter had talked me into it – but it struck me now how I would much rather go up to the Meadows that evening and lie down on the grass beneath a tree.

'D'you know, Luisa,' Mrs Baxter said as she prised a sandwich from her lunch box, 'this is my twenty-fifth year here. I've been eating my lunch in this room for twenty-five years.'

'Wow: twenty-five years?' I said.

It seemed an impossible number of years to have worked *anywhere*. Even to have *lived*. *How could that just happen?* I wondered. *How could that number of years just be allowed to flop and lollop along? You could probably make salt dough models in your* sleep. *You could probably teach* Fun with Phonics *with your eyes closed.*

'That must feel like quite an achievement,' I said. 'I mean, you must have taught hundreds of children.'

'Generations,' Mrs Baxter replied, opening up a little pot full of Ritz biscuits and sliding a couple in between the slices of her sandwich. 'Did the children ask you about your hair this morning, by the way?' she added insouciantly, changing the subject in one deft move.

'My hair?'

And I pictured myself – as I might appear at that moment – to the other teachers in the room: I was a peculiar, fretful flamingo, sitting there with my carton of juice and my sandwiches.

'It's just that it's a little . . .' Mrs Baxter continued, '. . . unexpected. And I wondered if any of the children wanted to know why you'd done it?'

I pierced the carton with its little plastic straw.

'Only Emily mentioned it, in fact,' I said. 'In Circle Time.'

'Ah, yes.'

I cleared my throat. 'She did also mention it', I confessed, 'while she was playing in the Home Corner with Jade and Lauren.'

'And what did you tell her?' Mrs Baxter asked. She seemed oddly intrigued.

'Well,' I said, thinking back to the conversation Emily and I had had. 'I just told her that some people dye their hair.' I sucked some juice. 'And I told them it was up to them if they wanted to dye it. And so I'd decided to dye mine pink. Only it was a mistake,' I continued. 'The pink colour. That turned out to be a mistake. And I told her I'm going to be washing it out over the next week or so.'

I trailed off. I did not go on to mention the conversation Emily and I had proceeded to have about the words 'dye' and 'die'. I did not say we'd touched on the subject of mortality: to die, as in to no longer exist. ('*Dye* is another word for colour,' I'd said. 'It's not "die" as in . . .' 'Yes, I know,' Emily had chirped back. 'My mummy dyes her hair, too, because she doesn't like all the grey hairs. She thinks they make her look like an old lady.') And a little picture came into my mind for some reason of Ed McRae and his T-shirt, that T-shirt I had loved because I'd thought it had said something about him: about his honesty and his alluring cynicism. *Life's a Bitch and Then You Die*. And I thought about those pills I'd swallowed, the one in the clinic and the one in my room at home. And about what had happened after that. And I thought about people not being as clever as you might once have believed; that sometimes they just wore T-shirts with other people's ideas on them.

'Oh, so did you not mean for it to turn out that colour?' Mrs Baxter asked lightly. 'Was the pink a mistake? Oh well,' she concluded, laughing, 'the best-laid plans of mice and men gang aft awry!'

I looked down at the foil-wrapped sandwiches on my knees. There was something about packed lunches that had always caused me to feel both pleased and gloomy. I don't know, maybe it was a hope over experience thing.

'Is it a problem then?' I asked Mrs Baxter. 'The colour of my hair? Is it', I ploughed on indiscreetly, 'something that's going to be yet another question mark on Mrs Crieff's form?'

Mrs Baxter frowned and did not reply.

'Oh well,' I said.

Along with the pineapple juice I had peanut-butter sandwiches that day, and one of my mum's gingerbread men and an apple. Lunch for a six-year-old. The Golden Delicious apple was neither golden nor delicious. The gingerbread man smiled its raisiny smile and hurt my front teeth when I bit its head off.

'Ooh: a gingerbread man!' Mrs Baxter said.

'Yes.'

'So, will you be making biscuits for the big event on Thursday?' she continued, settling back more comfortably with her lunch.

And for a moment I didn't know what she was talking

about. *Big event?* Then I remembered: Mrs Crieff's end-of-term jamboree. Her celebration of another school year successfully concluded, after which we could *all relax*. On the wall behind Mrs Baxter, to the right of her head, there was even a poster about it that one of the children had recently designed: a picture of an enormous fairy cake beneath crossed wooden spoons. It looked like something heraldic.

> *Come too our jumberlee*
> *for old scool uniforms,*
> *tombowler, toys, food and madgic!*

'Well,' I said, 'my mum's making a few things. She's really the . . . biscuit-maker in our family.'

Which was true: a week or so earlier, I'd made the mistake of showing my mother Mrs Crieff's letter about the jamboree, the paragraph where she'd said how wonderful it would be if '. . . mums, dads, grandparents and carers could spare the time to grab a spoon, don an apron and rustle up a batch of fairy cakes or flapjacks . . .' And my mother had obliged! My mother, who wasn't remotely connected with St Luke's, apart from the unfortunate fact that I worked there. She'd made twenty-four fairy cakes and eighteen slices of chocolate fridge cake. She'd already bagged them up and put them in the freezer, ready for me to take in.

'Well, that's very kind of your mum,' Mrs Baxter said.

'Yes,' I said. It was. And also a little depressing. *Mrs Crieff doesn't deserve your gingerbread men, Mum!* I'd felt like saying when my mother had taken them out of the oven, still smiling at 180 degrees. *Save your biscuits for someone else!* The whole event seemed to have become a slight obsession for Mrs Crieff. '*We feel the jamboree would be an appropriate way for us to leap forward into the summer holidays!*' she'd written laboriously in her letter. Which was how she wrote her letters: they were always full of words like *appropriate* and *leaping forward*. The school library had already benefited earlier that year from the kind donation of *one* parent, she'd continued coyly, and the proceeds of this particular fund-raising event would be going towards new gym equipment for the school. She'd asked people to make a big end-of-term effort: to rifle through their children's clothes drawers; to beg, borrow or steal bunting and balloons; to rustle up cakes and biscuits. They were full of *rustling up*, too, her letters, and *rifling through* and *moving forward*. Though I suspected she didn't really condone begging or stealing.

'I might make some rock buns if I get time,' I said to Mrs Baxter, glancing up at another sign on the wall, just to the left of the jumberlee one. *Besides rain and snow*, it said, *think of other 'weather' words for what falls from the sky.*

Mrs Baxter sighed and blinked. 'I'm going to make some of my Melting Moments,' she said. 'I'm famed for my Melting Moments.'

'Are you?' I replied, and I started to laugh. The words Melting Moments just struck me as funny. That, and the weather that falls from the sky. But then I stopped because Mrs Baxter wasn't laughing. 'So,' I said. I looked down, and then up, out of the high staffroom window, at the pale-grey summer air. There were more seagulls flying through it now, blown in from the coast. The weather felt . . . it was hard to know what it felt like. Something was changing, though. Something was beginning to change.

'By the way,' Mrs Baxter said after a while, with renewed dignity in her voice, 'don't forget you and I will be needing sandwiches tomorrow, too, Luisa. For the Waterways trip. It's amazing how often the classroom assistants forget to bring lunch,' she added ruefully, making me wonder again about the errant, enigmatic Miss Ford.

'Don't worry, I'd never forget my lunch!' I blurted before I could stop myself. 'Lunch is the best bit of the day!' Which was true, as far as I was concerned.

But Mrs Baxter was not in the mood. It was the last week of term and she still had her report cards to write and her appraisal forms to fill in, and she didn't need sarcastic nineteen-year-old classroom assistants adding to her problems.

'Just thought I'd mention it,' she said, and she stood up, brushed the crumbs from her cardigan and left the room.

*

I got up too after a while; after everyone else had gone. I plodded quietly over to the sink in my sensible shoes. I tipped some coffee granules into the 'I'm a Mug' mug

Stella Muir had once given me, shortly before we parted company, adding hot water from the urn and milk from the dregs of Mr Temple's milk carton. Then I took my coffee back to the turquoise seats, sat down and watched the steam rising from beneath the lid of the urn. Someone had left a pile of homework sheets on the table beside my seat. I picked up the top one and read it while I sipped my coffee.

Our trip to Holyrood Palace
   I liked our trip to Holyrood Palace. My favrite bit was playing hide and seak in the sentry boxes and also wen the guide put on a big hat and tol us how Rizzio was killed 56 times in front of pregant Mary.

There was a picture beneath, of a man being stabbed. Being killed fifty-six times. There was a scarlet fountain of blood and Mary Queen of Scots looking on, huge-stomached, her mouth a felt-penned chasm of woe.

'Right: upwards and onwards,' I heard Mr Temple saying in the corridor, as a burst of bright white sunlight suddenly lit up the room and made the steam from the urn look briefly ethereal.

I sat and thought about ghosts; the ghosts of things.

7

Mindy Moo seemed more real to me, sometimes, than the people I'd just spent the day with at St Luke's. More *there*. I always liked it when Emily mentioned her, because her name sounded like one I'd been familiar with once, a long time ago. *Mindy Moo* sounded like someone I'd known and liked. Standing at the bus stop after school that afternoon, I thought about something I'd read once in a book at school – a tradition gypsies used to have, when naming their children. They gave them three, in total, the book had said: there was the baby's official name, and then its family name and then the name whispered into its ear by its mother. That last name was something known only by the mother and – in some subliminal way, I supposed – the baby. There was something nice about that tradition, I'd thought. Names could be like that, though; they could be funny. Also, they could give people a character they didn't ac-tually have. *Stella*, for instance, had once sounded like a bright, uncomplicated name to me. Just as *Ed* had been a salt-of-the-earth name, an honourable name; manly and a good laugh.

I was never late, going home: punctuality was never a problem at the end of the day. I had to wait almost ten minutes before I saw the 42 bus heave itself mirage-like around a distant bend at the bottom of the hill. A maroon rectangle, advertising student bus passes. *Just the ticket for your Uni days.* It trundled past the chemist's, moved on past The Gift of Time gift shop, with its faded fish mobile hanging motionless in the window, then stopped at the bus stop before mine. I waited while some silent figures plodded up and down its steps like people in a Lowry painting, before it launched itself back into the road.

'Single, please,' I declared, getting on board, and I dropped my change into the machine.

The bus seemed to be full of old people that afternoon. People of my age had all been whisked away, like the children in *The Pied Piper of Hamelin.* I sat down beside an old woman in a green polyester turban who glared briefly at me before turning her gaze out of the window. In the seat in front sat a woman with a toddler. The child was standing on the woman's knees. She was wearing big, jangling sandals, the kind Stella had used to call *Jesus creepers.* 'I'm not a climbing frame, Crystal,' the woman said mildly to the child, but it made no difference: the child was just clambering, her little fingers creasing her mother's summer blouse. 'Mummy, make your knees a lap, Mummy, make your knees a lap,' she complained. They were on their way home, I supposed, from some crèche or playschool or toddler group. I'd heard some of the mothers at school talking about toddler groups. I pictured the noise and the thick-wheeled plastic trikes and the snacks. Halved grapes and chopped bananas. Nescafé and Bourbon biscuits.

'Mummy, Mummy, Mummy,' the child trumpeted, her sandals' crêpe soles threatening to rip the fabric of her mother's skirt. 'Mummy, Mummy, Mummy!'

'Oh, Crystal!' sighed the woman.

She reminded me of someone Stella and I had once used to observe through the windows of our old school bus: a woman we'd used to call The Mummy Woman, because she'd always seemed such an epitome of saintly motherhood. She'd stood at the corner of Cumberland Road every day, surrounded by infants – and Stella and I, sitting high and superior on the bus, had always used to shriek when we saw her. *'Look – there she is! There's the Mummy Woman!'* She had been shortish, this woman, late thirties, with a weary face and a practical padded jacket, and always with this huge entourage of small children. *Who in their* right mind *would sacrifice themselves to a life like that?* we used to think. We'd counted them once, the children: there were five of them, not including a baby strapped to the woman's chest and a larger baby, often yelling its head off, in a buggy. What on earth was she *doing*? What was she *doing* with her life? She was like the old woman who lived in a shoe. And we were the girls who were not going to get trapped. 'Excuse me, this is my stop,' said the old woman beside me, as if it *was* her stop, in some way.

'Sorry,' I replied, standing up to let her past.

'Mummy,' the little girl was still complaining, 'Mummy, make your knees a lap! Make your knees a lap, Mummy! Mummy –'

'Boo,' I said, as I sat down again: I couldn't resist it. And the little girl stared at me, wide-eyed, like some sort of marsupial, then slunk down to hide beside her mother.

This was, I felt, a small achievement. And now I considered just carrying on past my stop – because maybe you could do that; maybe you could sail straight past where you were supposed to be going, and by doing this, alter the course of your life.

I never had so far, though. Sailed on. I'd always just hopped off and gone home. Our nearest stop was at a place people from my old school used to call God Squad Junction – a crossing where four square, greyish churches confronted each other, like people having an argument. *There Is Hope*, it said on a noticeboard stuck in the front garden outside one of the churches. And there was a picture of a rainbow, an arc of pure beauty. I remembered there'd been a poster just like that at my old school, too, stuck above the door of our exam hall.

We lived only five minutes away from the bus stop. It was just an unfortunate fact that Mrs Crieff did, too. There was nothing to be done about this, of course – but, still, it was not a relaxing walk. I strode resolutely along the pavement that afternoon, speeding up as I neared her front gate. Fortunately, Mrs Crieff was never in. She was always still up at St Luke's at that time of day, working hard. As I hurried past her front gate I pictured her perched in her office on her blue pneumatic chair. She had a very upright way of sitting which always seemed like a reprimand to people who slouched. There she was, I imagined, sitting upright and working out who to keep and who to fire; there she was, collating and ticking and assessing. And there I was, the assessed, the unpunctual, the unfocused Miss McKenzie, schlepping home. Three times during the course of a recent meeting Mrs Crieff had used the words 'stepping stones'. But the stones *she* meant were not pretty resting points in a river, they were places from which you launched your next move.

The oddest thing about Mrs Crieff's house was that her front lawn was made from fake grass. I'd clocked this before I'd even known she lived there, and had wondered who on earth would have a fake lawn in their garden instead of the real thing. It was only evident up close: from the distance of my bedroom window you couldn't tell. My mother and I had had a laugh about it from time to time on our way home from the shops. Who could be so divorced from nature, we'd wondered, that they could bear to confront *that* every time they opened their curtains in the morning? And then we'd discovered that, well, Mrs Crieff could.

'I suppose it never needs mowing,' my mother had conceded politely. 'Maybe that's why she had it put down. I suppose she's a busy woman.'

And we'd both just stood and gazed at it for a moment, lost for anything further to say. The lawn was made from the same material that you saw sometimes beneath cuts of meat in butchers' shops or on indoor football pitches. It was a searing, impossible green. A blackbird had settled on it as we watched, bounced its beak against it and flown off again, puzzled. I'd seen that happen a few times since then: Mrs Crieff's conning of the blackbirds. The plastic had begun to fade a little now, though. It had turned a kind of greenish-blue, like algae on a pond; and hurrying past, it was hard not to gawp. Mrs Crieff also had quite a few garden ornaments. Positioned near the front door there was a stone-effect mushroom about the size of a toddler, several white plastic flower urns and a half-size concrete fox. Sticking up from the flower beds were two moles – the top halves of them, anyway – wearing spectacles and hats. And stationed at an angle near the gate there was a small, white, wheel-less wheelbarrow, within which sat a grey fibreglass rabbit. I was oddly drawn to it, this rabbit: I suppose I almost wondered if it would ever, one day, become real and hop away. As I scuttled past that afternoon I noticed that a new sign had been hung around Mrs Crieff's front gate. It said *I Live Here*, and beneath these words there was a picture of an Alsatian dog. Which was something else that made me wonder about Mrs Crieff and her choices.

*

My mother was in the front garden when I got home. She was standing there pruning the roses. And as soon as I saw her I wanted to run into her arms. My mother was the only sane person I knew in the whole world. The only kind person. The still centre. But I didn't, of course, run into her arms. It was a Monday afternoon in June, blue and overcast but otherwise undramatic, and I had not been brought up to be theatrical, I'd been raised discreet and stoical. I couldn't help thinking, though, that I must have disappointed her, not having a nice boyfriend and a rented flat and a proper set of things to do.

'Hello, darling,' she called to me down the path.

'Hi.'

We had big yellow roses in our garden – the kind you see sometimes in municipal flower beds – but we also had the smaller, scented, more disease-prone types with names like Madame Eglantine and Queen of Denmark. Also some great big ones the colour of a pink winter sky. My father had planted all the roses when we'd first moved to the house. I think they were meant as a kind of peace offering to my mother, who'd never (she'd once told me) particularly wanted to move to Pumzika. She'd always wanted to live in a flat in the centre of town, with wide, painted doors, and a balcony and a big kitchen and a room of her own.

'Good day?' she asked as I opened the gate and plodded up the path towards her. 'How was Mrs Baxter? And Mrs Crieff?'

'Oh, their normal selves,' I replied, pulling a tiny leaf off one of the rose-stems and squashing it between my fingers. I didn't really want to talk about my day at St Luke's, I just wanted to let it recede into the past, just like the children did, when their mothers asked them what they'd been doing that day. 'Things,' they would say. Or, 'Nothing.'

'So, what did you to today?' my mother asked, as if she could read my mind.

'Nothing much to report, really,' I breathed out, deciding not to mention my meeting with Mrs Crieff. 'Apart from one girl having a massive nose bleed at lunchtime. It started at lunchtime and it just went on and on.'

'Oh dear.'

'It stopped in the end, though. We began to think we might have to take her to A&E or something because it just wouldn't stop, but then it did, just as we were about to phone her mum. Oh, and Joe fell off the boat.'

'Joe fell off a *boat*?'

'In the playground. Not a real boat.'

My mother frowned. 'Was he OK?'

'Yeah, he was fine. His head swelled up for a while, which was quite worrying. The top of his nose went all sort of puffy, and I wondered if –'

– my mother was looking at me a little anxiously –

'– if he might have to go to A&E too, but it was probably some protective sort of response; the swelling . . . It calmed down in the end. And he was fine.'

My mother waited. She seemed to think I might have something else to say. But I didn't.

'Well, good,' she said, in her sensible voice – the voice that was a shield which had always protected me and my father from anything too bad, which had always prevented our lives from straying too far into chaos. Or admitting that they might be about to.

'. . . hmm, and what else happened?' I mused, hearing the familiar, slightly sour note appearing in my own voice – I had developed a tendency towards sourness that summer – 'Oh yes: the lollipop man told me another one of his jokes.'

I watched my mother clip one of the big yellow roses near its base – one of her Queens of Denmark – and place the stem into a wooden trug.

'He tells me jokes quite a lot,' I added, 'when I meet him at the crossing.'

Quietly, my mother bent and pulled a chickweed out of the ground. She was wearing her cut-down red Wellingtons and her spotty gardening gloves. She looked as if she was thinking about all the ways I had disappointed her.

'Do you want to hear it?' I asked.

'Go on then.'

'So, a bear walks into a bar, and the barman goes, "What would you like?"'

'Hmm,' said my mother.

'And the bear doesn't say anything for a moment. Then he goes, "I'll have a glass of orange juice, please."'

My mother looked up.

'And the barman goes, "Why the long pause?"'

'Sorry?'

'"Why the long paws?"'

My mother didn't speak for a moment. She stood up straight and looked almost a little tearful. Then she said, 'Yes, but surely you got that in the wrong order?'

'Sorry?'

'The pause. Or you should have paused or something. Or not mentioned the glass of orange juice. And should lollipop men be telling jokes about bars?'

'I know,' I said. 'That's why it's funny. He's funny, the lollipop man. He's a laugh. He doesn't take life too seriously.'

My mother's frown increased slightly.

'That's the way he told it to me, anyway,' I said. 'And I thought . . .' – but I could feel something sliding away now, something failing to amuse my mother, or even me – 'I thought', I said, 'that it was somehow funnier like that. The way he told me.'

'Oh.'

'He told me another one, too, the other day. A doctor, doctor one.'

'Right,' my mother said, flatly.

'Doctor, doctor,' I ploughed on, 'I keep thinking I'm invisible.'

My mother looked at me, waiting for the punchline.

'Next, please!' I said.

I thought it was funny, too, that joke. It was the funniest joke I'd heard for a while.

My mother placed her secateurs on top of the yellow roses in the trug, then lifted it up. *"Trug" – isn't that a peculiar word?* I'd said to her one afternoon, a few days earlier. But at least a trug was useful, I supposed, now. At least it wasn't Mrs Crieff's wheel-less wheelbarrow.

'Shall we go in then?' she said.

And we proceeded down the sidepath, through the back door and into the kitchen. 'Oh, by the way,' my mother added, putting the trug down beneath the table, 'I made some more cakes today for your jumble sale.'

And she went to the sink to fill the kettle.

I leaned against the side of the fridge.

'The jamboree, you mean?' I said. 'Really?'

'I just thought they could maybe do with another

batch from someone. I mean, I shouldn't think many of the mums have got time to bake, have they, in the middle of everything else?' she continued, over the noise of rushing water. 'And it's a pretty funny week to be having a jumble sale at all.'

'Jamboree,' I said.

'Whatever it's called.'

I didn't reply. I looked at the wall opposite and noticed that the Family Organiser had already been turned to July's page. There was a recipe for *Smoked Seafood Dip* and some advice on stemming the flow of blood from a wound.

'Mrs Baxter makes Melting Moments,' I said. 'Apparently she's famous for them.'

'Is she?'

'You don't have to make cakes for the jamboree, Mum. I mean, there's no obligation.'

'I know there's no obligation, darling, I just feel like it. I like making cakes,' she said, sounding slightly hurt. 'And it's for a good cause.'

'I'm not sure a load of gym equipment is much of a good cause,' I replied, not in the mood suddenly to be conciliatory, or even nice: sometimes, when I got home, something happened to me and I started behaving like a bad-tempered nine-year-old. 'I mean,' I said, 'since when is a gym horse a good cause, exactly?'

'Better than a poke in the eye with a sharp stick,' my mother retorted. Which was true, of course. A gym horse was definitely better than a poke in the eye with a sharp stick. It wasn't even one of her expressions though, it was one of my dad's. *We are all living a lie*, I thought, and I sighed and looked across at my old framed picture on the wall.

Happy Days Are Coming.

'So what sort of cakes have you made, then?' I asked.

'Another batch of gingerbread men. Look – there they are on the cooling rack. They're bigger this time because I found another cutter. I'd forgotten all about it and then I found it at the back of the drawer. It's that one we bought in Bakewell years ago.'

'Oh,' I said, and I looked across at the table top. There were twelve new gingerbread men lying there, twelve apostolic gingerbread men. *Tonight one of you will betray me* . . . One of them had a face that reminded me of Ed McRae's. Spacey and cruel, one eyebrow raised. 'Mum, I've got a question,' I said.

'What's that, love?'

'You know some children have imaginary friends? You know, invisible friends that they play with?'

'Yes?' She sounded a little wary.

'Well, did I ever have any? When I was little?'

My mother's face suddenly brightened, as if she was pleased to be asked a question about my childhood – an altogether happier part of our lives together.

'Why do you ask?' she said.

'No reason, really. Just, there's this wee girl at school who keeps telling me about this imaginary friend she's got. Her name's Mindy Moo. The friend, that is. She's this cool kind of . . . girl. And today, when Emily was playing in the Home Corner, she . . .'

'*Mindy Moo*,' my mother interrupted. 'Well, that's quite a name!' And she stopped talking and gazed off, into space. 'Well, I suppose you did have Shonky,' she said, after a moment.

'Sorry?'

'Yes. For a while there was this character you had called Shonky.'

'Shonky?'

'Yes. I don't know what she was, really. I don't know if she was a person or an animal or what. But I suppose *she* was an imaginary friend. She was definitely female, anyway. She was a she.'

I didn't know what to say. I had no recollection of Shonky at all.

'Yes, she used to loom quite large in your life for a while,' my mother continued, a look of fondness in her eyes. 'She was always following you around. Sort of . . . trailing around behind you. And then she just . . . disappeared. You stopped talking about her. I suddenly thought 'Luisa doesn't talk about Shonky any more, and she was . . . gone.'

'How funny,' I said.

'Yes: "Shonky's here," you used to say, sometimes in the funniest places! Sometimes when we were in the supermarket or somewhere, or when we were getting changed for your swimming lessons . . .'

She paused.

'She went on holiday with us one summer. Don't you remember? She came camping with us when we went to Wales. Slept in the tent with us.'

My mother put the lid on the kettle and plugged it in at the wall. And I stood and watched her and tried to remember.

'It's funny,' I said after a moment, 'because Shonky's an actual word, isn't it?'

'Well, yes. But *you* didn't know that, did you? You just made it up. You were three. And you used to like making up words.'

'Shonky,' I said. But all that came into my head, for some reason, was a little picture of Mrs Crieff and her plastic lawn.

'We used to like having her around,' my mother said. And she suddenly looked rather sad.

I walked over to the table, sat down, and tried to recall the space my imaginary friend had once occupied in my life. I suspected that I would have believed in her more than I'd ever believed in, say, God. She would definitely have been more *fun* than God. God never went swimming with you, for a start, or camping, despite what some people might say. 'Shonky,' I said again. But it was impossible to summon her up, or who she had been.

'It's difficult to know sometimes, isn't it,' I began, 'when something's made up and when it's real. Or even when . . .'

But my mother had surfaced from her reverie.

'No, I don't think so, particularly,' she said. 'Anyway, shall we sort out tea? Maybe you could spin the lettuce for me.'

Because she had that ability: to snap out of fond recall. It was a skill she had. A kind of pragmatism.

'Oh,' I said. And I looked up, and out through the window, as if she might be standing out there, my old friend Shonky. She wasn't, of course. There was just the camper van belonging to our neighbours Audrey and Donald Faulkner. *Sirrocco Breeze.* It was slowly reversing past the side wall of our house. It crunched noisily into a new gear and trundled off down the road.

I found the lettuce in the salad drawer. Then I went to the sink, dropped some leaves into the salad spinner, ran water over them and whirred them around. When you turned the handle fast, the salad spinner made a noise that sounded like the trains on the London Underground. That accelerating, whirring noise that got commuters from A to B.

'So I think I'll have a bath after tea,' I said, letting go of the handle and watching the salad spinner continue on its own, like a zoetrope. 'I'm going to try and sort my hair out.' It was the first time I'd mentioned the disaster of my hair, since I'd dyed it. 'I thought it was one of those wash-in, wash-out ones,' I explained, as if this might, in some way, make my decision seem more normal.

'Did you?' my mother said, airily, from the other side of the room. And she glanced quickly across at my hair, where it was coming loose from a kirby grip.

*

I was in bed extremely early. It was still light outside, and would be till nearly eleven. I sat up against my cloud-print pillows and listened to a blackbird making its warning call from the branches of our cherry tree. I read an old copy of *Cosmopolitan*, dated November 1992, when my life had been something else. But they were always the same anyway, those magazines. They always said the same things. There was a picture on the cover of a startlingly perfect young woman, probably about my age but different in most other respects. Her hair was a successful kind of tawny colour and her teeth, revealed in a joyful smile, were dazzlingly white. She looked as if she had some important job writing advertising copy or working for a TV station. She would definitely have a boyfriend and at least three close girlfriends she had lunch dates with. I turned the page. *Things happen after a Badedas bath*, it said, over the picture of a young woman draped alluringly in a bath sheet. When I was small I'd used to wonder what was meant by that Badedas slogan: by 'things happening'. I'd thought it might be something like Christmas presents or a sudden, exciting fall of snow. The magazine smelled of old perfume, which depressed me but also gave me, at the same time, a curious sense of hope. And it occurred to me that perfume might be designed to do exactly that: it might intentionally have a kind of double edge. Then I read an article I'd read at least five times before, about losing two pounds a week through keeping a calorie-counting diary and only eating, as far as I could see, nuts and yogurt and fish. I read another article called 'Make Time for *You!*', which was all about disguising your imperfections with the deft use of concealer, spritzing your face with lavender water and practising yoga for inner peace. Then, just before nine, I turned off the light. I think I must have fallen asleep pretty quickly. And at some point that night, I had a dream about Stella Muir. She didn't look like Stella, she was just this vague, floating presence – the kind that turns up in dreams – all spirit and no substance. But I knew it was her, and in the dream she was called Shonky.

'Hi, Shonky,' I said in the dream.

'Hiya,' Shonky replied.

'What happened to you? Where did you go?' I asked.

But Shonky didn't reply. She'd just come round to my house with some little pots of paint, for some complicated, dream-like reason. She'd brought dozens of colours, with names like burnt umber and vermillion and cerulean blue. We were supposed to be painting some picture. But she'd forgotten to bring any paintbrushes.

'So how are we supposed to *paint* anything?' I asked. I was pretty annoyed with her. 'How are we meant to paint our pictures now?'

8

I walked past Emily Ellis's mother the next morning as I was heading through the school gates. She was leaning over Emily's upturned face, wiping toothpaste marks from the corners of her mouth with a paper hanky.

'Look at you!' she was saying. 'Honestly; look at you!'

'But I can't look at me, Mummy,' Emily replied. 'People can't look at their own faces.'

Mrs Ellis paused.

'You're absolutely right,' she said.

And her own face suddenly became rather blank, as if all the thoughts in it had momentarily gone AWOL.

Mrs Ellis was nothing at all like her husband. She was actually one of the few people at St Luke's I ever felt any connection with. There was just something about her that seemed oddly familiar – probably be-cause she looked as if she didn't want to be there either, she just looked as if she'd wandered into the playground by mistake. She wore a white trench coat and a pair of high heels, and that was pretty much all I knew about her, apart from the fact that she owned a purple VW Beetle with a sticker on the windscreen that said *Purple Bug*. Also, there was the fact that she was pregnant.

Probably about six months *gone*, I'd heard some of the other mothers say in their hushed little groups in the playground – which always made pregnancy sound like a kind of madness. As in *Maud Gonne's gone maud*, a joke my old English teacher had once told us. We'd been reading Yeats – '. . . *tread softly because you tread on my dreams . . .*' – and that was what he'd come up with.

Maud Gonne's gone maud.

Ha ha ha ha ha ha.

Anyway. Sometimes I'd see Mrs Ellis standing there in the playground, her stomach already this big *fact* in front of her, this *gone-ness*, and I would feel sorry for her. And I would try not to think of the day I'd put those little yellow pills into my mouth and swallowed them down.

'Well, I hope you have a nice day, sweet girl,' she said now to Emily. And she put the paper hanky back into her pocket.

'Is it long or short?' Emily asked.

'Is what long or short?'

'The day. Is it going to be long or short?'

Mrs Ellis hesitated.

'Well,' she said, 'I think it's probably going to be medium-sized. And then there's the trip of course, isn't there?' she added. 'To that Waterways place.'

I saw Emily frowning at this unsatisfactory explanation. She frowned across the grey playground, focusing her gaze on the set of monkey bars at the far end, which Mrs Crieff always referred to, excitingly, as 'the adventure playground'. The only thing you could do with the monkey bars, really, though, was to revolve around them, like a cotton reel on a spindle, and sometimes fall off them altogether.

'You always say things like that,' Emily said to her mother.

'What? Things like what?'

'Things that are upside down and funny.'

'Upside down and funny. Oh dear.'

'You're not thinking straight today, Mummy, are you?' Emily tutted.

If I had been a different sort of classroom assistant, I might have intervened at this point. I might have swept in, as Miss Blythe from 1C would have done, or Mrs Richards from 1A. I might even have cracked a world-weary joke, as Mr Temple did. '*Oh, Emily,* I might have chuckled, *'it's like Twenty Questions sometimes, isn't it, Mum?!'* Because, at St Luke's it was OK to call the mothers Mum. You could call the mothers Mum but you couldn't call the fathers Dad. It was just one of those things.

'But how long are we going to be at the Waterways Visitor Centre? And why aren't you coming? And how long is a medium-sized day?' Emily was insisting as I edged mutely past. Then she began to twist one of her mother's protruding coat buttons around, between her fingers. Mrs Ellis frowned and prised her daughter's hand away. *How the hell should I know?* she looked as if she was thinking. *How long is a piece of string?*

'What it is, sweetheart,' she said after a moment, 'is it's a day you spend at school – well, some of it today at the

Waterways place, actually; and then you come home. For tea.'

Emily's frown deepened.

'But why? Why because you have tea at home? That doesn't make sense! And anyway, I always have tea at home. And why aren't you coming to the Waterways place? Some of the other mums are coming!'

'Oh, Emily.'

Mrs Ellis's attempt at motherly serenity had completely unravelled now. She just looked upset. She was wearing her trench coat and high heels as if she was on some professional assignment, but her shoes needed a polish and her coat had a sticker of Dumbo on the pocket, and beneath it, there was this baby.

'I'm going to be late if I don't go,' she said, mainly to herself. 'I'm going to say goodbye now,' she added, stooping to kiss Emily's cheek. 'Have a lovely time on the trip.'

'Oh, but I wish I could go with you!' Emily exclaimed, lunging forward and hanging onto her arm.

And for some reason, this sudden outburst sent a little shiver down my spine. I was just reminded, I suppose, of the days when I'd used to say goodbye to my own mother in the playground; of the way I'd missed her as soon as she'd walked away. How I'd wanted to go wherever she was going, in her white knitted hat and her camel coat and shoes!

'I wish I could stay with you too,' Mrs Ellis was saying, freeing her hand, finger by finger, from her daughter's grasp. 'But I'm sure school . . . will . . . be . . . great,' she gasped. 'Go and join your line now. Bye bye, sweet girl.' And she turned and headed for the gates.

I watched her go. She half ran, despite being pregnant. She legged it so fast she almost stumbled over a scooter that had been locked to the school railings, causing about half a dozen concerned-looking men to come hurrying to her assistance. When she turned back to wave, though, Emily was already walking up the ramp into the Portakabin. Resigned. She was sandwiched between Zac, the plastic-cow boy, who looked white as a sheet and was probably going to be sick, and a girl called Skye, whose cardigan had rainbow buttons on it, secured two holes away from where they should have been.

'Walk nicely up the ramp,' boomed Mrs Baxter, standing at the door of the Portakabin, and I fell in, at the back of the line. It was like being at the end of the plank.

'. . . well, you should come and see our bathroom: it's got ivy growing through the actual window frame . . .' I heard one of the mothers saying to another as I approached the ramp.

'. . . and I found myself standing in the hallway this morning going "Shoes and teeth",' another woman was saying. 'I was just standing there going "Shoes and teeth, shoes and teeth" like a bloody parrot! And nobody was even *listening*!'

Bolting the door behind me, top and bottom, I wondered where Mrs Ellis had been going in such a hurry, and what she was going to spend her medium-sized day doing; because mothers' days, between *drop-off* and *pick-up*, were pretty short. I thought, too, of the contribution she was planning to make to Mrs Crieff's jamboree on Thursday. Of the sausages on sticks, while everyone else would be turning up with their empire biscuits and their butterfly cakes. Maybe, in Mrs Ellis's condition, the smell of baking made her feel sick. Or maybe sausages on sticks was just a good response to have; a good, two-fingered, two-sausage-fingered retort to Mrs Crieff's heart-warming plans.

*

I had left my Walkman at home that morning, but I was still not being impressive: I was still not the first one in. I *should* have been, considering the chat I'd had with Mrs Crieff the previous day. I should at least have been *second*. Certainly, I should not have been *last in the line*, behind all the children.

'Punctual as ever, Miss McKenzie,' Mrs Baxter said briskly when I appeared in the classroom doorway. She was sitting in her chair, the register open on her lap, and had already begun calling out names. Now she looked up at the enormous wooden teaching clock on the wall, as if it might inform us all of the actual time.

'Sorry, Morag,' I said, above the children's heads. 'It's just the bus went this strange route again this morning. It was . . . just a bit all over the place, for some reason.'

'You're a bit all over the place, my love,' Mrs Baxter retorted *sotto voce*, as I headed past her. We were, after all, supposed to be talking about respect that week: 're-spect' was the Word, just as yellow was the Colour.

I sat down and looked around. The room looked oddly blank, and after a moment I realised it was because most of the children's pictures had been taken down off the walls; they had been spirited away overnight. I wondered if the janitor had done it, or perhaps Mrs Crieff, working late. There was now just a series of pale rectangular spaces on the walls, where the day before there had been paintings. The beady-eyed figures with enormous heads and sticks for limbs were gone. The 'I Am Healthy' series of florid-hued swimmers in bright turquoise squares of water. Even the animal prints and the posters about Golden Rules and Healthy Eating targets had been removed. There was a pile of them on Mrs Baxter's desk, waiting to be placed into folders or, possibly, the bin. And the children, sitting in their circle on the floor, all seemed tired. They were all dragging themselves towards the shallows of Friday morning, and appeared to have little strength left. There'd been far too many *fun* things going on recently, Mrs Crieff had muttered during the staff meeting the previous week – there had been dozens of birthday parties, for instance, brought forward so they wouldn't have to happen in the holidays; and the children had been arriving at school ashen-faced and with consumptive-looking dark rings around their eyes.

'Now,' Mrs Baxter said when she'd finished taking the register, 'we've got a busy day ahead of us today, haven't we, children?'

'Yeeesss,' droned the children.

'And we've just got time now, before we head up to assembly, for our song. Are we all ready to sing our "good morning" song?'

'Yeeesss.'

And she turned towards the large, clunky tape recorder she kept on her desk.

'Here we go, then!' she said, pushing a button and causing some merry electronic notes to bounce out of the machine. It was 'Peter Rabbit Had a Fly Upon His Nose', Mrs Baxter's favourite. We always sang it to the tune of 'The Battle Hymn of the Republic'.

*

We reassembled, ten minutes later, in the hall, for Tuesday assembly. Mrs Crieff was already there by the time we rambled in. She was waiting by the stage microphone with that stiffly patient look she had. Often at assemblies there was a reverend or a rabbi or a humanist, but Mrs Crieff had had to step into the breach that day. The whole week was just going to be funny like that, she'd already told us; it was going to be funny and different. Ends of terms always were.

'Good morning, children,' she said now into the microphone after we'd all gathered a short distance from the stage, the children sitting on the cold parquet floor, the teachers on their bendy plastic chairs. And then she just stood for a second, hands clasped, and waited for hush. She was wearing her turquoise power suit again,

I noticed, the one made from a kind of bouclé material. Her steel-grey hair looked newly trimmed.

'Good morning, children,' she said again as the noise of small voices abated, 'on this lovely sunny morning, on this very last *normal* assembly, in fact, of . . .'

'*Yessss*,' growled some P7 boys, skulking like assassins in the shadows behind me. Mrs Crieff stopped, peered in their direction and gave one of her cheerful, magnanimous smiles. The boys grew quiet. Mrs Crieff stood still and smiled and smiled and waited for absolute calm. The boys were silent. And then she resumed. 'Now, I thought that today, children,' she said, 'as it's such a lovely, *bright* day, and as it's our last *normal* assembly of term, we should all sing the "Golden Rules" song.'

Everyone regarded her a little blankly, some with their mouths hanging open. The smallest children had to tip their heads a long way back to regard her as she spoke because of where they were sitting, right at the foot of the stage. The angles didn't really work.

'But we've just been *singing* a *song*!' I heard John Singer mutter, a few feet away from me.

'Miss Almond?' Mrs Crieff ploughed on, seamlessly, from the stage.

And Miss Almond, kind, cowed Miss Almond the librarian and thwarted musician, began some introductory chords on the piano in the corner of the hall, leaving no one any further space or time in which to complain. *School hasn't changed a bit*, I thought, as I stood up and drew breath: it was still full of people singing happy songs about kindness and goodness. When I was at primary school it had usually involved God or the more mysterious *Lord*, but it was still all the same.

The 'Golden Rules' was a song Mrs Crieff often chose.

Gold is the colour of the summer sun,
Gold is the colour of the stars that peep,
Gold is the colour of the badges we earn,
Gold is the colour of the rules we keep.

I always suspected she'd written it herself. It was to do with the way 'sun' and 'earn' didn't quite rhyme; also because half the words had to be squashed to fit. It had accompanying hand gestures, too: spread-out fingers to indicate the sunshine, and patting the chest to indicate a well-earned sticker.

'Now. We sang that song this morning because I think there's never any harm', she said when the song came to an end, 'in remembering the Golden Rules. Is there? Even when we are going into the holidays. *Especially* when we are going into the holidays!'

She looked down at the children sitting on the floor and at the staff in our positions of servitude on our bowing plastic chairs.

Golden Rules don't work like that though, do they, Mrs Crieff! I felt like shouting out into the stillness that had suddenly overcome the room. *I mean, we had rules at my old school and we had a motto, too* – Per Ardua ad Astra – *and look where that got me!*

I didn't, of course: I just sat there, my mouth shut.

'Lovely,' Mrs Crieff continued into the microphone, as people began to fidget again and rearrange their positions. 'Because, you know, the Rules might be coming down off the walls this week, but they should stay in everyone's hearts over the summer holidays, shouldn't they? They should stay in our heads and our hearts the whole summer long.'

Outside the hall there were still quite a few mothers hanging around the playground, their conversations floating upwards and in, through the opened windows. Somebody was talking about head lice – about a comb you could get called the Nitty-Gritty; somebody else was talking about camping in France. A couple of women standing very close to the window were discussing the marriage breakdown of a friend, and another, larger group was laughing about their children's manly swimming instructor, and how they wouldn't mind being rescued from the water by *him*. Mouth-to-mouth resuscitation would be OK, they said, if it was *him* doing it. They were quite raucous, particularly now it was nearly the end of term. They were quite demob happy.

Mrs Crieff, standing at the microphone, suddenly paused at the noise and the subject matter, and rolled her eyes. She tried to look charmed – amusedly fond of those *chatty mums* disturbing the final assembly of term! – but she was evidently just irked. *For God's sake!* I imagined her yelling. *Haven't you got* homes *to go to?* And I pictured her striding across the hall to slam the windows shut.

'Miss McKenzie, are Mrs Crieff's rules the same as God's rules?' John Singer asked me as we were all returning to the Portakabin again twenty minutes later. And he slipped his hand into mine. It was a warm, slightly damp hand, which a lot of the other children tended to reject. Mrs Baxter and I were really the only people who held his hand.

'Well, I suppose, in a way, yes,' I replied. 'God's rules are quite like Mrs Crieff's. If you believe in God.' *And Mrs Crieff*, I wanted to add.

'But who is God?' he asked.

'Hmm,' I said. I didn't feel qualified to talk to anyone about God. God had been a big disappointment, as far as I was concerned. God was the person, if He existed, who'd picked me up out of the life I'd planned and plonked me back down in the wrong one.

'Well,' I said, 'do you know about ghosts?'

'Yes, I know about ghosts. Like the ghosts in *Scooby Doo*.'

'Well: not exactly. I mean, God is a bit like a ghost, in a way. But a good ghost, not a *Scooby Doo* one. He's like a cross between a ghost and a friendly sort of floating . . . presence. He's like a cloud. And also a bit like Father Christmas,' I concluded, fretfully. 'That's what I think, anyway.' And I stopped talking.

John Singer stared up at me.

'So will God bring me presents?' he asked.

'Hmm,' I said.

That was the trouble with working in a school. Sometimes you could say something useful, and sometimes you found that, within the space of two sentences, you were telling people a load of old rubbish. You were likening God to Father Christmas or a Hanna-Barbera character. You'd got yourself into some complicated piece of nonsense. And it was hard to get out of it again.

Circle Time was short that morning – a speeded-up version – because of the trip to the Scottish Waterways Visitor Centre. Mr Innes, the minibus driver, would be driving through the gates at ten o'clock sharp, Mrs Baxter told us, after we'd all briefly sat down again on our mats in the Portakabin. And so unfortunately there would be no time that day for Talking Ted to get passed around. We would just have to hear everyone's news when we got back. There would only just be time, in fact, to sing one more tune – to sing, quickly, our own class song –

S'time-terstarter-brannnew-day,
Brannew-day,
Brannew-day,
'S'time-terstarter-brannew-day
Wivall-our-frens!

– and to visit the toilets before everyone would have to traipse outside yet again and get onto the minibus. Life, really, being a succession of songs and little journeys.

'Miss McKenzie, can you oversee toilet trip?' Mrs Baxter asked in a slightly airless voice as she stood beside our shelf of papier mâché owls. I looked across at her. One of her eyes was bloodshot, and there was a fine sheen of perspiration across her nose.

'Sure,' I said.

'Thanks.'

'Not a problem.'

'OK, everyone: toilet time,' I said, raising my voice, and I went and stood at the doorway to the toilets, the girls' cubicles on the left, the boys' on the right. I had to make sure there was no queue-barging, and to remind each child to wash their hands.

'And don't forget to use soap!' I warned doomily, peering down at my own fingernails which, I realised, were pretty grimy themselves: I hadn't scrubbed them for a while, I reflected. I couldn't remember the last time that I'd used our little wooden scrubbing brush at home. My standards had slipped since the days when I'd painted my fingernails and perfected French manicures with Stella Muir.

'You always say that about the soap, Miss McKenzie,' said Eve Russell, one of the little girls standing at the basin. 'You always say that,' she said, turning a sliver of green soap dutifully around in her small hands, 'but I never do forget the soap.'

'Well, the *reason* I tell you', I replied bossily, 'is because it's important.'

'Germs!' agreed a couple of the other little girls.

'Exactly.'

'Do you know, Miss McKenzie,' observed John Singer, who was peering at himself in the low mirror in the boys' half of the toilets, 'I could only see my eyes in the mirror last week, but now I can see my nose too.'

Which somehow seemed a more significant observation than anything anyone had to say about soap.

'Now, I want everyone to be as quick as they can, walking out,' Mrs Baxter was shouting as my little group clattered back to go and stand with the other children in the corridor. 'It's like an oven in here today,' she added, to no one in particular. Which was true. The corridor was the hottest part of the Portakabin, and it was not where you'd choose to be for any length of time. A lot of things in it appeared to have finally given up the ghost that week. The sunflower seedlings the children and I had planted were all flopping hopelessly against the window in their empty yogurt pots (*'What was the result of your experiment? There was too much sunlight'*), and the lentils and pasta shapes were falling off their collages.

'Less chat and more moving,' said Mrs Baxter; because there was an increasing volume of little voices now – almost the sense of a slightly out-of-hand party – and she was trapped there in the middle of it. She was leaning against the *Welcome to Our Classroom* board with a slightly martyrish expression on her face. *Our colour this week is: Yellow*, said the board. If she'd been a saint, she'd have been Sebastian.

*

The minibus was not, in fact, a minibus at all. It was a huge bus, bright white, with the words 'Jimmy Steels Coaches' emblazoned across its side. 'For goodness' sakes,' Mrs Baxter sighed, emerging into the daylight at the top of the Portakabin ramp. The bus was waiting for us by the kerbside, the engine on and the door open. The driver, a small, grey-haired man sitting on the little round driving seat and staring straight ahead, looked irritated already. And I had to resist a sudden urge to sneak down the ramp, sleekit as a seven-year-old, and just run away. Just run and run. It was ten past ten on a Tuesday morning in June and a slight, splashy summer rain had begun to fall, and I would rather have been anywhere, almost anywhere else.

'Good morning, Mr Innes,' Mrs Baxter called cheerily to the driver, across the playground.

'Mor'.'

He looked crumpled and worn-out, as if life was a huge washing machine and he had been the washing inside it.

'JI-MM-IE STEA-LS COA-CHES,' John Singer observed, coming to stand beside me.

'Very good,' I said. 'Well done.'

Mrs Baxter smiled, breathed in and briefly closed her eyes. Then she looked down at the little group of children pushing and shoving their way down the ramp.

'I don't see a nice neat crocodile,' she said, her voice booming up and down the morning streets. 'Where is our crocodile?'

*

A volunteer mum was going with us on the trip that morning. There was always at least one volunteer mum.

She had come to join us in the playground: she was Topaz's mother and her name was Mrs Legg. It was the sort of name Stella and I would have had hysterics about, just as we would once have laughed at Mr Temple pensively stroking his beard. I couldn't do things like that any more, though, not now that I was the sensible, grown-up Miss McKenzie.

'Hi, Mrs Legg,' I said in my classroom assistant voice as I reached the bottom of the ramp.

Mrs Legg didn't appear to hear me; and I knew straight away that she was going to be one of those mothers I could not relate to. Who did not relate to me. There were quite a few of them. Mrs Legg was a woman whose collection of zipped holdalls and wipe-clean lunch bags and Wet Wipes I knew I would never achieve if I ever became a mother; not in a million years. And even if she'd been my age she would still have been the sort of girl who had all her pencils sharpened and ready and had passed all her exams with positive, life-enhancing grades. The gulf between us was impossibly wide.

'Have you been on trips with the school before?' I asked as we advanced up the line for the coach.

She finally turned and looked at me. 'Sorry?' she said.

She had that look on her face: a kind of weary prag-matism that some of the mothers seemed to adopt. A grudging tolerance of oddballs and losers. She was there to deflect the incoming waves, and I was one of the waves.

'Have you . . . been on trips with the school before?' I repeated, hanging onto my smile.

'Oh.' Mrs Legg frowned, and gave a little shiver. Despite it being a June morning, she was wearing a jumper bearing a recurring pattern of woolly sheep. 'I go on all the trips,' she said. 'I've got three older ones, further up the school. I've got a daughter in P6 and twin boys in P3.'

She spoke as if I should already know the circumstances of her life. But I didn't. And I couldn't think, either, what to say to her about her many children. I couldn't work out if it was a boast or a cry for help.

'Come on, Toby, pick your feet up,' she observed to Toby Cameron, and she moved away from me and further up the line.

Mrs Baxter had the register with her, a big black folder pressed flat across her bust. She held it open while she counted everyone up the steps.

'All present and correct,' she confirmed, as the door closed behind us and Mr Innes put the coach into gear. And it suddenly struck me, as we swung out onto the road, how terrible it would be if we *hadn't* all been present and correct and had actually left someone behind. Some child sitting beside the coats, or in the Home Corner, or wandering alone, across the vast grey playground. My heart tightened at the thought of it. What would we have done, when we'd noticed their absence? What would we have done, as responsible adults? It almost brought tears to my eyes just thinking about it. And I thought how I'd once pictured myself when I'd first got the job at St Luke's: how I'd envisaged a sort of golden scene in which I was a caring, practical young woman pointing out the wonders of nature – a catkin branch, a ladybird, a leaf – to a group of enchanted children; or singing nursery rhymes to the accompaniment of my own guitar, my fingernails scrubbed and short, my long hair illuminated by some bright, benevolent light streaming in through a window. Well, my nails were short and my hair was long, but those were about the only things that fitted the picture.

The inside of the coach smelt of rubber flooring and extinguished cigarettes and vanilla-scented Magic Tree.

'Miss McKenzie, have you got the wherewithal for people being sick?' Mrs Baxter asked as I was edging past her up the aisle. Which was a question that brought me to my senses.

'Yes, I have,' I replied, 'I've got it with me. I've got everything with me in the emergency bag.'

Because I was in charge of the emergency bag that day, a blue denim holdall the size of a medium-sized suitcase. I had packed it the previous afternoon. Its contents included Wet Wipes, plasters, Calpol and a large cardboard container with a rim round it, known as the 'sick bowl'. The sick bowl looked like an enormous grey trilby.

'Good-oh,' Mrs Baxter said.

We were like pilots, going over procedures for the flight. I don't know what we would have done in a real emergency, but it was OK because we had a cardboard bowl with us. It was all very *procedural*. *If Mrs Crieff could see me now*, I thought, *she would have no cause for complaint. She would be able to tick that box on her appraisal form.*

'So: I'll go and sit up at the back, Mrs Baxter,' I said.

'That's where you're meant to be sitting.'

'OK.'

And I plodded on.

The coach, with the door tightly shut, had altered its character. It had become grey and cavernous. And now that it had begun to move, it was filled with a low humming sound, like the noise from a ship's engine. There was the potential, I felt, as I located a seat near the back, to develop a swift, significant headache, if not actual nausea. Most of the children had paired up before they'd even climbed aboard, their friendship unwavering, unassailable. A few had wavered and pushed and asserted their rights, while others had joined forces, creating little parties of four or five. And then there was John. There were twenty-nine children in the class, and John was the twenty-ninth. I watched him make his way towards me, like someone heading for the least-bad option.

'Hi, John,' I said, as he sat down in the seat beside me.

''Lo,' he said, peering through the window. *This always happens to me*, he looked as if he was thinking.

'So, this is exciting, isn't it?'

'Hmm.'

'John smells,' some of the other children used to say sometimes, which was true: he often did have a smell of grubbiness about him, of unwashed clothes and infrequent baths. 'He smells of squashed spiders' webs,' I'd heard a little girl shuddering once, which was one of the

176

strangest and saddest insults I'd ever heard. Seeing the others teasing him was like watching a duckling being attacked by herring gulls on the canal. We intervened – of course we did – but there were always ways around intervention.

'Have you –' I began – but before I could say anything else Mrs Baxter's voice suddenly rang out.

'MISS MCKENZIE, CAN YOU SIT WITH JOHN?' she bellowed, her words ricocheting down the length of the coach; and I saw John sigh again and blink his eyes behind his glasses. I cleared my throat.

'Yes: I *am* sitting with John,' I shouted back, and all the children in the seats around us turned and stared.

Poor John. Johnny No-Mates. *One day it will be OK*, I felt like saying to him. Although, actually, there was no guarantee of that either.

I stowed the emergency bag as well as I could beneath my feet. It was quite bulky. The sick bowl made it quite difficult to deal with.

'Well,' I said to John, 'it's nice to be out of school for the morning anyway, isn't it? Going somewhere new.'

'It's not new to me. I've been before, with my mum,' he replied, still staring through the window.

He didn't help himself either sometimes, it had to be said.

*

We all had our particular parts to play that morning. Mrs Legg was stationed in front in the role of reassuring mother, Mrs Baxter was in the middle, her steady hand on the tiller; and I was at the back, above the wheel arch. I was always at the back of the coach on school trips. Once it had been because I was a rebel: it had been where Stella Muir and I had sat on our way to school, in the days when we'd peered out at the Mummy Woman standing on the pavement. We'd used to play a game, too, called Sweet and Sour: if you waved at people outside and they waved back, they were sweet; if they didn't, they were sour. But that was then: that was where we'd been supposed to sit *then*, and what people had expected us to do. Now it felt as if I was in the wrong place. The whole bus felt like the wrong place. I was one of only five people on board who was above the height of three foot ten. And there was no Stella with me. There was no Stella and there was no Ed McRae – there wasn't even Mary Wedderburn or Linda Daniels, and there was no sense of being where I should have been.

'Miss McKenzie, can I eat my Babybel?' John asked, just as we were swinging out onto the main road. I looked down to see that he had already pulled his sandwich box out onto his lap. It was a green plastic thing the size of a small attaché case and covered with muscle-bound superheroes. Inside, a foil-wrapped packet of sandwiches was partly opened, and the sandwiches were falling out and spilling their contents. 'My dad packed my lunch today,' he said.

'Oh.'

There was a bruised apple covered in buttery crumbs

and a pot of something called Yoplait, leaking a pinkish liquid.

'You shouldn't really eat your lunch before we get there, John,' I said. 'Or there'll be nothing to look forward to. I think you should put the lid back on now.'

'Ohhh!' John complained, but he did as he was told. He put the Babybel back in the box and clipped the buckle shut.

'Good boy,' I said, as he folded his arms and peered out of the window again. Once, I would never have spoken like that in a million years. And it still surprised me, how obedient children could be when you told them something in clear, unambiguous terms. How resigned to their fate. It worried me too, a little. It made me think of the ways people can follow the wrong leader.

'So,' I said, sighing and leaning back, and the coach rumbled on, through the rainy summer day. The seats were orange and dark blue tartan. *Moquette.* And everything was slightly muffled – voices, conversations, thoughts. It was like falling down the back of a settee.

'Grace, when we go over bumps my tummy goes blue,' I heard one of the little girls saying in the seat in front.

'Well, my head goes orange and yellow,' Grace retorted. 'Does *your* head go orange and yellow?'

Yes, I thought.

*

We'd only driven a few hundred yards up Melville Drive when Mrs Baxter got to her feet again and came swaying down towards the back of the bus. She was wearing a green and blue cagoule which rustled every time she moved her arms. She always wore practical things on trips, whereas I often forgot to put anything sensible on apart from the clothes that had just occurred to me on getting out of bed. That day for instance I was wearing a long purple hobble skirt and an off-white blouse, both of which I'd bought two years earlier in Topshop. The blouse was the one I'd been wearing when I'd told Ed McRae the Bellamy's veal pie anecdote. It was something I should have thrown away.

Mrs Baxter moved up and up the bus and finally arrived at my seat.

'Miss McKenzie, when we get there,' she whispered theatrically above John's head, 'the plan is to split up into three groups. You can have six, Mrs Richards and Mrs Legg can have seven each and I'll have the rest.'

'OK,' I whispered back, trying to inject a note of snappy enthusiasm into my voice.

'It's more manageable that way,' Mrs Baxter added, her eyes round and slightly more bloodshot than before. 'As you'll remember from that trip to the zoo.'

'Right. Sure.'

The zoo trip had happened the second week I'd been at St Luke's. We'd looked at some parakeets, a sea lion and a lemur and its child. Apart from that, the day was mainly a blur in my mind: just a woolly cave of temporarily missing children, an absent giraffe, a lot of penguins, a sarcastic shop assistant and a cafe with jungle murals on the walls.

'So I suggest', Mrs Baxter continued *sotto voce*, gripping onto the top of my seat as we rounded a corner, 'that you and Mrs Legg have the . . .' – she paused – '. . . easier ones. And I'll have the more . . .'

'Difficult ones,' I said. Beside me, John sat as motionless as a rock.

Mrs Baxter looked at me.

'I wasn't going to put it like that,' she said. 'However.'

And she peered out through the window, to see what point of the journey we had reached.

'There's a lot to see and not much time to see it,' she said, as if she was making a statement about life. 'But I think one thing everyone will want to do', she added, 'is look at the ducks on the river.'

'Have we brought bread?' I asked, like some Russian agent meeting a colleague for the first time on a park bench. I felt this was a sensible enough question, though, if we were talking about ducks.

Mrs Baxter wrested her gaze from the view.

'Bread?' she said. 'Oh, no! Bread would be asking for trouble.'

And she swayed back down to her seat.

*

Stella Muir and I had got on a big white coach once, and gone on a trip. The memory of it came back to me suddenly as I sat there. We'd gone down the A1 all the way to Whitby, a couple of weeks before beginning our Highers. It seemed incredible to me now: that my life had once encompassed going on a weekend's holiday to Whitby with Stella Muir; that we'd ever been close enough, or ever thought we were. But we had been, I supposed, just as I had once been in love with Ed McRae. 'It'll be a pampering session,' Stella had said, 'a pre-Highers treat. We deserve it. You especially, Lulu,' she'd added – which had been about as far as she'd ever got to acknowledging what had happened to me.

We'd chosen Whitby because we were skint and there'd been a £16 return deal on at Thomas Cook. Also, you could buy jet jewellery dead cheap there, and Stella's mother knew someone who had a holiday flat in the town. (Mrs Muir was one of those people who'd *known* people; my parents had never known people like that.) And so that was where we'd gone. The flat was huge, situated in a white Victorian villa on a hill leading down to the bay. The ceilings were so high that they'd almost roamed off out of focus.

'It's quite like Ed McRae's house, isn't it?' Stella had remarked when we'd first walked in. And then she'd stopped talking.

It *had* been like the McRaes' house, actually. It was the same kind of age and size, anyway, and there was a grand staircase and cornices in all the rooms, cornices and curlicues – although these ones had seen better days. *Unlike* the McRaes' place, a lot of the features of this house had not been well-maintained. The big front door, for instance, had been painted bottle green circa 1978, and when we switched on the lobby light, the bulb had immediately extinguished itself. We'd walked around for a while, opening doors and looking in all the rooms, and I'd tried not to think of Dracula arriving on the cliffs, which we could see through the living-room window; of him turning up one winter's night, malevolent, black cloak flapping, at Whitby Abbey. It was cold. Every room suffered from damp and there were odd bits of rubbish and a lingering smell of old cigarettes; and the holiday was already going wrong.

'Oh my God,' Stella said. 'I had no idea Mum's friend was so unhygienic.'

We pictured some dodgy old man staying there before us, chain-smoking Embassies all day long with the thin green curtains drawn and the television on. Pinned around the walls of the flat were a lot of notices hand-written by Stella's mother's friend. They all began with the word 'Please' –

Please switch off lights!
Please switch off immersion heater!
Please close front door quietly!

– but they were not friendly notes.

I'd wondered how many other people had read them, and what they'd done with their lives after leaving Whitby; how their lives had extended beyond the lights and the heater and the front door, like tendrilling plants seeking more light.

'I mean, what a bloody rip-off,' Stella said as we sat in the kitchen that evening, eating peanuts. 'Greedy cow. I knew we should have gone to Scarborough.'

And she'd made a point, after that, of leaving all the lights on, and the heater, and slamming the front door when we went down to the beach in the mornings – which was small and greyish and didn't live up to Stella's expectations either. I suppose a lot of things did not live up to Stella's expectations.

We did at least have a huge room each. Stella had a red futon in hers – quite new, in fact – although my bed was high and lumpy and covered with a torn peach candlewick bedspread. My room *did* have a compensatory balcony and a view, beyond the abbey, of the sea, although when I'd opened the thin little French windows on our first, breezy morning there and stepped out, I'd discovered another note. It was stuck to the railings with insulation tape:

Please do not stand on balcony. It may not hold your weight!!

So in the end, although Stella didn't have a balcony or a view, she was the one who'd ended up with the best room. Mine was also the one with the worst wallpaper and which had smelt the most strongly of cigarettes, and its fixtures and fittings were the strangest jumble of oddities. For instance; attached to the cold tap of my little green hand basin, there'd been an orange rubber nozzle. And when I'd stood there at night brushing my teeth I'd wondered what it was for. What was its significance? What was the purpose of an orange rubber nozzle on the end of a tap?

'What do you think this nozzle thing's for?' I asked Stella as she was walking down the hallway to the bathroom, a toothbrush in her mouth, a sponge bag swinging from her wrist.

'How the hell should I know?' she replied through a mouthful of toothpaste. A lot of the conversations we were having by then were like that.

Ed would have had a better answer than that, I thought as I lay in my lumpy bed that night. *Ed would have been the right person to have gone away with to Whitby.* Because I still loved him, even then; I suppose reality had not yet caught up with my emotions. Perched above my head, there was a short, wood-effect bookshelf, and on it were four things: a mildewed thriller called *All at Sea*, a dead housefly on its back, a plastic pixie in a long green hat, and a small wooden boat. And I remember thinking that if I considered these objects for long enough – the dead fly and the book and the pixie and the toy boat – if I really thought about them, then their existence might make some kind of sense. Because there must surely be some plan, I thought, some method, some way of reaching the right answer about things. Surely everything had some reason for its existence. Or even for the lack of it. On the other side of the room, on a wooden chair, there was a patchwork cushion with some of its octagons missing; and I considered whether there might be some spiritual kind of connection between those missing octagons and the octagonal tiles that were absent from the little fireplace in the corner of the room. I didn't mention it to Stella – my theory that all things must, in some way, be connected – because we had already moved too far away from each other by then – if we'd ever been close. And probably there was no connection, anyway, to be made between one stupid, arbitrary thing and another.

'What a bloody dump this place was,' Stella said on the afternoon we left. It was a bank holiday Monday, and we were sitting opposite each other in the kitchen, eating Marmite spread over the remaining slices of a Sunblest loaf.

'Yeah,' I said.

Because it was, and there was nothing else to say. Stella had spent the whole weekend on the little grey beach, wearing a sarong and a new jet necklace she'd bought in one of the gift shops and turning a beautiful pale brown, while I'd suddenly been beset with hay fever for some reason – hay fever at the beach! – and had had to wear dark glasses all the time. There were now two faint circles around my eyes, making me look like a panda in reverse. I looked drained. Gothic, I suppose, in keeping with Whitby and its legends.

A couple of weeks after we returned home, Mrs Muir told Stella that the gas fire in our holiday flat had been condemned by a health-and-safety inspector. It was discovered to be leaking out carbon monoxide. The tenant after us had complained of nausea and confusion and terrible fatigue. Apparently, he'd been so tired one morning he'd got on the wrong train at Whitby station and had ended up at Robin Hood's Bay instead of Newcastle. Someone had come round from the gas board, Mrs Muir said, and tied a sign to the heater that said, *DANGER: DO NOT OPERATE*. 'So that's why we were always too tired to get to the beach before midday!' Stella told me on the phone.

'Life's a beach and then you die,' I replied.

And there was a moment's silence.

Despite this, though – despite the carbon monoxide poisoning and the unravelling of our friendship – I'd always looked back on that weekend with a peculiar kind of fondness. I suppose it was one of the last few weekends when my life had appeared to resemble something normal; had still been heading in the direction people expected it to go. Though I already had a hunch that before long, it wouldn't. That I'd be sitting in an exam room one afternoon, my head suddenly full of nothing.

*

It didn't take long to get out of town now rush hour was over. After a while Mr Innes turned on the radio, loud, and we proceeded down the road listening to 'Fanfare for the Common Man'. Inspired by the drumbeats and the electric guitars, Mr Innes accelerated as we approached a wider, emptier stretch of road. He was a fast driver – reckless, even, I'd begun to feel – and we were flying down the hill now. The coach shot down the tenemented streets, past pleasant villas and delicatessens and cafes and gift shops, and hurtled on, back up another hill, around a corner and down. I put my hand up to the top of the seat in front of us and glanced through the window. The weather outside was beautiful now the rain had stopped: it was a perfect summer's day we were bombing through. At the bottom of the next hill we hung a right (as my old geography teacher had used to say) and found ourselves in a slightly less aspirational part of town. The Victorian villas had made way now for 1930s bungalows like ours. Bungalows on hills. We whizzed past things – glimpses of things, blurs at the window. A man stood in his garden, nailing a wooden post into the ground. A toddler wheeled by on a low plastic trike. A woman was hanging washing up on a whirly line: pillow cases and towels and a blue flowery nightie. We turned up Bartholomew Road, past a car showroom and an empty swing park, and headed on in the direction of the dual carriageway. There were road signs now for the Scottish Waterways Visitor Centre: a picture of a round-headed man walking purposefully along a brown background; and it made me think of all the day trips I'd been on with my parents over the years; of all our visits to castles and stately homes with our thermos flasks and sandwiches and hard-boiled eggs. And I felt bad, that I had not absorbed more information about those places. That I had not benefited from being educated. That I had let my parents down.

'Look,' Mrs Baxter said, pointing through the window at something. But nobody did look.

Nearing Lockharton Hill we began a new descent that took us past more chalets and bungalows and maisonettes. Then we turned left and left again, the roads becoming narrower and narrower, until they were almost too tight for a coach to get through at all. *Shouldn't we have chosen a different route?* I wondered, as we barged past residential pavements full of elderly people walking dogs and clipping their privet hedges or pulling golf trolleys along. But the driver didn't seem to care. He was Tam O'Shanter on his grey mare. He *was* the common man the fanfare had been written for. The electric guitars sang out as we swerved around a bend, the roof of the coach breaking some small branches off someone's cherry tree.

I felt slightly sick.

'Look at the people playing golf!' I exclaimed to John as we turned right, past a golf course; and as if this was worth pointing out – the sight of a lot of middle-aged men wearing bright white shoes and swinging golf clubs on a hill.

John peered through the window. He didn't say 'Golf is a good walk spoiled,' but he looked as if he was thinking it.

On the radio, 'Fanfare for the Common Man' ended and was replaced by Supertramp singing 'The Logical Song'. Supertramp was a band I felt Mr Innes would have eaten for breakfast. In a mirror angled above his head I watched him tut, lean forward in his seat and switch the music off. Then, one hand on the steering wheel and gazing intermittently through the windscreen, he clattered around in a little compartment on the dashboard, pulled out a cassette and put it into the tape player. There was a short silence, then the sound of more intermittent drumbeats. It was Meatloaf: it was

'Bat Out of Hell', and it seemed to inspire Mr Innes even further. *We're probably doing 60*, I thought, as we began to head through a kind of woodland. *We're doing 60 in a 30 mph area.* And I couldn't quite dispel an image from my mind of our coach lying on its side in a ditch, its wheels spinning, the windows on one side buckled and smashed.

'We're going fast, aren't we?' I said, hanging onto John's sleeve as we spun around another corner.

'I like it,' John said. 'It's fun!'

And at least the speed meant that we were, quite suddenly, there: almost miraculously we had arrived, uninjured, at the entrance to the Visitor Centre.

'Don't stand up until the coach has stopped moving,' Mrs Baxter announced, standing up. Because that was what you could do when you were a teacher, you could do the opposite of what you said.

Mr Innes pulled the coach abruptly into a lay-by opposite the building, switched off the engine and just sat there, motionless as a stone. There was a sudden hush. Then the children stood up and peered into the coach aisle. They seemed quite neatly divided into the pale and traumatised and the raring-to-go.

'Say thank you to Mr Innes,' Mrs Baxter instructed as we squashed our way out of our seats into the aisle and began to plod towards the steps. 'Thank you, Mr Innes,' obeyed a child, glancing nervously at him as he sat there, vulpine in his leather jacket, his hair slicked back, a packet of Raffles sticking out of his top pocket. And this, unfortunately, opened the floodgates.

'Thank you, Mr Innes,' all the children repeated, one by one, as they filed past.

'Thank you, Mr Innes.'

'Thank you, Mr Innes.'

'Thank you, Mr Innes.'

'Thank you, Mr Innes.'

'Thank you, Mr Innes.'

Until the stiffly magnanimous smile slid off Mr Innes's face altogether.

*

Once we were all assembled on the tarmac, Mrs Baxter did another head count. There were still twenty-nine children. Then we all got into our preordained little sub-groups. Emily Ellis was in mine, because she was one of the easy ones. John Singer wasn't, though. As soon as he'd got off the coach, Mrs Baxter swept over and grabbed his hand, as if executing some well-rehearsed piece of choreography. John silently accompanied her, like someone accepting the hand of fate.

'See you later, John,' I said, feeling oddly responsible for him.

'Yeah,' he said, 'bye.' And he was gone.

'OK, you lot,' I heard Mrs Legg announcing behind me.

Mrs Legg, of course, had been allocated her own child – the sweet, fairy-like Topaz – plus six of Topaz's friends. They were all wearing glittery hairbands and flamingo-pink anoraks, and they were all overexcited.

They set off hand in hand, in a wide, skipping line. Mrs Legg, in her sheep jumper and salmon-pink leggings, walked a staunch, responsible course in the middle.

'Keep to the inside of the pavement,' I heard her boom as they walked away – a sentence which, for a moment, didn't even make sense to me.

My group was the last to get going: there was a lot of faffing, somehow, going on with my group. And I suppose I felt a little confounded, anyway. I'd only ever done one trip with the class, which had been the semi-disastrous one to the zoo. And despite being forty years younger than Mrs Baxter and at least twenty years younger than Mrs Legg, it seemed, that morning, that I wasn't able to make such speedy decisions as them, or to use the right expressions or to move as quickly. I felt weighted down. Watched by someone, and found wanting. And I had the *easy* group! My group was the easiest one of the lot.

'Has everyone got their lunch?' I asked, in an effort to sound like a classroom assistant.

'Yeeees!' they replied, holding their sandwich boxes aloft.

'Good. So, off we –'

'But Mrs Baxter said we should leave them in the cafe, though, Miss McKenzie,' interrupted Ruby Simpson, the girl who'd once brought a haggis in to Show and Tell. 'So we don't have to carry them around all morning.'

'Ah. Good plan.'

'That's what Mrs Baxter said,' Ruby confirmed, and

she gave me a look of solemn appraisal. She was a composed child. Her hairband was bright red and had a yellow butterfly appliquéd on it. The only thing separating her from a useful, well-paid role in society, I felt – something in architecture, say, or medicine or geography – was an interlude of about sixteen years.

'Mindy Moo's here today, Miss McKenzie,' Emily Ellis whispered, slipping her hand into mine as we set off, and I felt strangely heartened by this. I'd hoped Mindy Moo would come. Why would she not want to, if it meant getting out of school for a while?

'So that means', I said to Emily as all of us – real and imaginary – plodded on towards the pedestrian crossing, 'that we've actually got eight people in our group today. If Mindy's with us.'

Emily considered this.

'No,' she said after a moment. 'You don't count them if they're invisible, Miss McKenzie. You don't count invisible people.'

'Oh,' I replied, defeated by the logic of this, because I suppose I did, in a way. Count invisible people.

'Mindy *is here*,' Emily explained patiently, 'but you don't *count* her! That would just be silly, Miss McKenzie!'

And now, apropos of nothing, she started to sing. We were all standing at the pedestrian crossing waiting for the lights to change, and there she was, this little girl, singing a song –

I like the sunshine,
I like the raindrops,
I like the blue sky,
I like the buttercups . . .

– when suddenly, from straight out of the blue sky, something splatted onto the sleeve of her coat.

'Oh, Emily, stop a minute,' I said, rummaging in my pocket for a packet of Wet Wipes – because I actually had some with me that day; I had attained that level of professionalism! *And maybe one day*, I thought, as I held onto Emily's arm and began to dab at her sleeve, *I'll go on car journeys with my own child, a tin of barley sugars and a damp flannel in a plastic bag. Just like my mum used to.* And maybe pigs will fly.

'Hold still, Emily,' I said, the Wet Wipe shredding a little against the fabric. Emily wore expensive clothes, but the bird muck on her sleeve just fell into line now with the mud already splattered there, and some pen marks, and a couple of yogurt stains.

'It's supposed to be a sign of good luck, getting bird poo on you,' I said, looking around for a bin to throw the wipe in.

'Why?' Emily asked, incredulous. 'Why isn't it bad luck?'

'Well, yes, I suppose that would make more sense . . .' I said, putting the wipe in my pocket and wondering if it would have been easier if I'd just told her the truth: that getting bird muck on your sleeve was not something to be

pleased about; that bad events could not always be transformed, Pollyanna-ish, into good ones. That life was not
like that at all.

'OK,' I said, 'let's get going.'

*

The Visitor Centre, directly opposite on the other side
of the road, was partly hidden behind evergreen trees. It
was constructed from wood and glass, and looked very
clean and Scandinavian. It was a nice design, built by
people who cared about the world. Maybe Ed McRae
would design buildings like that one day. He'd once giv-
en a talk at school about *organic design* – 'this design
evolved organically' he'd said, casually flipping a trans-
parency onto the screen of an overhead projector – and
I hadn't known what he was talking about. But maybe
he'd been talking about something like this.

The sub-groups had all caught up with each other
now. The sun came out from behind a cloud and shone
benevolently down on our heads.

'We are not stopping for ice creams,' Mrs Baxter announced, leading her little entourage to the double doors,
and the rest of us all rambled after her like sheep. Mrs
Baxter was one of those people you followed. *However
much I try*, I thought as I walked behind her, *I will never
be able to speak like that. I'll never be able to say 'We
are not stopping for ice creams.'* I would never have those
leadership skills, or that certainty about things.

Indoors, the slatted floor made an expensive wooden

noise as we clonked across it in our four pairs of big shoes and twenty-nine pairs of little ones. And then we all came to a halt again.

'One last head count!' Mrs Baxter said, standing at the front of the procession; and for the third time since we'd left the playground she began to count in twos, pointing at the children as they gazed placidly up at her.

'. . . and John: twenty-nine,' she said in conclusion, and she turned and headed for another set of doors, this time leading into a room called the Interactive Zone. She'd already told me, a few days earlier, that her group would be the first to look around inside the gallery. We'd discussed it in the staffroom, over our mugs of coffee: 'We'll do the exhibition first,' she'd said conspiratorially, 'while you and Mrs Richards and Mrs Legg have a wee wander up the river. That way', she'd added, 'we won't all go crashing into each other.'

'OK,' I'd replied seriously, unwrapping a Blue Riband biscuit. Sometimes, everything was serious.

'So: we'll reconvene at eleven fifteen right *here*, beside *this*,' Mrs Baxter announced now in a loud voice, placing her hand on top of a large bin. It was blue and shaped like a dolphin, similar to the frog one we had at St Luke's, its mouth wide open to receive empty drinks cartons and banana skins and cigarette packets. I always felt sorry for those bins. I suppose I had a bad habit of anthropomorphising things.

'So, off you go, everyone,' Mrs Baxter proclaimed. 'And let's all stick to the path and enjoy ourselves!' Which sounded to me like a contradiction in terms. And, surrounded by her group of *difficult ones,* Mrs Baxter strode in through the automatic doors of the Interactive Zone. There was a momentary burst of birdsong and croaking frogs and a babbling stream, and then the doors swept shut again and the sound was cut off.

I felt suddenly, oddly, alone. Like someone about to lead some doomed expedition. Like Scott of the Antarctic, or the lookout on the *Titanic.*

'OK, kids?' I heard Topaz Legg's mother urging a short distance away, and her little pink-anoraked group began to wander off too, out through the doors and towards the river.

'So,' I said to Mrs Richards, 'are you going next or shall we?'

'I think . . .' she began. And then she trailed off. She looked down at the children in her group. Her group contained three children needing the toilet. They were probably going to be some time.

'We'll see you out there I expect, Luisa,' she concluded doubtfully. And she herded her children towards a sign depicting one of those stick-people wearing an A-line skirt, opened the door and let it shut gently again behind them.

'Any of you lot need the loo?' I asked my group, reflecting that that was what I *should* ask on trips like this: it was one of the checklist things Mrs Crieff talked about. But they didn't need the toilet: they all insisted on this, and I was certainly not going to boss them into it – because there was a fine line, I'd begun to realise, between pretending to be bossy and actually becoming so.

'OK, then,' I said, 'if everyone's sure . . .' and we all headed off through the exit, in the wake of Mrs Legg's party. I tried to encourage the crocodile mode of walking – three lots of two, holding hands – but nobody took any notice. The narrow, gravelly path was awkward, and I just couldn't do commands the way Mrs Baxter did.

'I wonder if there'll be any frogs,' I said, as we were clattering across the wooden bridge over the river.

'Oh, are there going to be frogs, Miss McKenzie?' they all cried instantly. 'Are there going to be frogs?'

'Well,' I said, taken aback by their enthusiasm, 'there might be. You know: it's a froggy kind of place here. And it's the right time of year.'

And we carried on walking. The skirt I was wearing that day, the tight purple hobble skirt I'd bought when I was with Stella once in Topshop, was a particularly stupid choice of clothing. The hem of it had already got covered in mud and I was having to take smaller steps than you should on a walk like that. I just seemed doomed, that summer, to turn something that should have been easy into something complicated.

'There might *not* be frogs, of course,' I said to the children as I hopped along, worried that I might be setting them up for a big disappointment. 'But, you know, there'll be lots of other interesting things to . . .'

'Owwhhh!' they all cried. 'No frogs!'

And I wondered how different my life would have been if, for instance, I hadn't bought my hobble skirt from Topshop. Or become friends with Stella Muir. Or if I hadn't got on that bus and gone to Ed McRae's party.

I wondered what I might have been doing that morning, instead of hopping along a muddy path and discussing frogs with five-year-olds.

The morning had become beautiful now. The shade under the trees was what a guidebook might have called dappled, and there were summer flowers – wood anemones and celandines and cow parsley and purple loosestrife – along the banks of the river. Little birds sang small, trilling songs in the trees. The river was brown but still clear, translucent: it was the kind of river my father had once told me you might see trout swimming in. An Asda supermarket trolley stood upside down, stricken mid-stream like a stranded cow, but apart from that it was pretty unspoilt. None of the children in my group seemed to be much of a walker: they were dawdlers, dreamers, stopping every few seconds to look at a tree or a flower, or to pick something up off the ground – twigs, leaves, flowers, pebbles. Emily seemed to be collecting pebbles; Ben and Solly were more interested in sticks.

'Shall we catch up with the others?' I said.

Because it was a little irksome, in fact, the waiting. The hanging around while everyone gathered things up from the path. Mrs Legg's group were already way ahead, and behind us I could hear Mrs Richards' group catching up. Feeling quite a sharp need, suddenly, to move, I saw an opportunity for diversion. I leaned over to the verge, where I'd seen some bright green cleavers growing, snapped off a stem, pulled a few of the sticky little side shoots off it and stuck them onto the sleeve of my shirt. My mother had shown me that when I was little; she'd shown me what a laugh you could have with cleavers.

'Tah-dah,' I said to the children, opening out my empty hands.

The children gazed at the cleavers stuck there on my arm like curious grasshoppers.

'How did you do that?' Emily asked.

'Well, they just, you know, stick,' I said. 'They're great, aren't they? They're called cleavers. They're kind of like Velcro.'

'What's Velcro?'

'Well . . .' I said. There was a story at the back of my mind about someone inventing Velcro after they'd fallen into a patch of burrs. Someone who had triumphed through adversity.

'You know your shoe straps?' I said, suddenly inspired. 'Well, Velcro is the bits of fabric that stick your shoe straps down. Like Solly's shoes, look' – they all turned and looked at Solly's shoes – 'or the fastenings on your coat, Ruby. You know: the bits that make that ripping sound. That keep things together. And that you can also. . . pull apart.'

The children weren't really listening now, though: I had already lost them. They had begun to pull some cleavers from the bank, and were laughing, and sticking them onto each other's clothes. I watched them for a moment, feeling old. Old and sad.

'When I was a little girl,' I said, 'my friends and I used to play a game with these. We called it Arrows. We used to throw them at each other when we were walking home from school, and they'd stick.'

Linda Daniels and Mary Wedderburn, I thought. Mary and Linda. We'd played that game.

'Arrows?' asked Emily.

'Yeah,' I said. 'We just called them Arrows. It wasn't dangerous, though. They weren't like real arrows, of course. They wouldn't have hurt you. But best not to throw too many,' I added hastily, because, already, the children had begun flinging the cleavers into each other's hair. And it would probably have contravened Mrs Crieff's health-and-safety rules. But it was too late now, of course, to take back the idea; it was something I, Miss McKenzie, had just taught them all to do.

'Oh, look,' I said, attempting now to *distract* them from the cleavers. 'I can see Mrs Legg's group. Can you?' Because every so often, rounding a corner in the path, we would catch a glimpse of the party ahead of us. We could see the bright pinks and reds of their coats in the distance. They were getting further away, though. Mrs Legg was flanked by two of the children and was having a conversation with them, some practical, informative conversation. She was saying something sensible that an adult would say to children on a school trip. She was not suggesting they throw cleavers at each other; and they were not running around with sticks. *Mrs Legg is better at this than I am*, I thought, *and she's not even getting paid.* And I was about to attempt that role once more – to dissemble professionalism, to say, 'Look how far they've got! Who's going to catch up first?' – when Emily Ellis suddenly stopped short in her tracks and gave a little gasp of surprise.

'Look!' she said.

She pointed up, towards the slope on our right, and higher still, upwards, into a sort of sunlit glade.

I looked. There was a swathe of bracken and ferns and some spindly trunked birch trees.

'What is it, Emily?' I asked. 'What can you see?'

'There!' Emily said. 'Look! Up there.'

I squinted into the sunlight. The sun had become quite strong and it was hard to see anything at all.

'Where? What are you pointing at? Is it Mindy Moo?' I asked; because I thought, perhaps, it might be. 'Is Mindy Moo up there?'

'Of course not!' Emily snorted in disbelief. 'Of course it's not Mindy Moo, Miss McKenzie. Mindy Moo's invisible!'

'Who is it then?' I retorted, stung by her put-down.

'There!' Emily said, still pointing. 'Up in the wood. Look.'

I looked. And there *was* someone there – I could see that – as the sun suddenly went in behind a cloud. There was a man up there. And he wasn't on his own. He was there with a woman. The two of them were standing in the ferns and bracken, halfway up the bank. And they were stepping away from each other; they were breaking off from a kiss.

'It's my dad,' Emily said.

My heart lurched.

'What?' I said.

'It's my dad.'

'What?' I said again.

They had begun to move now, the lovers – Mr Ellis and the woman. They were clattering and branch-snapping down the bank towards us, and there was nothing we could do. We all just stood absolutely still and watched them approach. They were blundering through the foliage now, struggling through the celandines and wood anemones, their clothes flecked with twigs and pieces of bark, their faces bright pink. Because they had seen us, and because they had nowhere else to go – where *could* they go? they couldn't just evaporate into *thin air*! – and so they both had to plod laboriously back down to the path and stop there, in front of us.

Nobody spoke for a moment. Nobody said a word. Mr Ellis looked angry though, it occurred to me. That was the only way you could describe him. The woman was calmer-looking, more resigned. She was also – more accurately, really – a girl. She was blonde, pretty, and about the same age as me. 'Hi,' I said to Mr Ellis in a cheery voice, as if we'd all just bumped into each other in Tesco's.

But he didn't reply.

'Hello, Dad,' Emily interjected. 'Hello, Miss Ford,' she added.

Because that was who she was. It seemed that she was Susan Ford. She was the girl who had not quite cut the mustard.

9

I remember putting my hand beneath my seat on the coach back and feeling a hard, smooth lump of chewing gum. I imagined it, a pinkish-grey blob stuck there secretly, months earlier, by some schoolboy en route to some dreary educational establishment.

I didn't want to think about Mr Ellis. I didn't want to think about him and the affair he was conducting with Susan Ford. But the seat backs confronting Emily and me were scrawled over with graffitied statements about love and duplicity, and it was hard not to think about them. There were a lot of words in particular beginning with C and F and B, and I had to hang my cardigan over them, in case Emily worked them out. She was good at reading. *And I can at least protect her from that*, I remember thinking. *I can protect her from that, if only for the length of a bus trip.*

'So, I didn't know my dad goes to the Waterways Visitor Centre,' Emily said after a while. And she frowned down at the bright pink picture of Barbie on her lunch box. 'I didn't know he *knows* it there.'

'Didn't you?'

I couldn't think how else to reply. I didn't know what to say at all, about the way we'd all stood there on that woodland path, speechless and hot with embarrassment, everyone covered in cleavers and bark, like some twisted version of *A Midsummer Night's Dream*.

'And I *definitely* didn't know my daddy is friends with Miss Ford,' Emily continued.

'Ah,' I said, feeling slightly sick again. I thought about Emily's mother, and about the space on Mrs Crieff's wall of fame where Susan Ford's picture had been, and I didn't know what to do with the knowledge I had just acquired.

'Miss Ford used to teach the Fantastic Foxes,' Emily said. 'She was nice. I was in her reading group.'

'Were you?'

'Miss Ford used to sing songs with us sometimes, too. She played the guitar. She played it better than Mrs Baxter.'

'Did she?'

We had been allocated a different driver for the journey home. He was calmer than Mr Innes. But there were still packets of crisps left to be opened, and drinks cartons that needed piercing with straws. 'Miss Mc-Kennn-zie,' the children began to call, 'Miss Mc-Kennn-zie . . .' and I had to step into role again, the role of a person who knew what she was doing.

'Do you have a boyfriend, Miss McKenzie?' Emily asked, as the coach began barging up a hill. 'I mean, do you have a special friend who's a boy?'

I paused in the middle of opening a packet of Mini Cheddars for Jade and looked at her. She was sharp, Emily, even though she was still so small that her knees didn't coincide with the bend of the seat.

'Well,' I said, 'I used to have a . . . sort-of boyfriend, I suppose, for a little while. A . . . sort-of boyfriend.' (*He was the father of my child*, I could have added. *He was, for a few weeks, the father of the tiniest, tiniest child.*) 'But', I concluded, 'I don't any more.'

Handing the opened packet across to her, I felt suddenly exhausted. Worn out. My head had begun to hurt: quite a distinct, sharp pain on one side. *They've left the wood now*, I thought. *Mr Ellis and Miss Ford.* And I couldn't help picturing them as they got into his shiny estate car and whizzed, quiet and chastened, back into town. Back up to the library or museum or park, perhaps, where they might have first arranged to meet. Or maybe they would be heading off somewhere else, like a hotel or a guest house. Or to a little pub to discuss a plan of action: a story to tell Mrs Ellis. Because there would have to be one now.

'I think Miss Ford looks a bit like Mindy Moo,' Emily said, dropping a Mini Cheddar on the floor.

'Really? Is that what Mindy Moo looks like? But doesn't she have dark hair?'

Because I don't know why, but I'd always thought Mindy Moo was a brunette. It was just one of those things, like thinking Monday is red, and Friday is green.

Emily shook her head.

'She's blonde,' she said simply.

'Oh,' I replied, and I felt quite sad, because it appeared that even Mindy Moo was not the person I'd thought she was.

'Well,' I said, 'I suppose Miss Ford's like Mindy Moo

in a way, because she's a bit of a secret, isn't she? A bit
. . . invisible.'

And I stopped talking and looked out of the bus window. It had begun to rain. Cheerily, we were passing a funeral parlour.

*

Mr Ellis had been the one who'd spoken first.

'What on earth are *you* doing here?' he'd said, as we'd all stood there on the path.

What are we *doing here?* I'd thought.

'Well,' I'd said, 'what we're doing, Mr Ellis, is we're on our end-of-term trip.'

And he had looked quite stricken for a moment, as if he'd just remembered something he'd promised himself not to forget. As if he was thinking, *Damn!* I watched as the colour rose up his neck, across his cheeks and up to his forehead, until he resembled someone who's stayed out too long in the sun. He glanced quickly across at Susan Ford, who did not return the glance. Then he gazed down at his brogues. Close up they were a maroonish brown. The holes in them reminded me of the pattern on my mother's tea strainer.

'It was a change of schedule, you see,' I continued. I couldn't quite bring myself to look at Susan Ford, who had, after all, once had the job I now had and who should, I felt, in an obscure way, have been on my side. 'It was originally going to be Monday,' I added. 'A long time ago, it was going to be Monday.'

'*What* was going to be Monday?' he snapped.

'The trip.'

'The trip?'

'Daddy,' Emily interjected.

'Yes: *wait*, Emily!' Mr Ellis barked, looking as if he wanted us all just to disperse into the surrounding air – me, the children, his lover, even his wee girl – to close his eyes and, when he opened them again, for none of us to be there.

'Anyway,' he said in a pained voice, 'this is . . . we were . . .'

But he didn't seem able to say what he and Miss Ford had been doing.

'Hi,' Miss Ford said suddenly, apropos of nothing. Maybe it was in lieu of something more hysterical. She had a nice voice actually, clear and steady and low.

'Hi,' I replied, as if we had just been introduced at some wedding reception. And then we all stood, unmoving, like people turned to stone. Miss Ford was wearing a belted green coat, one I recognised as coming from the Clockhouse range at C&A; it was the same as one I'd tried on once during a shopping trip with Stella – who'd said it didn't suit me. *That kind of green,* she'd said, *just isn't your colour.* And then a few days later she'd gone back and bought one herself.

So, what on earth do you see in Mr Ellis? I felt like asking Miss Ford. *And did you know about his wife? I suppose you know he has a wife? And I suppose you know she's pregnant?*

But I didn't say this because Emily was standing right

there, with her five schoolfriends and probably her one imaginary one, too. 'Susan and I work together up at the university,' Mr Ellis explained now in a tight, airless little voice. 'In the tropical diseases unit. We're here this morning to . . . research waterborne diseases.'

To which nobody responded at all.

'Well, *we* were just talking about cleavers,' I said. Because any sentence seemed reasonable now, after his tropical diseases one. 'I was just telling Emily', I continued, 'that when I was her age I used to play a game with some friends of mine . . .'

'Yes, a really funny game!' Emily interrupted. 'Called Arrows.'

And at this, the expression on Susan Ford's face finally began to crumple, and I saw that she was actually close to tears. I felt my heart thud with a curious, unexpected kind of sympathy.

'It's called Arrows, Miss Ford,' continued Emily, who was looking at her too, 'because they look like arrows. And it's a really funny game. They stick to your sleeves, these funny bits of grass. They're like tiny sticky horses' tails, Daddy. Or like little green sticky caterpillars –'

Mr Ellis seemed unable to reply. He couldn't even look Emily in the eye. I thought of his wife, wiping toothpaste off Emily's face in the playground that morning; and of the way life can hurt you sometimes, from out of the blue.

Maybe he's a good lover, I conjectured, as the coach lurched and rumbled on. Or maybe Miss Ford was just bored. Maybe that was all you needed to be, to start an affair. Perhaps their eyes had met one day during some show about the Vikings or ancient Egypt, or at some parents' consultation evening. Or maybe he'd brought Emily to school one morning, his wife at home and newly pregnant and suffering from morning sickness. (*Chop, chop, Emily, get a move on…*) And there she'd been: Miss Ford, young and lovely in the winter sunlight.

'She's pretty, isn't she, Miss Ford?' Emily said, sliding her finger along the black trim of the coach window.

'She's OK.'

'She's got nice hair.'

'Hmm.'

'My dad never goes for walks with my mum. They don't go for walks apart from when they're walking down our path in the mornings. My mum used to be my dad's girlfriend. But now she's his wife.'

'Ha ha ha!' I laughed, in my big, classroom-assistant way. 'Ha ha ha!'

And then I stopped laughing in case I began to cry, because a kind of sorrow had sidled into the space behind my ribcage and had just stuck there, and I didn't want to cry about two people I didn't know conducting a love affair in a wood. Or about the fact that, just as we were all turning to leave, I'd seen big tears finally begin to run down Susan Ford's face. She'd suddenly looked full of remorse. *But really*, I'd felt like snapping, *it's a bit late for that now, isn't it, dear? The damage has already been done.*

'I don't think my dad should go for walks with Miss Ford if he doesn't go for walks with my mum,' Emily said.

'No,' I replied.

'I liked her hair grip, though,' she added, pragmatically. 'I'd like a silver hair grip like that. Do you ever wear hair grips, Miss McKenzie?'

'No,' I said.

'I've got some with rainbows on and some with cats' faces and some just glittery ones.'

And folding her hands together in her lap, like a very young and small old woman, she peered out of the coach window.

We came to a halt at some roadworks. There was a man standing on the road holding a red sign that said *STOP*. Lying in the back of a van, parked up on the pavement, was a green one that said *GO*. Out of the corner of my eye I saw a lorry, *Forsyth's Fresh Fruits* printed on its side, reversing out of a side road and holding up several cars. People began to beep their horns.

'Miss McKenzie, Ben's feeling sick,' Mrs Baxter proclaimed, advancing up the aisle. 'Have you got the wherewithal?'

'Oh God,' I replied, glancing up at her. Mrs Baxter looked a little woebegone herself, I couldn't help thinking. A little frazzled by the circumstances of the day, even though I was pretty sure *she* hadn't clocked her former colleague crashing through the ferns with Mr Ellis. Her left eye was even more bloodshot now, and her hair needed a good comb.

I reached down, unzipped the emergency bag with all its supplies – all its Band-Aids and hankies and sprays – and dragged out the upturned cardboard trilby.

'Here it is,' I said, capably, getting to my feet.

Mrs Baxter peered at the bowl.

'That's not what you should have brought,' she said.

'Sorry?'

'That's a sick *bowl*. That's not supposed to leave school. We don't use the *bowls* on buses. We use *bags*.'

'Oh.'

Mrs Baxter looked unimpressed.

'A bowl's too awkward to deal with on a bus.'

'I suppose it is,' I said.

'Well, off you go: the bowl will just have to do,' Mrs Baxter sighed. 'You'll know next time.'

'If there *is* a next time,' I quipped.

'Yes,' she said.

And I stopped talking and proceeded down the aisle towards Ben. He looked pretty green.

IO

Someone spoke to me as I was heading for home across the playground that afternoon. Someone hailed me. 'Spring has sprung,' someone proclaimed, and I turned and saw that it was the lollipop man.

'Spring has sprung,' he said again, striding across the tarmac in his peaked hat and his rustling fluorescent jacket, 'da grass is riz, I wonder where da boidies is . . .'

Even though spring had actually sprung weeks ago; months ago – we were already past the summer solstice and into the second half of the year! 'Good evening,' he added, doffing his cap – he was off his head, sometimes, the lollipop man – he was like the Mad March Hare, and he always talked to you as if he didn't have a care in the world. 'Had a good day? Heading off anywhere nice this fine afternoon?' he queried.

'Not particularly, no,' I said, because I'd had a pretty terrible day, and I was going nowhere except home.

The lollipop man was not deterred, though.

'. . . da boid is on da wing . . .' he carried on as I headed towards the gates. '. . . but dat's absoid . . . I always taawt da wing was on da boid . . .'

And he suddenly closed his eyes against the bright

sunshine and held his arms out wide. They were performances, his conversations; they were speeches to anyone who would listen.

'See you tomorrow, Ron,' I called. In a different life, he would have been a saxophonist in a nightclub or a comedian in New York. I don't think he would ever have chosen to be a retired accountant from Buckstone. The thing about some people, I thought, as I set off along the pavement, was that they could get away with pretending to be someone else. They could lie without even thinking they were lying. I didn't have that ability, though; or, if I did, it was a daily struggle to maintain it. I knew, for instance, that I wouldn't be able to keep quiet about what I had seen in the woods. I wouldn't be able to lie. It was nothing to do with morality or niceness because I wasn't moral or nice; it was just that my thoughts were beginning to feel almost tangible somehow, almost visible, the way I'd imagined them when I was little. They were like speech bubbles above my head, and there was no guarantee I could keep them a secret indefinitely. *Do you like jelly fruits, Luisa?* I could still recall my Great-Aunt Ina asking me once when I was about five, advancing towards me with a great, battered box of York's Fruit Jellies. And despite nodding and prising a pretend orange segment from the crinkly black case, I'd been convinced she would see a big 'NO I DON'T LIKE JELLY FRUITS' sitting there above my head. That was the way I felt now. I thought about what Mrs Crieff had said to me at the start of the week: *If there's anything you want to come and talk to me about, Luisa, relating to your work here – anything at all – then do come and tell me.*

And I knew I would have to.

*

The doorbell rang that evening, just as I was on the point of leaving to walk up to Mrs Crieff's house. I felt the bones of my ears move. I felt them twitch, like a rabbit's ears turning at the sound of a potential predator. Just this wee, primitive instinct. I'd mentioned that to Stella once, when we were sitting in the dinner hall, assailed by the sound of scraping chair legs and crashing plates. 'Stella,' I'd said, 'do you ever feel your ears moving just the tiniest of fractions when you hear a sudden noise?' And she'd looked at me and said, 'You're weird, Luisa, do you know that?'

'I'll get it,' I called out to my parents now, who were both sitting in the living room watching the six o'clock news. 'Unemployment', I heard the newscaster announce in a solemn, almost reverential voice, 'has been reported today to have risen to two and a quarter million . . .' I stood up, whacking my thigh as I did so against the corner of the kitchen table, and headed out into the hallway. I half hoped that it might be Mr Ellis at the door. Because if *I'd* been Mr Ellis, I would have tried to explain myself, I thought, as I hurried down the hallway; if it had been *me*, caught in the woods with some girl who was not my pregnant wife, well, I would at least want to try.

It wasn't him, though, I saw as soon as I opened the door: it was a man selling fish.

'Fresh fish?' he asked in rather a merry way.

I looked at him.

'Fish?' I repeated, as if the word were some necessary part of an English sentence.

'Fish. Fresh. From Newcastle,' he said.

Which was where he was from, he went on: he was from Newcastle, and he'd driven up that afternoon with a van full of fish.

'Oh,' I said.

'No need to look so pleased,' he replied. He seemed quite hurt, as if he really cared what I might think. I suppose the expression on my face can't have been that welcoming.

'Sorry,' I said. Because I was; and it wasn't his fault that he was the fresh-fish man from Newcastle; it was just the way it was. He was quite young, it occurred to me. His face was pale and his eyes were roundish and greenish. There was a delicate curve to his jaw, and only the faintest suggestion of stubble. He looked as if he should be doing something more dynamic with his time than flogging fish from the back of a van. He was wearing a pale-brown coat a bit like an old-fashioned grocer's coat and big yellow Wellington boots, and he told me he was selling that very morning's catch. His uncle had caught them, he said, and they were very fresh. 'Really?' I said. Because some of the fish he was holding out now for my inspection appeared to be vacuum-packed kippers. They even had a flower-shaped blob of butter with them inside the packet.

'Tell him we don't want any fish, Luisa,' I heard my

father yelling rudely from the living room: he'd had a few run-ins before, I knew, with the fresh-fish man from Newcastle. And with his uncle. And he was right, I supposed: we probably didn't need any vacuum-packed kippers. So I smiled, apologised, and closed the door. *I wouldn't mind turning into a vermillion goldfish*, I thought. I just thought it suddenly. And then, after waiting half a minute – after I'd heard his van start up and drive away – I opened the door again. 'Just going out for a sec,' I called out to my parents, and I started to run. I ran down our path, out through the gate, onto the pavement and down the road towards Mrs Crieff's house. I just ran, my heart thudding. I suppose it was something about the fish – or the lying about it – it was something about all the lies we tell each other – that had caused it to thud like that.

*

I'd never gone right up to Mrs Crieff's before. To house number 25. And when I got there I felt quite unnerved, even by the shape of the 25 nailed onto her front gate. By the metallic edges of it. I hoped, as I pushed down the gate latch and stepped onto the path, that the Alsatian, the *I Live Here* dog, wasn't lying in wait somewhere behind the trellis. It seemed to be the sort of trellis – bright orange and woven and splintery – behind which a belligerent dog might lurk. Mrs Crieff's plastic grass looked even more unnatural on this side of the fence; and positioned near the front door there was, I could see now, a trough filled with very unbelievable-looking flowers.

I proceeded up the path, past the wheel-less wheelbarrow and the flowers and the fibreglass rabbit, and tried to imagine what I would say. Up close, the lawn had a blueish tinge to it, like a Polaroid photo left out too long in the sun. If I'd painted a picture of that in art class, I thought, Mr Carter might have suggested it was the wrong kind of green. Or maybe he'd have asked if I was going for something abstract.

The path was less ambiguous than the grass. It was a smooth length of pure concrete, ending at Mrs Crieff's door. And now I was there, approaching the door, it seemed like the wrong place to be entirely. It struck me that it was a very ordinary evening, far too ordinary for revealing a scandal about one of the parents at the school. It was a Tuesday evening in late June and there was the sound of the ice-cream van now, playing 'Greensleeves' at the far end of the street, *and I shouldn't be here*, I thought: *I should go home*. But I suppose even home had developed a strange kind of double edge.

There was no discernible ringing sound after I pushed the bell, but almost instantly, from somewhere inside the house, came the sound of barking. Then I heard Mrs Crieff's voice.

'Sultan!' she shouted, and at a small upstairs window framed with hairspray cans and a Toilet Duck bottle the slats of a venetian blind were briefly parted.

I stood and waited, my heart tight and small, and regretted that I had rung the doorbell. I could hear Mrs Crieff plodding downstairs, followed, I presumed, by

Sultan the Alsatian, and there was nothing I could do. I couldn't run away, like someone playing Knock Down Ginger, I'd never make it back to the gate in time. All I could do was prepare a sunny expression and wait, all my convictions – my reasons for being there – already evaporating and gliding upwards into the still, hot air.

'Sultan!' Mrs Crieff yelled in a high voice as she reached the bottom of the stairs. Through the wobbly glass of the front door, I could make out a dark red carpet and a pedestal table with some kind of pot plant on it. And now the wavering shapes of a middle-aged woman and a dog appeared alongside the table, meaning there was no possibility of flight now, only, potentially, fight. I felt a little faint, a little bloodless. *I should not have come. Why did I come?* Into my head flitted a kind of dream of other places I had been to in my life, other doors I'd stood on the wrong side of. That had been the wrong places and the wrong doors.

'Who is it?' Mrs Crieff's shape called, moving closer to the glass in the front door.

'It's Luisa McKenzie,' I croaked.

Mrs Crieff was fiddling with the door-chain now. Her form was becoming more distinct. 'Be quiet!' she called, making me wonder for a second if she was talking to me. Then the dog stopped barking, and she opened the door.

'Hi,' I said.

'Oh,' said Mrs Crieff.

The dog was not an Alsatian at all; it was a Jack Russell. It was the canine equivalent of the wee man in *The Wizard of Oz*, pulling levers behind the curtain.

'Sorry to interrupt your evening,' I said.

Mrs Crieff looked at me as if she couldn't quite remember who I was. I suppose she'd probably blanked me out after she'd got home that afternoon.

'What brings *you* here?' she asked incredulously, as if I'd just arrived from some long-distance journey and didn't *really* live just seven doors away from her. The Jack Russell was looking at me, too. And now, with a synchronised turn of their heads, they both glanced up the path, as if expecting to see some sort of posse standing at the gate, some group of individuals waiting to whisk me away.

I could feel my heart jumping.

'Well,' I began – and my mind began to whirl through the sentences I'd imagined saying on my way down the hill. But now I couldn't think why I'd been so determined to go there: it was almost as if I'd forgotten, suddenly, how to be anywhere at all.

Mrs Crieff waited, an expression of immense tolerance on her face. At her feet, Sultan sighed and flopped down onto the hall carpet, exposing a fat, pink, nippled belly.

'I'm sorry to bother you out of school, Mrs Crieff,' I said finally. 'It's just . . . there was something that happened today, when we were on our school trip, that I really felt I should mention. Just a worry, I suppose. Something that . . . occurred today . . . which . . . I thought . . .'

'Oh?' interrupted Mrs Crieff.

'. . . should be brought to your attention,' I continued.

'It's just that it involves . . . somebody's happiness. A child's happiness at school. And I just . . . remembered that you said . . . I . . .'

'Are you referring to Jonathan Singer?' Mrs Crieff said, in slightly sepulchral tones.

And I stopped talking.

'No,' I said.

Mrs Crieff was peering at me, bug-eyed, and I didn't know how to continue. I didn't know what to say about John Singer. I worried about him; I worried, of course, on his behalf – but I didn't know what to say about him to Mrs Crieff.

'It's actually about someone else,' I resumed, feeling my face growing hotter, 'it's just something I felt I should maybe . . . but you know, actually,' I heard myself rambling as Mrs Crieff stood there, silent as stone, 'I probably shouldn't have come. I mean, I suppose it's . . . probably something that can wait till tomorrow.'

And I came to a halt and gazed down at Mrs Crieff's lawn. It looked quite psychedelic in the early evening light. And I pictured my life drifting on like this: of standing in places I didn't even want to be standing in, at the ends of conversations I didn't even comprehend.

'What an amazing lawn,' I said; because I had to say something. 'My mum and I . . . we've always thought, you know – *Wow!* – when we've walked past your garden. That would be a really . . . you know . . . low-maintenance lawn to have.'

Mrs Crieff remained silent for a moment. She looked at me. She seemed suddenly bigger and wider, like a bull standing at the gate of a field, breathing steam through its nostrils. Then she said

'It's called Permaturf.'

'Is it?'

'It's a great time-saver.'

'Yes,' I nodded. 'Well, we definitely thought . . . I mean, my mum and I . . .'

'Now: I'm actually getting ready to go out this evening, Luisa,' she interjected. 'Me and Mr Crieff. And our taxi's going to be here in about ten minutes. So what is it you actually came to say?'

I breathed in. *What would it feel like to walk on that lawn? I wondered. Would it be springy? Or tickly? Or tough? Maybe it would even be therapeutic, like one of those beds of nails . . .* And then I told her. I told her everything I'd seen that day; everything involving Emily Ellis's dad and the affair he was having with my predecessor Susan Ford. I mentioned the unhappiness that I felt sure was heading in Mrs Ellis's direction and, surely, by extension, Emily's. And I reminded Mrs Crieff of the Golden Rules we were all supposed to stick to – to be honest, I said: to be kind and to tell the truth. Which was what I had decided to do.

Mrs Crieff waited for me to stop talking. Then she said, 'I know about Susan and Mr Ellis.'

'Oh,' I said.

'I already know.'

'Oh,' I said again.

'But, really, what can one do?' she continued. 'We can't get involved – it's a private affair. It's outwith school hours. And Mr Ellis, as you know, is a very generous member of the PTA . . .'

Something, some understanding I'd been trying to suppress, began to bubble up now, to rise and expand like some monstrous dough. Like the porridge in *The Magic Porridge Pot*.

'Do you know how much he has donated to the school this year?' said Mrs Crieff.

The books. I thought of the books Mr Ellis had donated to the school. The *Biff and Chip*s and the series about the universe.

'Well,' I said, 'no, I don't know.'

'Let's just say', Mrs Crieff said, 'he made it possible for the P5s to go to the Cairngorms for a week last March. And also, of course, there were all those books for the library.'

'Ah.'

'Ours really is not to reason why, Luisa,' she said. 'Miss Ford is no longer with us, after all,' she added, as if Susan Ford had died. 'And Mr Ellis is a well-respected man.'

She was already closing the door. There was already more door between us than space. The Jack Russell had got back up again and was already slouching towards the dim, unknowable reaches of Mrs Crieff's house. Out of the corner of my eye, I suddenly saw Mr Crieff – the briefest glimpse of him, anyway – slipping through a doorway at the end of the corridor. He looked quite thin and waif-like. A husk of a man. He was wearing a baggy, diamond-patterned jumper and a pair of beige trousers.

'Why, though?' I blurted, as the gap between me and

Mrs Crieff narrowed even further. 'Why is he well respec-
ted? And why is ours not to reason why, Mrs Crieff?'

'Because it's private,' she snapped, receding into her
hallway. 'And it's none of our business.'

But I couldn't stop thinking of the way Mr Ellis was
being allowed to get away with it – of the way some men
just got clean away with things – and I felt, quite suddenly, something peculiar happen to my heart, a small,
unexpected anger growing wilder and wider by the
second.

'It's just, you told me once, Mrs Crieff,' I heard myself
saying, stepping closer – almost door-stopping, like
someone going round the houses selling brushes and furniture polish – 'you said that if there was ever anything
bothering me, relating to St Luke's, I should come and
talk to you about it. And that *did* bother me. You know:
what I saw this afternoon *has* bothered me.'

The door opened again, just slightly. Mrs Crieff's face
appeared in the gap.

'It's like that poem you've got in your office,' I said.
'*Speak your truth quietly and clearly,*' I added, aware
that whatever it was I'd been keeping quiet myself, keeping under wraps, had just been released, like a greyhound
let out of a trap. '*And listen to others,*' I continued, '*even
the dull and ignorant; they too . . .*'

– Mrs Crieff glared –

'. . . *have their story . . .*'

Mrs Crieff breathed in and then out, a small, peculiar
smile appearing on her face.

'Yes, well two can play at that game, Luisa,' she said,

and I felt my confidence faltering. 'For instance, *Keep interested in your own career, however humble; it is a real possession in the changing fortunes of time.* I know those lines off by heart.'

'Hmm,' I said.

'And I'm afraid to say, Luisa,' she continued in a low voice, 'that there will almost certainly have to be consequences now. Especially if you breathe a word of this . . . relationship . . . to Mrs Ellis . . .'

'But the thing is, Mrs Crieff, it's about . . .'

'. . . because it states quite clearly, in the confidentiality clause of your contract, doesn't it, that you must respect the . . .'

'But, Mrs Crieff . . .'

'. . . privacy and confidentiality of . . .'

'But she's *pregnant*, Mrs Crieff! Isn't she! Mrs Ellis is *expecting a child*!'

Mrs Crieff glowered at me.

'More fool her!' she said. 'She should have thought a bit more about that one, shouldn't she!'

And she shut the door.

*

The phone was ringing when I walked back through the kitchen door of our house. I picked it up straight away.

'Good evening, madam,' began a woman's voice in an immediate, breathless rush, 'I'm calling this evening because De-Luxe Living is currently offering £500 in vouchers to install showrooms in your area . . .'

'Are you?' I said. I felt as sad as I had ever felt. I'd felt a kind of sorrow for a long time – it had followed me around like a ghost for nearly a year and a half – but that evening, for some reason, was the first time it had really got me.

'. . . and I wondered', the woman continued, 'if I could have just two minutes of your time, madam, to ask two very simple questions. Just to see if your house qualifies?'

I hung onto the receiver and couldn't think what to say about the two very simple questions. I couldn't think what to say about our little house. Our little house in the suburbs; the place where I'd gone to hide.

'So, question one,' the woman began. 'If money was no object, madam . . .' – she'd adopted a brisk, optimistic tone now, like a person reading someone's tea leaves and seeing something promising in them – '. . . if money was no object, would you redecorate your bedroom, your bathroom or your kitchen first?'

I felt tears coming into my eyes, welling up like water rising in a basin. Soon the water would begin to spill over the edge.

'I think it would have to be my bedroom,' I whispered.

'Your *bedroom* was that?' the woman asked, a slight note of irritation creeping into her voice.

'Yes. It would have to be my bedroom,' I said, 'because it's the only room in the house that's mine.'

'*Sorry?*' the woman asked. 'Are you not the owner of the property, then?' she snapped.

'No, I'm not the one who pays the mortgage,' I said. 'I'm only nineteen. I'm . . .'

But she had already put the phone down.

11

I don't remember anything about that Wednesday. Wednesday happened; it came and went. Some days are like that. I suppose I must have got the bus to St Luke's and back, but my mind was somewhere else completely. I don't remember anything apart from the blue of the sky.

*

The jamboree was going to kick off at eleven on the Thursday. The only other things that kicked off, as far as I knew, were arguments and games of football. Mrs Crieff had told us about the day's programme during a staff meeting the previous week. '. . . the Infants' Magic Show, however,' she'd said, 'is going to start slightly earlier. Because Magic Bob has to get away by twelve for another event.'

Which had struck me as quite un-magic – the fact that Magic Bob should have to bow to the demands of ordinary time. *If magicians have to do that*, I'd felt like saying, *what hope is there for the rest of us?* And I'd pictured Magic Bob arriving at the event – at the birthday party, say, of some ailing octogenarian – and locating a coin behind their ear, or an egg. *Hey presto!* And I'd wondered how old you'd have to be before you didn't find magicians like that really annoying.

*

I didn't see Mrs Crieff when I walked in that morning, but the sign on her door proclaimed her to be *IN* and her silhouette was there, behind the slats of her venetian blind. She was like the big bad wolf in the forest, or the troll that lurked under the bridge, waiting for the billy goats to scamper across. I wondered, as I walked past her office bearing three Tupperware boxes full of my mother's gingerbread men, what she was doing in there; how she was occupying her time before the start of the jamboree. She was probably devising the best, most expedient way to sack me. And even though I didn't want to be there any more, the thought of not being there seemed even worse. I would miss the children – I realised that suddenly – and I would miss Mrs Baxter and Mrs Regan and the lollipop man. I might even miss the sight of that lonely, silver birch tree and the frog-shaped rubbish bin.

I had to take the gingerbread men to Mrs Regan's office along the corridor. I zipped past Mrs Crieff's like a scalded cat and knocked on the door.

'Come in,' called Mrs Regan in her gentle voice.

She was sitting on a black swivel chair, stuffing a small yellow T-shirt into a plastic bag. On a shelf above her head was a snow globe containing the Eiffel Tower; and a mug that said *I've been to Stirling Castle.*

'Hi, Luisa,' she said.

'Hi.'

On the floor at her feet was a stack of green lever-arch files, and behind her, piled up in a cardboard box, were a lot more yellow T-shirts. I had no idea what they were for – some sporting event, perhaps. Or maybe they had been kindly donated by Mr Ellis.

'I've got some gingerbread men,' I said, as if this was a totally normal statement.

Mrs Regan glanced at the Tupperware and didn't reply. She was busy dealing with the yellow T-shirt and the plastic bag. After she had finished sticking a length of Sellotape across the top of the bag, she looked up with more focus, and smiled.

'So, what have we got here?'

'Gingerbread men,' I repeated, feeling a mild despair, already, at our lopsided conversation. 'They're for the jamboree,' I added. 'Flapjacks and gingerbread men.'

Which sounded, I thought, like a song Julie Andrews might sing.

Mrs Regan peered more closely at the boxes.

'Well!' she said. 'You've certainly been busy, Luisa.'

'Actually,' I replied, 'it was my mum who made them. She was the one who . . .'

– and all of a sudden it seemed quite an effort to talk at all: to come up with anything sensible – or even that made any sense – about biscuits or jamborees or anything else. Mrs Regan's office was just a room filled with lever arch files and pot plants and plastic bags. It might, once, have been part of some grand

Victorian vision, but it was really just as impermanent as everything else. Nothing lasted. Nothing was what you thought it was. Nothing and nobody. And I felt, suddenly, all the confidence I'd ever had draining away from me like blood from a wound and dripping into dark pools around my feet. I *had* tried: I had tried for over a year to say the right thing and do the right thing, and now I wondered what the point had been. Nothing appeared to have made any difference. Whatever I said, it seemed as if Mrs Regan would just continue to sit there smiling and stuffing T-shirts into bags and saying 'Someone's been busy.' And in assembly the next day, we would all still sing the same songs about being honest and faithful, and Mrs Crieff would talk about the importance of telling the truth. I thought about Mrs Ellis, pregnant and duped, and I felt weightless, bloodless, adrift. *Help me, Mrs Regan! help me!* But Mrs Regan, in common with everyone else, would not know what I was talking about.

'Someone's been very clever with the icing,' she said, regarding the little sugary jackets my mother had twirled onto the gingerbread men that morning; it had taken her so long that I'd nearly missed the bus again. 'Someone's got an artistic touch.'

'Yeah, my mum's keen on baking,' I replied. 'And she thought the jamboree was a worthy cause.' *Although I can't think why. I mean, for all we know, maybe Mrs Crieff's going to embezzle the proceeds and get on the next plane to Luxembourg.*

'Well, that's very kind of her,' Mrs Regan said. 'People

have been very kind,' she added with a sigh. 'Look at all the fairy cakes people have been bringing in.'

And she gestured to a huge, rectangular mountain of Tupperware balanced on a trestle table in the corner of the office. They were all full of cakes. Leaning against the plastic walls of their containers, the tanned, shadowy forms of cupcakes and millionaire shortbread slices appeared almost sinister.

'Between you and me and the doorpost, though,' Mrs Regan whispered, 'this is not the easiest week to have a jamboree.'

And then she yawned. She stretched both pink-cardiganned arms into the air and yawned with quite unexpected abandon.

'However,' she said.

'Mrs Regan . . .'

'Anyway, Luisa,' she interrupted, snapping her mouth shut again like something hinged, 'I'd better get on. I've all these T-shirts to do. Then I've to put all the chairs out in the hall.'

She gazed, blank-eyed, at the cardboard box full of T-shirts. Perched in a wire tray beside it, I noticed, was a stack of St Luke's letterheads, all proclaiming the school's *Honest and Faithful* credentials.

'You'll be wanting the Tupperware back, presumably?' she said, as I was turning to leave.

'No rush. I'll pick them up later. Better get going.'

And I legged it out into the corridor. I didn't know what to say. I didn't know how to console Mrs Regan about all the T-shirts and the plastic bags. 'Mind how you go,' said the lollipop man, returning from crossing duty and almost colliding with me. He was still carrying the huge yellow and white lollipop that always seemed in danger of clonking small children on the head.

I was on snack duty that morning. It might be jamboree day, but I still had to do the snacks. So while Mrs Baxter read *Sam and Susie Go to the Dentist*, I went into the kitchenette to begin preparing the food. There was at least something a little calming about being in there. Standing at the sink, I put on my white nylon apron, washed my hands and tied my hair back. Then I checked the menu that Mrs Baxter had stuck up on one of the cupboard doors.

Wholemeal toast fingers
Raisins
Juice

Thursday had never been the most interesting snack day. *Wholemeal toast and raisins* always sounded more like something you might scatter on the ground for pigeons. Friday was the best day, when the children had *cheese cubes and melon slices*, like something at a 1970s cocktail party. But we weren't doing snacks that Friday: by then, we'd already have run out of time. And God only knows, I thought, where I might be then. At the Jobcentre, most likely, filling in a claim form.

'. . . Sam is a little bit scared,' I heard Mrs Baxter informing the children as I was getting out the tub of raisins, 'but the dentist is a very nice man. He tells him it is important not to eat too many snacks between meals . . .'

Oh, but is he? Is he a very nice man? I felt like exclaiming from behind the preparation surface. *Because sometimes, children, in my experience, nice people are really not very nice at all.*

And I placed a smile on my face and headed out of the kitchenette. I walked across to the octagonal tables and put a plate at each of the eight sides. I returned to the kitchenette and came back out again with two plastic jugs filled with diluted orange juice. I poured the juice into twenty-nine colour-coordinated cups and placed two fingers of toast and a small scattering of raisins on each plate. Then, when Mrs Baxter had concluded the dentist story and told everyone how important it was to 'brush their teeth' and 'not to snack between meals', I stepped forward.

'Snack time, everyone,' I shouted.

'Yessss!' said the children.

'Go with Mrs Baxter to wash your hands,' I added bossily – *I have become bossy*, I thought – 'and then come and sit down quietly.' Sitting down quietly was, of course, something else adults didn't always do. As was hand-washing and eating healthily. 'It's important to eat healthily, children,' I'd heard Mrs Baxter announce once as the children sat dutifully eating their oatcakes and grapes. And a couple of hours later, in the staffroom, I'd seen her tucking into a sausage roll and a can of Pepsi.

'They're really sitting nicely these days, aren't they?'

Mrs Baxter observed fondly as we stood, arms folded, watching the children eat. 'They're gaining quite nice wee table manners.'

'Yeah,' I said.

But I couldn't help thinking that, while gaining in some ways, they might be losing in others. For a start, they were all kitted out these days like tiny business people, in their stiff grey skirts and trousers and inflexible white shirts. Some school-uniform manufacturers, I'd heard, put Teflon in the skirts and trousers, to make them harder wearing. *Teflon!* The stuff they put in *saucepans!* Also, I felt sure they'd once had more enquiring minds. For instance, they'd used to ask a lot of questions about God. *Who is God? What is God? Where does God live?* But they'd lost that, ever since Mrs Crieff had started inviting Reverend Johnston into assemblies.

'Mrs Baxter . . .' I began.

'Hang on a minute, Luisa,' Mrs Baxter replied, running to mop up some spilled orange juice.

*

Mrs Crieff made an appearance shortly before eleven that morning. I was sitting at one of the little tables stringing beads onto a shoelace with Solly and Zac when I heard her voice.

'Just poking my head round,' she said, and my ears twitched, the way I'd once described to Stella Muir.

'Hi, Mrs Crieff,' I heard Mrs Baxter reply blandly, and I turned my head and there she was, standing in the doorway, looking resolute. She didn't look at me.

'Just poking my head round,' she said again, 'to see if we're all set to . . . head across in a minute.'

I clutched the little plastic beads I was using. I couldn't quite meet her eye, either, because if I did I knew that both our heads would fill with the vision of me standing on her doorstep the evening before, quoting the *Desiderata*; of what I'd told her, and of what she'd replied.

'Are you not all meant to be tidying up now, Mrs Baxter? And heading across to Room C?' Mrs Crieff asked across the heads of the children.

Mrs Baxter, who had been gathering up abandoned toast crusts, frowned slightly.

'What time d'you make it, then, Mrs Crieff?' she asked.

'Well,' Mrs Crieff said, still avoiding me, the peculiar, inappropriate, underachieving Miss McKenzie surrounded by beads. 'Well, I make it gone quarter to.'

And she turned in the doorway, positioning herself at a curiously oblique angle, so I could no longer see her face, and squinted up at the clock. *I am the fly in the ointment*, I thought. *I am the spanner in the works*. I did not represent one of her stepping stones – or maybe I did, in the sense that I was about to be stepped on.

'Is it gone quarter to? Really?' Mrs Baxter said mildly, and she glanced at the little gold watch on her wrist. Then she looked briefly over at me. 'I make it quarter to by my watch, don't you, Miss McKenzie?'

'Yes,' I agreed, not bothering to look at my watch.

'Well maybe my watch is a bit slow, then,' Mrs Baxter

conceded. 'Sorry to hold up proceedings, Mrs Crieff. We'll be with you in two ticks.'

'Super,' Mrs Crieff said, as if she'd just reluctantly remembered the Golden Rule: *We are patient.* 'No immediate rush,' she added. 'Take your time.'

And she turned to leave. She was wearing olive-green again that morning: that blameless colour that I knew I would always associate with her now, just as I'd always associate sea urchins with glass display cabinets and the music of Steeleye Span.

'Oh, and who's got a hat to wear?' she said, just as she was heading into the corridor. Because the previous week she'd suggested the P1 children might like to decorate some paper hats, in which to attend the jamboree. It was one of those odd ideas she had sometimes. *We might,* she'd said, *all like to cut some cartridge paper into hat shapes, and to glue sequins and streamers onto them.* 'Well, that's an idea, Mrs Crieff,' Mrs Baxter had said, tight-lipped, looking as if impromptu millinery was the last thing she wanted to spend her morning doing.

'We're going to put our hats on later this afternoon,' Mrs Baxter said now. 'At home-time.'

'Super!' Mrs Crieff said again. And she looked up at the staff coat hooks on the corridor wall, where Miss Ford's coat must once have hung. Then she looked momentarily at me. It was the briefest of glances. Then she turned on her shiny heel and walked away.

I watched as she hurried past the Portakabin window, across the tarmacked playground, past the wooden boat and the tree and the monkey bars. Past the Golden Rules.

She hurried on. I wasn't sure where she was going, but she was making swift progress towards it. All the children lining up at the door watched her too. After a moment she started to run.

*

We had to walk, of course.

We all walked through the assembly hall to get to Room C, where Magic Bob was going to be, that morning.

'Walk in a straight line, children. No stopping,' Mrs Baxter instructed everyone, but it was impossible not to slow down a little to gawp at all the stalls that had been put up since we were last in the hall. There were a lot of them: dozens of trestle tables to negotiate and bric-a-brac to contend with. Stacked high on the tables were piles of old cast-offs – toys from the 70s and 80s – and home-grown herbs in plastic pots and cardboard boxes full of paperbacks. There were old boxes of Lego and Meccano and Stickle Bricks, and stacking cups, and Barbies with busts, and Tiny Tears dolls that would cry if you squeezed them. The trestle tables were the kind I remembered from my days in the Brownies: the kind that looked flimsy but were virtually indestructible; makeshift tables that would just go on and on across the decades, supporting fairy cakes and old books and tombola gifts in school halls up and down the country. And standing behind those tables there would always be the volunteer mums. The members of the Parent-Teacher Association, selling tray bakes. Kind people, like my mum and Mrs Ellis. Mum-ish people, Mummy Woman people, who knew what to say and how to be. And I would never join them.

Standing behind the table nearest my little group was Mrs Legg. She was wearing a yellow dress and a very white cardigan with a pattern of pretend diamonds scattered across the front, in a fountain-like spray. In her hands she had a Crawford's biscuit tin marked *Petty Cash*.

'Hi, Mrs Legg,' I said.

'I'm manning the bric-a-brac, for my sins,' she replied.

'Are you?' I said, because I couldn't think what else to say; about bric-a-brac, or sins. I looked down at Mrs Legg's table, wondering if there was anything I could say about that, instead. It bore an assortment of silken-haired pink horses and elderly plastic gonks. A battered, boxed bath-gel set had been plonked beside a set of fern-scented Morny soaps, one of which was missing from its container. And it all made me think, suddenly, of the contents of my own bedroom. Of all the stuff I'd hung onto. There was a tin with the initial 'L' on it, a tiny rose-patterned teapot, a set of cork coasters and a melamine tray depicting a smiling Labrador. There was also a 1970s edition of *Jonathan Livingston Seagull*. I picked it up and peered at the picture of the seagull on the front.

'There's always copies of that at the school fete,' Mrs Legg observed, the biscuit tin tipping slightly in her hands so that all the coins in it slipped noisily from one side to the other.

239

'What's it about?' I asked.

'A seagull, I presume,' Mrs Legg retorted.

'Unless it's a metaphor,' I said.

'A what?'

'A metaphor for something else,' I said. 'Something that's *like* a seagull.'

And I put the book back down again. My sentences had begun to sound quite strange, even to me.

'What's *like a seagull*?' Mrs Legg said crossly, 'apart from a seagull?'

'I don't know,' I replied. 'OK: let's go,' I added, addressing my little group of children, and we moved on towards Room C, past the temptations of other people's old junk. It was in fact quite hard to move particularly fast, because there were an awful lot of people in the hall, now: a couple of hundred, it seemed to me. A multitude of goodness and kindness. At the stall next to Mrs Legg's there was a big group of people buying and selling tombola tickets and offering each other small, crumbling cakes in zip-up plastic food bags. There were chocolate cherry cakes and millionaire shortbread slices and cream-filled ginger snaps and, yes, there were my mother's gingerbread men! – I could tell because of the piped buttons and ties – and I felt a strange kind of affection for them, a kind of longing. I felt an odd desire to scoop them all up and rescue them, like little evacuees.

'Are you OK, Miss McKenzie?' Mrs Baxter asked as I pushed on with the children, past the cake stall. 'Anything wrong? You look quite . . . pale.'

'Do I?' I asked, alarmed that my anxiety had begun to show on my face. It was just that all around me there seemed to be a converging kind of sea. Half the city was there that morning, it seemed to me, and the sound of voices had completely drowned out everything else. It was the sound of goodness, the noise of niceness: everyone at St Luke's was so *nice!* And standing above it all on the stage at the back was nice Mrs Crieff, *one of the best heads in town*, smiling and laughing and parrying questions. There she was, raising funds, meeting targets, stepping across the stepping stones. There she was, *veritas et fidelis* personified.

'Miss McKenzie, will there still be some cakes left after the magic show?' a small girl asked me.

'I –' I began.

'Ah! The all-important question!' Mrs Baxter interjected, in the kindly sarcastic voice she reserved for such occasions. *I can't even do that voice*, I thought. I could do kind or sarcastic, but I couldn't do both. Not at the same time. And I watched Mrs Baxter sailing on.

*

A thin, middle-aged man was standing in the doorway of Room C when the children and I eventually surfaced from the waves. He was holding a holographic clipboard and wearing a top hat and a rotating bow tie with flashing lights. His waistcoat had stars on it. Evidently this was Magic Bob.

'Good morning, kiddiewinks,' he said to the children,

and my heart sank. Behind the hat and the bow tie and the waistcoat, Magic Bob looked quite truculent and bored. He had a sallow complexion, as if he'd spent far too much of his life in school halls and community centres, the curtains drawn against the sunlight. His mouth was set into a thin, bitter-looking line.

'Ding, ding,' he said, suddenly reaching out towards Emily Ellis, who was standing beside me, and pulling one of her plaits. Emily looked up at him with astonishment. We both did.

'Sorry. Was that rude of me? Was that *de trop*?' Magic Bob asked, letting go of her hair and turning his attention to me. 'Hello, what have we got here?' he added. 'A flamingo?' His eyes were a very flat, unsmiling blue. 'What's with the pink hair, love? Fell out with someone at the salon? I think I'll have to call you Miss Flamingo! Is this Miss Flamingo?' he asked the children clustering around me in the doorway.

They all looked at him, uncomprehending. He was a very peculiar man – that was all there was to it – and now he started whistling the tune of some song I'd heard on the radio occasionally, a quite nice song about pretty flamingos that didn't suit him.

'I'd prefer it if you didn't pull the children's hair,' I said. *And the song you're whistling doesn't suit you*, I felt like adding, *it's too nice for you*. Magic Bob stopped whistling and gave a brief, theatrical sigh.

'Oh dear,' he said. 'Slapped wrist for Magic Bob!'

I did not reply.

'Come in, then, if you're coming,' Magic Bob continued. 'The show's in here. On with the show, that's what I say. Are you with the bride or the groom?' he asked me.

What? What was he *talking* about?

'Sorry?' I said.

'Joke, love. Maybe I've just done too many weddings recently.'

I looked at Mrs Baxter, who was still on the hall side of the door. She looked utterly blank.

'Now: important question. Is there going to be some party food later?' Magic Bob asked Emily, bending down slightly and lowering his voice. 'Personally I always like the savoury food best at parties, do you, sweetheart?'

Emily frowned slightly. 'Yes,' she said, 'I like all the savoury food. I like all the cakes and jellies and biscuits.'

And Magic Bob straightened up. 'Well, clearly I'm speaking in tongues today, aren't I?' he snapped. And a few of the children, pushing their way through the doorway, gazed up at him again. They looked as if they were trying to work out the discrepancy between the magic of their dreams and the Magic Bob of reality, and for the first time since I'd worked at St Luke's I felt like putting my arms around them all, Mother Hen-like, to shield them from harm.

'We're certainly not going to get into the room four abreast are we?' Magic Bob snapped. 'If you'll pardon the expression!'

'*Sorry?*'

He regarded me, a faint, combative smile on his lips. Then he took a pen from his pocket and ticked a piece of paper on his clipboard. For the briefest of moments, I thought it might be one of Mrs Crieff's staff-appraisal forms.

'Right,' he said, walking into the classroom, putting the clipboard down on a desk and clapping his hands together. 'What's going to happen now is: you, Miss Flamingo, and you, Mrs Teacher, and all the little folk have to file up the left-hand side of the room.'

'Why?' I asked.

'Because all the P2 lot have to go up the right side in a minute, see? So we can fit everyone in. I have to do the show for the P1s and the P2s together, yes?'

It was beginning to feel like a sort of military ordeal. The only time I'd ever been to a magic show was when I was thirteen and had been a Girl Guide. There'd been something called a Circus Skills Weekend, which had taken place in a grey pebble-dashed church hall on the edge of a town I could no longer remember the name of. All I could remember was a lot of green teacups and someone named Geraldine, who had worn mauve lycra leggings and spun a lot of plates.

'So, keep to the right, kiddiewinks,' Magic Bob barked to some P2 children who'd begun to ramble, confused, through the doorway. 'Jesus, it's like herding cats,' he muttered. 'And you're supposed to be leading them, Miss Flamingo, aren't you?' he added, in a louder voice, grabbing hold of my arm and pushing me through the doorway.

'OK, Mrs Teacher?' I heard him say to Mrs Baxter behind me.

'Fine, thank you, Magic Bob,' Mrs Baxter replied with icy dignity.

And then I heard John Singer piping up. John Singer, as bold as brass.

'Excuse me,' he asked, 'are you supposed to be the wizard?'

There was a moment of total silence. I looked over my shoulder and saw the last vestige of jollity fall from Magic Bob's face. It was a distinct sort of falling away. 'Am I *supposed* to be the wizard?' he barked. '*Supposed to be?* Well, I don't see anyone else round here with a box of tricks, do you, young man?'

And resuming his smile, he ruffled John Singer's hair.

*

Room C looked quite different that morning. Someone appeared to have gone into it overnight and decorated it. Maybe Mrs Regan or the janitor or the lollipop man, or some people on the PTA board. Maybe even Mrs Crieff. The whole room was draped with bunting now – yards of starry triangles strung up beneath the swinging rectangular lights. Paper stars had also been stuck to the walls beside the Golden Rules. *We are honest! We are kind! We are patient! We are fair!* Three white sheets, stapled together and hung up against the whiteboard, had the words *Welcome to the Magic Show!* written on them in blue paint.

'Well,' Mrs Baxter said in a flat voice, 'someone's made an effort.'

I walked further into the room and stood beside the teacher's desk. There was a large black, fabric-covered box sitting on it that had *Property of Magic Bob: This Side Up* inscribed on it in marker pen – and I wondered what it might contain. Some wands, perhaps, or silk scarves or trick flowers or loaded dice. Beside the box stood a Tupperware tub full of yet more flapjacks, and a plastic cake stand bearing six small meringue nests. They appeared to have escaped from the hall.

'Wow,' said a child, looking up at the bunting and the stars and the stapled sheets.

'Yes,' Mrs Baxter said, drily, 'indeed. But I think every-one needs to sit down now, though. Magic Bob has told us he wants us all to sit down.'

Although Magic Bob himself was, I suddenly realised, nowhere to be seen.

'Sit down, everyone,' Mrs Baxter commanded in his absence, raising her voice. 'I want everyone to find a space and sit down on their bottoms.'

And almost instantly, everyone did. The children formed an instinctive little semi-circle on the carpet. I pulled out one of the plastic chairs from a small, leaning stack and went to sit near the door. Mrs Baxter sat a few chairs away from me, closer to the window. She seemed rather quiet suddenly. 'Where is he?' I whispered across to her after a moment. 'Where's Bob?' Because he was still nowhere to be seen.

Mrs Baxter sighed and leaned forward in her seat.

'I'd love to tell you', she said in a low drawl, 'that Magic Bob has disappeared in a big puff of smoke. But he's actually in the stationery cupboard, Luisa.'

'The stationery cupboard?'

'Yes. I think he's waiting to leap out or something.'

'Is that what he normally does?' I asked.

'Apparently.' Mrs Baxter moved back again in her seat. 'He's preparing his act in there.'

*

It was very hot now, even hotter than it had been in the Portakabin. On the other side of the windows the sky had turned a dark blueish grey, and the fluorescent lights above our heads were the kind that hummed, low but constant, until within a short while your head started to hurt. From some loudspeakers set up on the other side of the classroom a song was emerging. It was Barry Manilow singing 'Could It Be Magic?' I recognised it from discos and wedding receptions; I remembered it being played at my cousin Kirsty's wedding. Nobody was listening to it really, though. Mrs Baxter was zoning out by the window, reading some leaflet about ballet classes she'd picked up from somewhere. Sitting in a little group at my feet, Solly and Topaz were discussing the cakes they were going to buy after the magic show, and Jamie and Aziz were fighting over a plastic hippo. And I just sat on my chair and felt like the person I'd been trying not to be all year: a girl in the wrong place, a girl who'd been waiting and waiting for the right place and might continue to wait, maybe for the rest of her life.

Then somebody said something.

Somebody whose voice I did not recognise leaned over to me and said, 'Excuse me, Miss McKenzie.'

I looked up. And it was Mrs Ellis. Oh God, it was Mrs Ellis! She'd walked into the room without me even noticing, and now she was standing beside my chair, her white trench coat failing to button across the bump of her baby.

'Would your lot like some song sheets?' she asked. 'Because I think we're supposed to be singing a song before the show starts . . .'

And my heart flipped like a frog. I opened my mouth, but no words came out. Mrs Ellis smiled briefly, a little quizzically, and I could smell the Polo mint she had in her mouth.

'. . . you see, I just noticed', she continued, 'that your lot don't have any song sheets.'

'No, they don't,' I said.

Which was all I could manage.

'Here you are, then,' she added, offering me some yellow sheets of paper.

'Thank you,' I said. Oh, and this was not the place to meet her! The place to tell her what I knew! I hadn't envisaged an encounter like this! Not here! It was not meant to be here, in Room C, waiting for Magic Bob to start his tricks!

'Do you think the children will actually be able to *read* all these verses?' Mrs Ellis said. 'I mean, Emily's still struggling with magic "E". Let alone', she added, 'Magic *Bob* . . .'

I was aware of the blood rushing up to my cheeks. I suppose it was just the way she seemed so bright, so upbeat, that made me feel so upset. Guilty almost – as if *I'd* been the one skulking around the woods with her husband.

I peered down at the song sheet I was clutching. It was 'Peter Rabbit Had a Fly Upon His Nose'.

'I hate this song,' I said. I just said it. Honest and true.

'Do you?' Mrs Ellis asked, surprised. 'It was always one of *Miss Ford's* favourites, I remember.'

My heart thudded.

'Was it?'

'Oh yes,' said Mrs Ellis. 'Miss Ford *loved* this one.'

'Really? Did she?'

And I tried hard not to summon up the image of Miss Ford standing on that woodland path with Mrs Ellis's husband, but it would not go away, it would not erase itself from my mind. And I knew that I was going to have to tell her; I would at least have to begin, whatever Mrs Crieff had said. Now or never: *speak your truth quietly and clearly* . . . I cleared my throat and began.

'Mrs Ellis,' I said, amazed at the joviality of my own voice, 'there was actually something, to *do* with Miss Ford, in fact – that I . . . well, that I . . . I'm not sure if you already . . . but I feel perhaps you . . .'

'It's OK, Miss McKenzie,' she said, putting her hand on my arm. 'I know.'

'Oh'

'Yes. I already know.'

'Ah'

We looked at each other. She was smiling, but there were tears in her eyes. They'd flooded in suddenly, as if she'd just tipped a whole bottle of Optrex into them.

'Emily told me,' she said. 'Last night. When she came

home. She told me all about that little encounter. But it's *absolutely fine*,' she continued, levelly. 'It explains a lot of things. She's done me a favour, in fact.'

'Right,' I said. 'Right.'

'We'll be moving out, of course,' she continued, looking right at me, as if to confirm this fact. 'Me and Emily and the baby. We'll have to wait till the baby's born, of course, and then we're moving out. It's not their fault – Emily's and the baby's – that they've got a father like that.'

I could feel the heat galloping across my face.

'Of course,' I said. 'Well, I . . .'

– but now there was an abrupt increase of volume in the room, and someone else was speaking.

'Magic Bob's coming out the cupboard,' shrieked Ruby Simpson. 'Magic Bob's coming out the cupboard!'

And I turned in the direction she was pointing, and there he was. There was Magic Bob. He'd sprung out of Mr Temple's stationery cupboard with a peculiar kind of flourish – with a flash and a bang and a puff of smoke. And he had a rabbit in a hat. A white rabbit sitting in a black top hat, very still and solid-looking.

'Oh,' I said. And I actually laughed.

Because it was quite an apparition. It was a very large rabbit. It seemed, in a peculiar way, almost larger than Magic Bob. Its eyelashes were as ethereal as frost, as strange as a photographic negative, and its eyes were exactly the same pink, it occurred to me, as my disastrous hair. It was looking around the room with something like disbelief, its fat little nose twitching. And

I couldn't possibly continue, now, with all the serious things I'd planned to say to Mrs Ellis.

'It's just occurred to me, you ought to have my seat!' I burst out to her instead, my heart thudding so hard I was amazed it couldn't be heard by everyone else in the room. 'What', I added, 'am I *thinking* of?'

Because if Mrs Ellis could be level-headed about her husband having an affair with Susan Ford than I supposed I would have to be. It was what being an adult seemed to be about – it was about being sensible and not overreacting. Everything could be explained, it seemed. Everything could be glossed over in some way, or made respectable. And in any case I knew that pregnancy could make you feel pretty tired; unwilling to take on any more than you had to. I'd been tired, and I'd been pregnant for less than a month. I certainly shouldn't be the one with the chair. 'Please take my seat, Mrs Ellis,' I said, feeling an urge to get away now; to move, at least. 'Or let me find you another seat. Because it looks as if the show might be going on for a while . . .'

And without waiting for her to answer I stood up and rushed forward to look for a chair. Though who would willingly sit in a Portakabin on a summer's day to watch a show like Magic Bob's, I wondered, as I looked around. Surely not many people would do that, unless they were being paid to, or felt obliged in some way. People like us, I supposed: mothers and classroom assistants.

'Thanks,' Mrs Ellis said, when I returned with a chair. 'That's OK.'

And she sat down. It was ridiculous, the subject we were not discussing. But we weren't.

'Can you all *see*? Can you all *see* who I've got in my hat?' Magic Bob queried.

Nobody replied.

'Who wants to know what she's *called,* then?' he persisted, tetchily.

'Whitey?' suggested Jade from her little space on the carpet.

'Bunny?' said Zac.

'Bugs?' said Eve.

'No!' Magic Bob retorted. 'Not Whitey, not Bunny and not . . . Bugs. Her name, in fact, is Beauty. And the thing about Beauty is, she does whatever I tell her. Don't you, Beauty? Look at the children, Beauty.'

We all watched as the rabbit shifted its position a little in the top hat and turned its face towards us in a rather bored fashion.

'And now look at me, Beauty,' continued Magic Bob. The rabbit slowly turned back and regarded him. 'Isn't she a good girl, children?' he said, hunting around in his left pocket for something – some prop from his collection of tricks.

And this, I think, was the moment when things began to alter. When a kind of unwinding began to happen. It was something to do with the rabbit, I think; it was to do with the rabbit, and with what Mrs Ellis said next.

'Miss McKenzie,' she whispered, turning in her seat to look up at me. 'There was actually something *I've* been meaning to ask *you*, in fact . . .'

'Oh yes?' I said in my sensible voice, my voice of mature discretion. 'What's that?'

Mrs Ellis regarded me.

'Were you ever', she said, 'a pupil at Rose Hill Primary?'

My heart jumped.

'Sorry?'

'Is your first name Luisa?' she said. 'And did you use to go to Rose Hill Primary about ten years ago?'

I could hardly understand for a moment what she was saying. I didn't see how she could have any connection with my life as a child who'd once attended Rose Hill Primary. And now I could almost see myself, as if looking down from a height: there I was, floating, puzzled, a few feet above the rest of the room. There I was, there in Room C – Miss McKenzie but not Miss McKenzie! Nineteen years old and five at the same time!

'I *am* Luisa, yes . . .' I said cautiously. 'And I *did* go to . . .'

'*I knew it was you!*' she exclaimed. 'Ever since you started working here I've been racking my brains and thinking, *Where do I know Miss McKenzie from?*'

Something in my memory started to shift; some vague haze that had hovered like a sea haar ever since I'd begun at St Luke's and first seen Mrs Ellis in the playground.

'Ah, but you don't remember me!' Mrs Ellis smiled.

And the haze cleared and something lifted, something moved into focus, and I knew who she was. She was Miss Gazall! She was my first teacher! She was the woman who'd pinned the 'Well Done' sticker on my jumper!

'Miss Gazall!' I said, which was all I could manage.

'. . . and now Beauty's coming round to see you all,' Magic Bob was droning away on the other side of the room. He'd begun parading the rabbit about, walking up and down the neat rows of crossed and outstretched legs, propelling the hat and its occupant around in a kind of low arc near the children's faces. 'Do you want to say hello to Beauty? Do you want to say hello to Beauty?' Because this was evidently part of his act – to introduce something nice before taking it away again. That seemed to be the magic of it. And as he came near Mrs Ellis I saw her placing her hands over the bump of her unborn child.

My nose had begun to run now for some reason, so I quickly wiped it against my sleeve. My eyes would prob-ably be pink, too, I suspected, pink to match the rabbit's eyes, as well as my own hair. I suspected I looked quite a mess. I didn't know what to say. But I would have to say something. So before my confidence ran out completely, I leaned towards Mrs Ellis again. *Miss Gazall.* I think I was planning to whisper something to her about bravery; about how much I admired her refusal to break down, and what a courageous woman I thought she was. But the words that actually came out of my mouth were,

'Mrs Ellis, you were the person who inspired me to paint.'

She looked up at me, bemused.

'I just have this really vivid memory, you see,' I contin-ued, flushing, 'of standing in front of this painting easel when I was about five . . .'

('. . . *Beauty's going to say goodbye now, everyone,*'
Magic Bob was boring on in the corner of the room. '*Say
bye bye to Beauty . . .*')

'. . . and wearing this artist's smock, and of you handing me this paintbrush and saying . . .'

'Really, love?' Mrs Ellis interrupted, the small smile
on her face growing wider, as if she was recollecting the
happier, more creative days we'd both once inhabited:
those *ars longa, vita brevis days.* 'Oh *no,*' she said, 'I
don't think that would have been *me,* Luisa. That would
have been someone else, if you're remembering the painting sessions. That person you're thinking of,' she said,
'would maybe have been your mum.'

I stared.

'Sorry?' I said.

'Yes, I bet that's your mum you're remembering. Because she used to be one of the parent helpers, didn't she?
Or maybe you *don't* remember. But she used to come
in on Friday mornings to help out with the painting. I
was always off on Fridays. And painting was a Friday-
morning thing.'

*

Something caught my eye, and I looked up. Magic Bob
had conjured up a blue silk scarf from somewhere, and
now he was in the process of flinging it over the rabbit.
I saw the rabbit turn briefly in the top hat, blink and
twitch its nose. 'Hey presto!' Magic Bob proclaimed, and
there was a silence as the scarf floated down. And when

he took it away, Beauty was no longer there. Beauty had gone. And something felt as if it was falling over inside my head; something was crashing and scattering like skittles. And I knew that I was going to have to leave, then; that my time at St Luke's was up. Time was altering, accelerating like some departing train, and if I didn't run and catch up with it, jump into it, it would just proceed without me. And I would be stuck indefinitely, living someone else's life. Living the life of Miss McKenzie, classroom helper.

'Are you OK?' Mrs Ellis said, peering at me with concern. My face must have been pretty blotchy by this time, I suppose, my eyes puffed up and sore-looking.

'The thing is,' I heard myself saying, 'I think I must have some sort of . . . allergy to the rabbit. I have an allergy, you see to . . . I mean, what happens is, my eyes just start to . . '

– and I turned ninety degrees and began to crash my way across the rows of outstretched legs, and towards the door.

'Excuse me,' I said as I went, aware of all the children peering up at me. 'If I could just . . . squeeze past, Zac . . .' I added, springing over the triangle of Zac's bent knees, hopping across an abandoned tambourine and a basket full of Lego, ploughing noisily straight through the Quiet Corner and finally, finally, reaching the door. 'Excuse me,' I said to the room at large, and I put my hand on the door handle, pulled it down and opened the door.

Turning for a second, I glanced back into the room.

Mrs Ellis was sitting there, seven months *gone*, her future already a date in her head. And Mrs Baxter was still by the window on the other side of the room with the leaflet about ballet classes on her lap. '*Where* are you *going*?' she mouthed at me, a look of utter bafflement on her face. But it was too late not to carry on.

'Is somebody leaving?' huffed Magic Bob, standing there with a long chain now of fabric sausages. 'Well, don't mind *me*!'

'No, I won't,' I retorted – because I'd always wanted to do that, to leave a horrible man on a high, sarcastic note – and I pulled the door wide open, stepped through, and closed it behind me. And then I started to run.

*

We were not far from the assembly hall, and as I ran along the corridor I could hear the older children beginning to sing. They had been practising this particular song for weeks: I knew this from the glum way Mr Temple had spoken about it in the staffroom. 'It's a bloody dirge,' he'd said once. It was supposed to be a song to celebrate our year at school, and to praise the wonderful jamboree Mrs Crieff had organised. But really, it *did* sound a lot more like a dirge.'The seasons's work is over . . .' I could hear them droning as I got nearer:

The summer days are near,
And now we meet together

To sing our goodbyes here.
Goodbye, goodbye, goodbye . . .

It was a song from a long time ago, one I'd sung myself once at primary school – one which my mother might have sung, too, it occurred to me – when we'd been sure of the world and our place in it.

With pleasant thoughts at parting
For friends both large and small,
With wishes bright and loving
We'll say goodbye to all.
Goodbye, goodbye, goodbye . . .

I turned left and headed down the corridor leading to-wards the staffroom. On either side of me I saw pictures that had not yet been taken down off the walls. Images of cats and birds and people; of cars and trees and houses and castles. *We Love Painting Pictures*, announced one by a girl called Chloe Davies, a pupil in Mr Temple's class. It showed a tree, a zebra, a cloud, a trumpet, a cat and the Eiffel Tower, and it had been hanging there all the time I'd been at St Luke's. I had never really looked at it. But now, as I glanced up, I saw how lovely it was, what a beautiful collection of things it contained.

The staffroom was where I'd left my coat and bag. I ran on towards it past the kitchens and their smell of Milton's and dank dishcloths, past a flash of steel pans and copper colanders and a row of hairnets hanging drably, dutifully, on pegs. I ran on, puffy-eyed, along the glazed walls of the library, past the gym hall and the space where Mrs Crieff's newly funded gym horse was going to stand, past all the piled-up rubbery crash mats and the stilled climbing ropes and the varnished wooden frames that reached a kind of nonsensical impasse at the ceiling. I headed past Mrs Regan's office with its permanent aura of Cona coffee and its filing cabinets and goggle-eyed pom-poms, past the janitor's office with its mops and brooms and floor polishes, the medical room with its disturbing clown wallpaper and tins of plasters and its metal bed on wheels, past Mrs Crieff's office, the sign on the door still declaring her to be *IN* despite the fact that I knew her to be out, at that very moment, standing on the stage and singing into the microphone. Then I reached the end of the corridor. I went to the staffroom doors and pulled them open – wrong one first so that they made a great clattering noise – and burst in.

The staffroom was empty. Almost silent. A radiator, unseasonably switched on beneath a window, made a ticking noise. A tap dripped slow drops of water into a sink. From the distance I heard the double doors opening in the assembly hall and the sound of a child's footsteps making a flat pattering sound on the corridor floor. The patter of size-one feet. And for a moment I heard Mrs Crieff's voice: she had gone up onto the stage at the end of the song to give a little talk. She was saying something about cooperation and hard work. About enterprise and team efforts and the school's motto, *Veritas et Fidelis*.

'. . . and what a testament to the Golden Rules . . .' I heard her saying in the terrible, Moses-on-the-mountain voice she adopted at times like that, and then the doors closed again.

I looked out at the playground. Heavy drops of rain had started to fall, like drips of paint falling from a brush. I saw mothers and children running across the tarmac to the shelter of the bike sheds, and the lollipop man crashing about with his *Stop! Children* sign, and one of the dinner ladies, running with long strides, the gracefulness of her run belying the terrible catering coat she wore. I thought of my mother, thirteen years earlier, walking towards my school on a Friday morning, her gloved hand holding an umbrella, her white hat on her head. Little puddles were already beginning to form in the playground's dented tarmac and the rain was hitting the Busy Lizzies in their pots. They *were* Busy Lizzies, they weren't Black-Eyed Susans. But their bright pink petals still bent in the rain. And the Portakabin still looked like a kind of ship, afloat on a hard grey sea. Bobbing in the distance, beside the school railings, I could see the frog-shaped rubbish bin, three abandoned scooters and, on the low brick wall, a pair of blue plastic sunglasses.

*

My bag was where I had left it earlier, hanging from one of the coat pegs. And as I walked across to unhook it, I saw something else there, half concealed beneath the hem of someone's coat.

A large black box.

It had a handle at the top and reinforced metal strips at the sides, and I knew straight away what it was, because I'd seen Magic Bob lugging it up the school steps that morning. It was his box of magic tricks. And I suppose if I hadn't had to retrieve my bag from the staffroom – or if I hadn't had to run there in the first place because of what Mrs Ellis had told me – then what was in the box would have remained a mystery. But I did, of course: I did have to run and get my things, and move the box to one side. And when I did and glanced down into it, I saw that sitting inside it was the white rabbit.

It was such a shock that I gasped. All alone, in the empty staffroom, I gasped at Magic Bob's abilities. He had managed, somehow, using a blue silk scarf and the words 'Hey presto', to transport a rabbit from a top hat in Room C to a box in the staffroom.

I put the box back down. I didn't know what to do.

'Hello, rabbit,' I said, after a moment. Which I suppose would have sounded pretty stupid if a person had been standing in the room listening. But they weren't.

The rabbit didn't register my presence, anyway; it didn't even seem to see me. It just sat there, its white whiskers stiff as nylon and quivering very slightly, its eyes an extraordinary pink, its nose a couple of centimetres away from the box's inside wall. Its coat was the purest white I'd ever seen.

'Hello, rabbit,' I said again.

And then – I don't know why – it was as if I'd been planning it for weeks – I suddenly *knew* what to do. I put my hands into the box, placed them gently around the rabbit's middle and lifted her up. I'd never held a rabbit before, not once in my whole life, and I wondered if she might kick or wriggle or try to get away. But she – I was sure she was a she – hardly responded at all: she just scuttered her big white feet against the side of the box, her claws making a dry, scratching sound on the cardboard. Apart from that, she was very compliant. I supposed Magic Bob must have trained her to be like that.

And now I moved fast.

Quickly, carefully, lowering the rabbit into my bag, I quietly zipped it up, leaving a little breathing space at one end. There – done. Then, my heart hammering, I picked the bag up, hung the strap over my shoulder, lay my coat over my other arm and turned to leave.

But now there was someone standing in the doorway. A child. John Singer. It must have been his footsteps I'd heard in the corridor, and there he was now, hovering uncertainly in the doorway on his way back to the magic show.

'Hi, there,' I said. He ignored this social nicety.

'Miss McKenzie, what are you *doing*?' he whispered.

And what could I say? What on earth could I say?

'Well . . .' I replied; and I paused, the bag hanging heavy from my shoulder. I looked down into it and could just see the tips of the rabbit's ears. 'Well, what I'm doing, John –'

And I tried not to think of the picture that might already be fixing itself in his head: an image of the day Miss McKenzie, a young woman who'd once worked at his school, had lifted a rabbit out of a box, lowered it into her bag and run out of the staffroom with it. I tried not to imagine the conclusion he might reach one day: that grown-ups' lives are not always the happy, ordinary things everyone had led him to believe – that they can flip sideways sometimes for a short time, or even a long one; that they can become something that fails to find its shape, its colours – a gyroscope spinning off-kilter, a picture pinned up too early, so the paint ran down the page.

'What I'm doing, John,' I said, hearing the teacher-ish note appearing in my voice for the first – and also the last – time, 'is I'm rescuing this rabbit. Because she really needed to be rescued.'

John regarded me. He stood very still, his eyes as round as planets.

'My mum used to read me about a rabbit,' he said. 'She used to read me about a rabbit called Peter. But she liked tortoises better.'

And that was when I worked it out, the difficult time John Singer had been having. I suppose I'd always known, in a way; I just hadn't wanted to think about it. And then I remembered how, during the childcare course I'd gone on, I'd been taught that you should always be quite matter-of-fact when talking to children about death. That was what *children* were, after all: they were matter-of-fact. So I said, 'I bet she was lovely, your mum. What was her name?'

His face went hot-looking.

'Her name's a secret,' he said. 'I don't tell people her name. But it floats in the air, above my head. Her name, and all the things I think about her. It sort of floats, like a cloud. And I hold onto its string.'

Something like ice at the back of my neck, like a cold hand clasped there, made me shiver.

'Not many people know about things like that, though,' John added. 'Clouds, with your thinking in them. So I don't really tell people. Because at school you have to be normal.'

And he turned and walked away up the corridor, to face the next twelve years or so of being educated.

He would cope, though. I felt he would probably cope OK.

*

It had stopped raining by the time I made it through the front doors, but I still ran, fast, obliquely, across the playground, avoiding the assembly-hall windows and all the teachers and children and parents, the whole lot of them, the rabbit bag slung over my shoulder. I ran even after I'd cleared the school gates: I just carried on, through the puddles that had formed on the pavements, up the road, past all the flats and houses and to the bus stop and a bus that would stop for me and let me on. I took Beauty home on the bus. It was home-time, anyway.

12

I didn't know what to do with the rabbit when I got back. I didn't know where I was going to hide her.

'Hi!' I called cheerily, turning immediately for the stairs. I was pleased to be home, in the way that an escaped convict feels pleased, or maybe a prisoner on parole. And as I crept along the landing to my room it suddenly occurred to me that the rabbit I had stolen couldn't possibly be the one that had been in Magic Bob's hat. Of course it couldn't! This one must have been a back-up, I realised, opening my bedroom door; a kind of understudy. This wasn't Beauty! I had stolen the wrong rabbit! At least, I hadn't stolen the right one.

My bedroom was quiet and stuffy that afternoon, the Velux window having been closed all day. It smelt slightly of the rows of half-empty coffee cups I'd left to accumulate on my windowsill, and of the sea urchin Sondrine had given me. And soon it would smell of rabbit. I put the bag gently down at the foot of my bed, walked across to the window and pushed it open a crack, averting my eyes from the sight of Mrs Crieff's back garden at the bottom of the hill. Mrs Crieff was someone I would have to face another day. Mrs Crieff and her plastic garden ornaments. I sat down at the end of my bed, lifted the bag up from the floor again and put it on my lap. I felt almost scared, as if it might contain something else entirely – something that had been magicked there in the rabbit's place, like a changeling. I unzipped the bag, looked down, and saw a broad, white rabbit's back. She was as there as any creature could be, solid, breathing, her fur as white as whitewash.

'Right,' I said.

And I put both my hands into the bag, placed them around the rabbit's sides – around her warm, rabbity girth – and lifted her out.

'Hi, Rabbit.'

The rabbit glanced at me with a sidelong, knowing kind of look.

I lowered her onto my lap and pushed my hands into her thick white fur. There was an undeniable weight about her, a warmth and a forgiving solidity. It had seemed almost impossible to believe, on the bus home, that I had a rabbit with me – that I had stolen someone's rabbit – but now that she was out of the bag she seemed to fill half the room. She was a problem, I supposed; a dilemma I had created for myself. Although, for the first time in months I felt something shift in the space behind my ribs, something realign itself. 'Hello,' I said, and the rabbit turned her head to look at me.

*

'What's this?' my mother asked when she came upstairs a little later, to find me. The rabbit was lolloping around the carpet by this time, and I was just sitting on my bed watching her. She really was a big rabbit. Her fur was exceptionally white. Her back legs, I calculated, were getting on for a foot long.

'Hi,' I said, and I felt myself blushing. 'This is the school's rabbit', I added. 'This is Beryl.'

My mother stood in the doorway.

'Beryl?'

'Yes,' I said, because I'd decided that if I was going to own a rabbit, I didn't want to own one called Beauty. I didn't want to burden her with a name like Beauty or Hope or Verity or Patience, which were far too challenging for anyone to live up to.

'Beryl?' my mother repeated. 'What sort of name is that for a rabbit?'

'It's named after a gemstone,' I said. 'Gemstone names are popular at the moment.'

'But for rabbits?'

'Yeah. Anyway, Mrs Baxter asked if I'd look after her over the holidays,' I said.

'You're looking after her?'

'Yeah. I thought; *why not?*'

My mother frowned – she could obviously think of reasons why not – and then she sighed and cast her eyes around my room – all the mugs and the books and the clothes on the floor.

'Doesn't she have a hutch or something? I mean, how did you get her home?'

'Oh, I just . . . you know . . . brought her back on the bus, in a kind of . . . pet-carrying thing. A sort of bag-type thing.'

'On the bus? In a bag?'

'Yes. It's just, they . . . wanted the hutch to stay at school. Because the jannie's going to clean them out over the holidays. All the hutches.'

'Really?'

'Yeah. All the hutches and cages. It's a health-and-safety thing'

I was almost beginning to believe my own lie now. I suppose the thing is, once you begin to tell a story, it's easy just to keep telling it. It's easy, even, to believe it. And in some ways I suppose I was being more honest about that rabbit than I had been for months and months about anything.

'They're doing the same with the hamsters,' I said. 'People are taking them home in cardboard boxes.'

And we didn't even *have* any hamsters at school. All we had, in fact, were Bobby and Billy and Bunty the goldfish, and I wasn't sure what was happening to *them*. 'Quite a few of the teachers have gone home with hamsters,' I said.

'I see,' said my mother.

Downstairs, filtering out of the living room, came the sound of the television. My father was watching the six o'clock news. It had just reached its halfway point, and an advert for Monster Munch had begun. 'Even big brave monsters get scared sometimes . . .' the voice-over was saying. And I imagined the advert, and my father watching it with his serious expression: a scene involving people in fluffy monster suits cavorting around a wood. It was one of those adverts, safe and homely and ridiculous, that I'd watched with my parents since I was small.

'Well,' my mother said, peering curiously at the rabbit as it lolloped across the carpet, 'she's quite cute, I suppose.' And she stooped down and touched the top of its head. We'd never, as a family, owned a pet. Not so much as a mouse or a guinea pig. Not even a goldfish brought back from the fair in a plastic bag. It was just something that had never happened, like siblings and long-distance flights.

'Yeah,' I said. 'The pink eyes are kind of . . . funny. But', I trailed off, 'that's not her fault.'

'Where are you going to keep her then?' my mother asked, straightening up again. 'I mean, you can't keep her in here, can you? In your room? Are we supposed to buy her a hutch or what?'

I didn't reply. I suddenly felt a little lost. A part of me wanted to confess; to prepare my mother, at least, for the fact that I'd just stolen someone's pet. That I'd taken something that wasn't mine to take at all. And my heart flipped over at what I had done.

'Isn't she quiet?' my mother said. 'Totally silent.'

The police might come, I thought. *They might turn up in a panda car or a van and cart me off to the cells.*

The rabbit had reached the far end of the room now and was sitting in a rectangle of sunlight coming in through the window. A few feet away, still pinned to my noticeboard, was Beate Groschler's old letter, and nearby,

John Singer's mad paper figure of me. *missmckenze*. And something made me sniff. Maybe it was the sunlight or maybe it was the rabbit's fur, but it made me put my hand up to my eyes.

'Are you OK, sweetheart?' my mother said. 'You seem a bit . . .'

And she stopped. She just stood there in the doorway, with the rabbit at her feet.

'It's just you've been a bit funny all week, haven't you?' she continued, as I sat with my hand still up at my face. 'Ever since Sunday. I've been wondering if it was maybe something to do with Stella Muir, after we bumped into her in Safeways. I thought maybe meeting her might have, I don't know. . .'

And now I could feel it, this great rush of sadness hurtling up from somewhere – some dark expanse. And into my head tiptoed all the ways I'd gone wrong; all the things I hadn't done and the places I'd not been to and the people I'd never met. All the ways. I got up from the bed, stepped over the rabbit towards my mother and put my arms around her. I put my head against her shoulder and closed my eyes. 'How close have I been, do you think,' I said into the wool of her jumper, 'in the past few months, to cracking up?'

I could feel my mother brush her hand across the top of my hair, my terrible pink hair, where the dye was already beginning to grow out. 'I would say quite close,' she said, after a moment. My heart was jumping. My eyelashes, when I blinked, caught against the angora fluff of her jersey. 'I suppose I've just found it hard', I said, 'to know what's right. You know – sometimes I think I've probably done all the wrong things. And sometimes I don't even know what the wrong things are. Or even the real things. You know: like making a card for Kirsty's baby. Maybe I should have made a card for Kirsty's baby.'

My mother paused for a moment. We both did. Paused for thought. Then she said,

'It's all right. I've sent Kirsty a card.'

'OK,' I sniffed.

'You never did anything wrong, sweetheart,' she said.

'OK.'

And, leaning my head in close, I felt some faint pull towards remembering – some memory, as slight but definite as a pencil line, of a woman who asked me something once, who put a paintbrush in my hand and asked me what I was going to paint.

13

A short notice appeared in the *Evening News* at the beginning of July concerning the loss of a rabbit:

A Disappearing Trick

Verity, a white rabbit which went missing from St Luke's Primary School last Thursday morning, has still not been found. The rabbit's owner, a popular children's entertainer who has been thrilling audiences with his magic tricks for the past twenty-seven years, said . . .

I considered lining Beryl's new hutch with the article, but then thought I'd rather look at hay. It might have been better, anyway, I thought, if the reporter had called the article 'Where is Verity?' or even, 'What is Verity? *Quid est veritas*, boys and girls?' Those would have been more interesting questions. There was no visit from the police. Catching rabbit thieves did not seem high up their list of things to do. On Monday morning, though, a man turned up at the door with a recorded delivery which I had to sign for. I took the envelope into the kitchen and opened it neatly, precisely, with the bread knife. I was in that sort of mood. Inside was a folded, pale-green form, edged with darker green, and with a lot of boxes to tick.

Please read the notes in Part 2 that accompany Part 1A, it said at the top of the form. *The notes give some important information about what you should do next and what you should do with Parts 2 and 3 . . .*

Paper-clipped to the front of the form, like an invitation to a summer soirée, was a St Luke's comp. slip, bearing a short, handwritten note. There was the fat owl and the motto, *Veritas et Fidelis*. The handwriting was Mrs Crieff's.

Dear Miss McKenzie,

Please show this to your next employer/college/ Jobcentre.

I have had a meeting with Mrs Ellis and will not, in circs, pursue events of last Thur.

P. Crieff

It took me a moment to understand the term 'in circs'. I thought for a moment of circuses: of Mrs Crieff in a Big Top, wearing spandex tights and a fitted scarlet jacket and holding a lion tamer's whip. And then I thought of Circle Time. Then I realised, of course, that Mrs Crieff was simply talking about *circumstances* – those difficult events, those situations it is sometimes hard even to write down in full, let alone to discuss. I read the sentence again, the way I used to read the Golden Rules on my way across the playground.

I have had a meeting with Mrs Ellis and will not, in circs, pursue events of last Thur.

I thought of Mrs Crieff with her fake lawn and her *Desiderata* and her Jack Russell. I thought of Mr Ellis with his series of books about the universe. Then I tore the comp. slip up in half, and then into quarters, then in eighths, then sixteenths, and then I put the bits of paper in the bin.

*

The weather continued sunny that July, as the weather-men said, when they appeared after the *News at Ten* bulletins with their new, improved clouds and their iso-bars and their warm fronts. They never had to pick the clouds up off the studio floor any more – they only had to move them with the click of a button – and I missed them a little, those old clouds, just as I missed our *Today the weather is* sign in the Portakabin. The sun shone, anyway, without help from the weathermen or me or Mrs Baxter or maybe even from God, and the swifts continued to flit through the warm air that rose up the slopes towards Pumzika. I spent a lot of July and August sitting in the back garden, the rabbit hop-ping around near me in the grass. The lawn was green and warm and scented, and the sky was blue and white. Beryl had quite a stretch of grass to run across, and a view of the Pentland Hills. It was a good view for a rabbit – a better view, anyway, than the inside of Magic Bob's top hat. I sat with a cup of tea at my elbow and a sketch book on my lap, and I drew some pictures of the hills – pencil sketches, mainly, and others with pastel and charcoal. And I felt like someone recuperating: like some pallid but rallying child who has been sent to a sanatorium in the Alps after a long illness. My hair began to fade after a while, from pink back to mousey brown, but the rest of my life started to become more colourful. For a start, I began seeing the fresh-fish man from Newcastle. Although he was a boy, really, not a man. He was only a year older than me. But he already knew that selling fish wasn't what he wanted to do with his life. Things happened after I met him, anyway. Things changed; and all those people I'd known at St Luke's – even the people I'd liked, like Mrs Baxter and Mrs Regan and the lollipop man – were people from my past already; were people I would not be seeing again. Even Mrs Ellis, my Miss Gazall, was someone who would alter now; who would come to her own conclusions and continue the way she thought best. Probably she would move on. Everybody had to, eventually.

'I'll only be keeping the rabbit for a few weeks,' I'd lied to my parents at first – although Beryl ended up staying at Pumzika a lot longer, of course; a lot longer than I hung around. Even so, she was still, in some childish way, my rabbit. My pet. She was the last vestige of something, I think; a kind of ghost, a spectre from some earlier life. The strange thing is, she made the house feel homely. Like home, just as I was about to leave it. And the last thing I did, an hour or so before I packed up my things and got in a taxi and waved goodbye to my father and to my mother (*Goodbye, goodbye, goodbye!*), was paint her picture.

Acknowledgements

Many thanks –

to Sarah Hosking and the Hosking Houses Trust for a 2010 residency in Clifford Chambers; to Janice Galloway for her timely encouragement and to my editor Hannah Griffiths and project editor Kate Murray-Browne for their sensitivity and patience. I should also like to thank Deborah Rogers for her enthusiasm, Jennie Renton and Lucy Scriven for their advice, and my parents and sister, who have always supported me.

The Royal Literary Fund have been extremely kind providers of a writing fellowship and I am very grateful to them, as I am to the Royal Conservatoire of Scotland and its students for giving me a job and music to listen to; and my friends for keeping me happy.

Finally, I could never have written this book (or taken so long over it!) without the patient understanding of my family. Thanks again.